THE TOWER of SONGS

By Casey Barrett

The Tower of Songs
Against Nature
Under Water

THE TOWER
of SONGS

Casey
Barrett

KENSINGTON BOOKS
www.kensingtonbooks.com

KENSINGTON BOOKS are published by

Kensington Publishing Corp.
119 West 40th Street
New York, NY 10018

All Kensington titles, imprints, and distributed lines are available at special quantity discounts for bulk purchases for sales promotion, premiums, fund-raising, educational, or institutional use.

Special book excerpts or customized printings can also be created to fit specific needs. For details, write or phone the office of the Kensington Special Sales Manager: Attn. Special Sales Department. Kensington Publishing Corp, 119 West 40th Street, New York, NY 10018. Phone: 1-800-221-2647.

Kensington and the K logo Reg. U.S. Pat. & TM Off.

Library of Congress Card Catalogue Number: 2019940161

ISBN-13: 978-1-4967-0974-5
ISBN-10: 1-4967-0974-8
First Kensington Hardcover Edition: September 2019

ISBN-13: 978-1-4967-0976-9 (ebook)
ISBN-10: 1-4967-0976-4 (ebook)

10 9 8 7 6 5 4 3 2 1

Printed in the United States of America

To my family, from the East and West

"You'll never be mentally sober."
—*Frank O'Hara, "On Rachmaninoff's Birthday"*

Prologue

*D*anny Soto opened the door to find Mr. Sun flanked by a pair of female bodyguards. He'd heard about the ladies, an eccentric quirk of this enigmatic tycoon. They accompanied him at all times. Each towered over her boss. Each wore tight black fatigues, her silk-black hair cut short across a broad forehead. They were both armed, with shoulder holsters strapped unhidden across their chests. Behind Mr. Sun and his guards there was a slight young man, standing imperious and stern. He was holding a wheelchair before him.

"There he is," said Danny, offering his wide smile and a quick bow of the head. "Come in, it's a pleasure to see you, neighbor."

Mr. Sun smiled. His mouth was full of twisted yellowed teeth. "Neighbors, yes. My neighbor above me, at the very top, Mr. Daniel Soto."

The men extended hands and shook as the group crossed the threshold. Without acknowledging his guards, Sun turned and guided the young man forward. "And this is my son, Edward. I hope his attendance is acceptable. He will soon be taking a role in my business, after he finishes his studies."

The younger Sun grasped Danny's offered hand in both

of his own and bowed in deference. He was maybe twenty-two, another weak fuerdai *being groomed to lead the family's next generation. Under normal—that is, American—circumstances, Danny would have ignored the punk, but he knew that would be a grave error. Like it or not, it was important that Danny included him with generosity in all they discussed.*

"It is an honor to meet a man of your success, Mr. Soto," said the kid. "Thank you for having me."

Always acknowledge and respect the elders first. Rote and phony as it was, Danny knew these social obligations of status and age must be adhered to at all times by these fortunate sons.

Edward pushed the wheelchair into the foyer without explanation.

"May I?" asked the elder Sun, motioning to the view.

"Please. Come, come."

Mr. Sun walked to the large cubed windows that extended in a row of six across the length of the double-height living room. He looked down at the darkness of Central Park, a blanket of black surrounded by the glittering lights of Uptown Manhattan. Danny joined him. He gazed upward, watched a plane descend over the East River. It appeared closer than the masses beneath.

"You are just a few floors higher," said Mr. Sun, "but it is different from here. So special, there is no one higher."

"For now," said Danny. He motioned to the construction below, down the block. It was already sixty floors and rising fast.

"Yes," sighed Sun. "Records never last, but it is still impressive. It must feel very good to know that no one lives above you—no one ever."

It was a record that would soon be broken. There were currently five towers in mid-construction across the world— three in the Middle East, one in India, and the one outside the window—that would surpass his. Yet for the moment Danny Soto and his family lived in the highest residential building on Earth—on the top floor, 1,396 feet in the sky. It was pure ego, he knew, another way for billionaires to keep score, after they'd accumulated more than they could spend, but to Danny and to others of his ilk, it meant something.

He was currently number 366 on the Forbes richest list, though those rankings were clueless. It was quaint the way a magazine presumed it was able to quantify such things. Many of the world's grandest fortunes were not even mentioned. Danny himself was worth far more than the insulting number they assigned to him. Yet no one on or off that list had ever lived in a place this high in the clouds that looked down on everything. All of Manhattan and everything beyond, he could survey it all from his home in a way that had never been done in human history.

Danny wondered who would buy the apartments on the top of these other towers. Probably a Saudi or Russian, he thought. Maybe Chinese, but of late they were having trouble getting their wealth out of the country. His sometime neighbor from the eighty-eighth floor, Sun Bin, had been one of the first to buy here, before the crackdown by the folks in Beijing.

Regardless of the owners' nationalities, most of these spots sat empty. Safe deposit boxes in the sky, that's all they were. They weren't homes, not like his. They shouldn't even count. Since they moved back to town from Greenwich, the Soto family—Danny; his wife, Nicole; seventeen-year-old daughter, Layla; and twelve-year-old son, Lionel—lived here. It was their primary residence.

The five others—the spread in Southampton, the London pied à terre at Trafalgar Square, the island in the Exumas, the lodge in Jackson Hole, the private residence in the Hong Kong Four Seasons—those were residences that were visited as needed. The Hamptons house was more for his wife and kids, the London and Hong Kong apartments for business, and the Bahamas place for the occasional family holiday. He couldn't remember the last time any of them went skiing out West. He probably spent more time aboard his jet than inside any one of those properties.

Yet this perch atop Manhattan was the only one that felt like home. *Same as tax evaders in Florida, in order to claim the record of world's highest address, you should have to prove your six-months-and-a-day residency to qualify. Shouldn't there be an asterisk?*

A ridiculous line of reasoning, there were so many ways of keeping score. The damn apartment cost him $96.1 million; it was 9,000-square-feet, which came to over $10,600 per foot, which made Danny a fool. When you started breaking it down it became more and more obscene. His wife's bathtub alone cost over a million. And the apartment didn't even have private outdoor space. The lower floors were selling in the five-to-six-grand-a-foot zone, still insane, but only half as preposterous as what Danny paid. Oh well, he was paying for the unprecedented views and the title—the world's highest apartment. A record soon to be broken, but whatever, in a few years it would prove to be a good investment. The market for these monster properties might have cooled, but what was a nine-figure price tag to multibillionaires? Mortgages were moot.

You paid cash, always through an anonymous LLC; pride of ownership was to be kept quiet. It was not only crass, it was unsafe to broadcast one's possessions at a certain level. Men like Danny Soto and Sun Bin understood this. It was Danny's mother, or to be precise, his mother's third husband who was responsible for the introduction. Because of the family connection, he hoped the usual time-sucking niceties of doing business with the Chinese could be dispensed with. The slow, fake, getting-to-know-you protocols drove him nuts, but his mother had taught him well. Danny might have been half gweilo, *but his mother, Eileen, was full Chinese, from Shanghai, a child of the Cultural Revolution who, through savvy successive choices in husbands, had risen high. She was determined to see her only son rise higher still. And he had.*

The group stood in silence, contemplating the city below. They waited for the host to speak. Sun's son, Edward, began to fidget.

"I'm sure this could have been yours," said Danny, "but it must have been hard to resist the eighty-eighth floor. I know how special that number is in your culture."

Sun nodded, once. "Very auspicious, yes, bā bā *the number of fortune." Then he turned to face Danny and asked in a gentle voice, "Would you like to sit?"*

There was quick movement behind him. There was no time to turn. Danny felt a sharp sting in his neck. Then a hood was forced over his head. His magnificent view replaced by blindness. The injection worked at once. Whatever it was, his adrenalized panic gave way to a spinning wooziness. He heard the sound of wheels behind him. The wheelchair, he remembered. He felt himself being lowered into it, unable to resist, his body as pliant as a puppet.

Before he lost consciousness, he sensed himself being wheeled away.

Chapter 1

It was the worst of July heat and I was taking a beating. I was getting tossed around the mat by a beefy young cop named Kingsley. He was a bright, ambitious kid from Lagos, Nigeria. Kings was bound for big things in the department, an NYPD poster boy for enlightened, diverse policing. There were more and more cops around the dojo these days, encouraged by superiors to learn a martial art in lieu of potential lethal force, when scared, overwhelmed officers reach for their pieces at crucial moments. My black-belted abilities were still eroded, and Kings had about fifty pounds of muscle on me. Every throw I attempted was swatted away. Aikido is supposed to equalize any opponent, but whatever the color my belt, I was still a joke to a guy like Kings. The beating felt good, just what I needed.

Afterwards, I hit my vape, exhaling as I stepped out into a blazing afternoon. My face burst with sweat, my t-shirt was sticky against my back, but it wasn't like the booze seeps. There was nothing to release but endorphins. My dojo, New York Aikikai, was over in Chelsea on West 18th Street, a short walk east to my apartment. On a day like this any outdoor movement was offensive. Manhattan in summer is for suckers, for those without the means or the control over careers to escape for more reasonable climates. Count me among them; I'd done a poor job saving what little I had after my latest breakup.

Newly single, another predictable bender had followed. Six weeks devoted to coke and whiskey and regrettable four a.m. decisions. Now, I was off the booze and riding the weed-only wagon. It seemed to be a trend among reluctant alkies these days. There are those out there, a great many, who will always have the need to feel *something*; a buzz-free life of total clarity is not an option. Light drinkers who'd never consider another substance, folks who can take it or leave it . . . who are these people? But whether it was whiskey or wine or just the maintenance beers, I could no longer deny the effect the alcohol was having. My liver needed a break.

I wasn't kidding myself that the change was permanent. I knew I would drink again, someday, but I was fit and energized in a way I hadn't been in years. In addition to my morning workouts at the pool, I had also returned to the dojo.

I'd received the proverbial call to wake up in a literal way, accompanied by a kick to the ribs. In the darkness after closing time, I'd passed out on my front stoop. Coherent enough to find my way home, but, somehow, I'd been unable to unlock my door and fall through it. I'd spent the early morning hours sprawled on my steps like a bum, unconscious in the February cold. Then it was half past eight and the sidewalks were full of the stroller brigades, moms pushing little sons and daughters off to preschool.

My new landlord-in-waiting was standing over me, disgusted and ready to deliver another swing of his loafer. His name was Kent, a real cunt, and evidently Mr. Petit's only heir. The owner of my brownstone was in his eighties and running out of whatever borrowed time he had left. For almost fifteen years, Gerald Petit had rented me his garden apartment for a song. I couldn't remember when he last renewed my lease. At this point I suppose I had squatter's rights. But ever since his hospitalization in the fall, his nephew Kent had been making regular trips from Jersey into the city. Sniffing around the property he lusted to inherit, like he'd ever cared about his bachelor uncle. He wanted me out. The moment the will was read I knew he intended to sell it for a few million. He'd turn off my heat, if necessary, and maybe try to buy me out for a few bucks. After I vacated like a rodent in the basement, a buyer would gut the place, strip it of every touch of period charm. Yeah, I'd seen that movie, been disgusted every time it aired.

The irony was that I was responsible for Mr. Petit still being alive. If I hadn't been coked up one morning at six a.m. last October, I wouldn't have heard him fall. He took a tumble down the stairs and broke his hip. I responded, called 911, the paramedics were there in minutes. After he returned home, now with a live-in nurse, I made a habit of visiting him in his parlor a few days a week. We'd never been close, but faced with imminent expulsion from my longtime home I started to ask him about my father. They'd been colleagues, before my dad's disgrace and imprisonment, and I suppose I wanted to learn what I could before he spoke no more. Of course, Kent the cunt took my visits as a cynical too-late ploy to ingratiate myself into the will.

It wasn't Kent's kick on the stoop that morning that put me on the wagon. It was the witnesses that accompanied it. My first sight as I regained consciousness was a young mother pushing a double-seated stroller. Her kids were maybe three, twins, a girl and a boy. The mother looked weary, like she'd slept about as well as I had. She was dressed in sweatpants, UGGs, and a puffer coat. The twins were bound up like a pair of bloated Easter eggs.

"What's the matter with that man?" asked the girl.

"Not everyone has a home," said the mom. "Not everyone is as lucky as you two."

She patted their heads and wheeled around us. Mistaken for the homeless, in front of my own home. If I believed in rock bottom, that might have qualified. Kent leered at me. *You will be soon enough,* his look seemed to say. I averted my eyes, offered no apologies, and unlocked my door. Then I emptied my apartment of all alcohol.

I braced for the withdrawal. Without professional help, I knew going cold turkey off the booze could kill. I accepted the risk. Made sure I had a refill of Xanax ready to soften the shakes and the dread. To my surprise, the first few days were rather pleasant. There was a certain joy in feeling my face un-puff; in the morning there was clarity, a weird sense of well-being. I was reminded of that old Sinatra line, how he felt sorry for people who didn't drink—when they woke it was the best they were going to feel all day. Old Frank might have been right, but I'd been waking with doom and shame for a long time. By the fourth day I was feeling smug about shaking off my habit without the terrors and seizures they warn you about.

A week in I wasn't so cocky. The whiskey whispers started and grew to a roar by my tenth sober day. I curled up on the couch, popped one Xanie after another, and binge-watched *Bosch* and *Jack Taylor* and *Wallander*. The shows didn't compare to the books, but I was in no position to indulge in the cliché when I couldn't focus on the page. When I managed to sleep, I dreamt of amber and hops and the sounds of loud barroom chatter.

It turned out my old friend, Page Six reporter extraordinaire, Roy Perry, was coming through his own bout of drying out. Coke was more his issue, but there's no such thing as a cokehead who's not also an alcoholic. He suggested I try smoking my way through. He said pot was the only way he'd managed to stay sober.

I called his guy, bought a few strains he recommended— Girl Scout Cookies, Gorilla Glue, Trainwreck. Times had changed since I dealt. Back when I was hustling around the city, before I got busted, I never knew a thing about Indicas or Sativas or THC content—pot was pot. It looked fresh, or it wasn't. Now each canister came with descriptions of the high and treatment suggestions, like a mobile pharmacy of greens. It all seemed too precious but fuck me if they didn't work as directed. It seemed I'd come full circle, a druggy journey home, back to the substance that got me started.

A few months later I was getting stronger by the day. I'd shed fifteen pounds. The definition was coming back to my chest and abs. My face had shape again, the whiskey bloat no longer. So what if I was dependent on the weed and the Xanies? I was rather proud of myself.

My workload increased. Perhaps word of my reformed habits got around. I was getting referral upon referral for divorce cases, averaging one per month, lining them up and knocking them down. I'd noticed a curious twist to my standard catch-the-cheating-bastard assignments. It used to be that I gathered evidence for the wronged wife, so she could divorce him and score the highest settlement possible. Now, more and more wives weren't after a divorce—they were determined to scare off the mistress. The *New Yorker* even ran a story about this burgeoning cottage industry. They called it "The Mistress Dispellers," reporting that it was now standard practice in China. A fine piece, though it failed to investigate its own backyard. This was not something limited to the Chinese and their *tai-tai* class. It was also common practice on the Upper East Side and in other pockets of our city with more money than love.

My latest assignment wrapped two days before. The client in question was a Belgian beauty named Kimberley; a former model married for a dozen years to a trust fund kid turned pseudo real estate developer. She had a four-bedroom loft on Bond Street, two kids in private school nearby, a staff of nannies and help, and an ironclad prenup that would have left her with ten million, should the marriage end for any reason. It had once seemed like a lot. Her husband, Cody, once seemed like a good man. Now he had a twenty-two-year-old girlfriend, an English tart who looked depressingly like Kim two decades earlier.

The girlfriend's name was Katie. She did a bit of modeling, but mostly aspired to influence people on Instagram. Kim was prepared to pay her off, but I convinced her it wouldn't be necessary. Katie just needed someone more tempting—cooler, richer, whatever—than her current married sugar daddy. With the help of Roy Perry's club connections, I managed to get her in front of Ian Kahn, a nightlife and hotel magnate, divorced and looking. He had a thing for blondes with a posh accent, if two of his four ex-wives were any indication. One night at Libra in the West Village we made sure he spotted her. He didn't stop looking until she looked back. Sometimes cupid's job is rather easy. Roy placed the item in Page Six: *Ian "Killer" Kahn's newest hot young thing* . . . Old playboy Cody was yesterday's news. Consider Kim's marriage saved, if not full of unbroken vows. She told me to stay in touch, adding that her husband was going on a golf trip soon, and her kids would be away at camp. If not with me, Kim would be exacting her revenge sex with someone soon, and she'd also keep the lifestyle to which she'd become accustomed. Maybe she'd ask her husband what he thought of Ian Kahn sometime, just to see him squirm.

Sin in the city, it seemed my job was recession-proof. As long as I stayed clean-ish and stuck with the impersonal cases involving affairs of the heartless.

But what fun is that?

I saw her waiting by my stoop and knew by the troubled look on her fresh face that this was about more than a marriage. She was somewhere in that discomforting range between late high school and early college, full of precocious arrogance and useless facts. She stood there in an expensive-looking red sundress, her black hair swept back in a high ponytail, her wide eyes peering over sunglasses that tipped at the point of a button nose. She straightened up as I approached.

"Mr. Darley?" she asked.

"That's right. Do I know you?"

I tried to step around her, down the steps to my apartment. She moved with me, blocked my entrance.

"No, you don't, my name is Layla Soto," she said. "I think you've met my father, Danny Soto, a few years back."

"Don't think so."

"He was Charlie McKay's boss," she said, "at Soto Capital, my dad's fund."

The name was not one I liked to hear. Charlie McKay, my old teammate, an Olympic swimming champion turned millionaire trader with a soul sold to Satan. The association had almost killed me on more than one occasion. It had also given me my fifteen minutes as an investigator, a D-list, days-long brush with fame.

"I think I talked to your dad once," I told her. "But I don't really remember, sorry."

Of course, I remembered him. He was a toxic presence,

a supercilious snake of a man dressed in black. I recalled how Charlie McKay had lusted for his approval after a profitable day in the markets.

"I also know Steven Cohen," she said. "He goes to my school."

If invoking the McKay name was a punch to the gut, mentioning Stevie Cohen next was a left hook to the jaw. I staggered and set a hand on my gate.

My ex, Juliette Cohen, had a son, Stevie. I still missed him, but Juls and I agreed that it was best for me to stay away. His therapy was not going well; the night terrors had not subsided. Thanks to a case I pulled them into, then eight-year-old Stevie killed a man. It was an act of astonishing bravery, saving my life and that of another, but it would take time for him to recover from the psychological scarring.

He may never.

"You're calling out the greatest hits. How's Stevie doing?"

She shrugged. "He's in fourth grade, I'm going to be a senior. I only know him because he's sort of famous at school, because of . . ."

"Because he killed somebody."

"I guess. He was out for a few months. Everyone was talking about it when he came back."

"So, what is it I can do for you, Layla? You writing a story for your school paper or something?"

She motioned toward my front door. "Would you mind if we talked for a few minutes?"

No way was I letting her inside my place. I was notorious enough around the neighborhood. No one was going to witness me leading an underage girl into my home, no matter how innocent or business-oriented the meeting.

"I'll give you five minutes," I said, "but not here. Why

don't we walk over to Piccolo around the corner? You can tell me about your dad over a coffee."

She glanced over my shoulder, then turned and scanned the street behind her. Her eyes were quick and mistrusting and full of worry. She covered them with her sunglasses.

"We need to speak in private," she said. "My father is missing. I think he's been abducted. I *know* it. He's been taken. Please, I think my whole family is in danger."

Chapter 2

I should have sent the kid on her way. Nothing positive could come of hearing her out. If someone snatched her billionaire dad, what was I supposed to do about it? Call in the feds? The best I could offer was false hope and bad advice.

We agreed on a walk around the block. She refused to speak inside any establishment where anyone might eavesdrop, and I wouldn't let her inside my apartment.

"I'm sure your family has security," I said. "Everyone at your father's level has it. Even if you don't see them . . ."

"Of course we have security," she said. "I've had an armed driver taking me to school since I was ten. If I could trust them I wouldn't be talking to you, obviously."

Obviously, says the exasperated teenager.

"What about the cops, Layla? That seems like a pretty obvious place to go."

She gave me the sort of withering look that only a sharp teenage girl can pull off. "That is the *last* place I would go," she said.

"And why's that?"

"Because whoever took my dad has a lot more power than the NYPD. There's nothing they could do. Besides make things worse."

"But you think I'll be able to make things better? Listen, just because you've heard of two cases . . ."

"No, I don't think you'll be able to make anything better," she said, stopping at the corner. "I think my dad is probably dead. I don't think I'll ever see him again."

She spoke with a cold certainty that was disconcerting.

"Then what do you want?"

"I want you to find out why. Because I think I know who's behind it."

"Who's that?"

"His mom. My grandmother, Eileen."

I didn't have anything for that. Layla lowered her head and continued walking the block. The heat didn't seem to bother her. I looked at the back of her dress—dry as can be. I was sweating like a hostage. My blood was not made for these climates. My t-shirt was drenched, my forehead dripping. I thought quitting drinking would help with my perspiration issues. Not as many toxins to sweat out and whatnot. That wasn't it. Behind her back I snuck another hit off the vape, waited for her to continue. We circled Third Avenue and approached my building. She stopped, looked back at me.

"My family is seriously fucked up," she said. "That's why I think you'll help me. Because you understand that part."

No argument there, kiddo.

She'd done her homework. In the twisted family sweepstakes, mine was hard to top. A father who might have become as rich as hers, until it emerged that his fortune was built on a half-bright Ponzi scheme. The only impressive part was how long he'd been able to maintain the charade. Now he was serving life in federal prison down in North Carolina. A mother who drowned drunk in a bathtub a few years later, then the only son, yours truly, a convicted felon . . . and that was before all the madness of my unli-

censed investigative practice began. The Darley clan knew
their way around fucked-up-ness. So, fine, I was listening.
I knew I should have turned my back on her, gone inside
and answered my next divorce inquiry, dispelled another
mistress, but that comment had me standing at her attention.

"Will you help me?" she asked.

"I doubt I'd be able to."

"But you'll try?"

"You'll be wasting your money."

"It's mine to spend," she said.

"You worked hard for it, huh?"

"I've done nothing for it, but it's still mine."

"For now."

"My dad might be missing, but he's not a crook," she
said. "I think my trust fund's pretty safe."

"So did I."

Sweating on the sidewalk, bickering with a rich teenager,
so much for dignity.

"Look, you'll be well paid," she said. "Just help me out,
okay?"

"For a few days, no promises."

"Really?"

"I've done worse for less."

She smiled at that. "Not to worry, Soto Capital treats its
employees well."

"Only as long as they keep performing."

"True. You *do* remember my dad, don't you?"

" 'There is no try, only do or do not,' " I said, recalling
my only conversation with the man. " 'And you will do it
until it is done.' "

"Knew it. Dad loves his *Star Wars*. That's his favorite
Yoda line. He used it on you?"

"He might have."

We returned to my stoop and stopped together. She

glanced up and down the block, hugged her bare arms around her body as if she were cold, then looked up into my eyes. "Thank you," she said. "I knew you'd say yes."

She turned and began to walk west toward Union Square.

"Hold up," I called. "I'm going to need some more information." I didn't add *and money*, though that was a rather motivating factor as well.

"Check your email," she replied.

I watched her hurry down the block before she turned right on Third Avenue and disappeared from view. I considered our encounter, wondered what I'd just agreed upon. I hadn't taken much persuading. It would be a nice check for not much work. I didn't intend to expend much effort. But not for the first time, I wondered about my latent death wish, the pull of self-destruction that was always there, lurking just beyond conscious thought. Over the last several months, off the booze, life had taken a turn for the better. I was strong and healthy and not quite as haunted. I was having success with my cases. Word-of-mouth was picking up. Now I could feel all that stability receding. It was as if the sidewalk was opening under my feet. The beast that resides beneath this cursed island was stirring again. Ready to pull me down once more into the murk.

The devil comes in many forms, most of them attractive. The well-dressed gentleman with a smirk and a promise— that was an old favorite. But sometimes he shape-shifts. Sometimes he—or she—may appear as a teenage girl, dressed in red, who speaks without emotion when discussing her surety that her father is dead. And what to make of her belief that it was her grandmother behind it, Danny Soto's own mother?

Check your email, she said, as if her visit to me was just a formality.

I unlocked my door and stepped inside the apartment,

breathing in the stillness. I missed Elvis. The hound had been dead over a year now. I knew it was almost time to return to a shelter and adopt a new guy, but I still couldn't bring myself to do it. I doubted whether I was fit to parent even a pup. Yet the silence of an empty apartment without a pet felt unnatural. It would never feel like home without an animal to greet you.

Alas, no dog, no booze, none of the creature comforts I'd loved for so long. I didn't get the itch to drink too often these days, but my meeting with Layla Soto left me thirsty. That should have been a sign in itself. I opened a sparkling water from the fridge, thought about packing the one-hitter. Before opening my laptop and checking that email, I turned on some music. Leonard Cohen. Since that baritone bard died I had become rather obsessed. His deathbed album, *You Want It Darker*, might be the finest self-composed eulogy ever written. It was something close to religion for the faithless. It put me in the proper frame of mind for whatever was waiting in Layla Soto's email.

It was sent from an encrypted account. The sender was listed as "Mirrasoft—LS," the subject line read SEE BELOW. I clicked the email open. It read:

Dear Mr. Darley,
Please review the attached content and video, which has been secured using Mirrasoft encryption. I will be back in touch shortly. When a blocked number appears on your phone, please answer it.
Regards,
Layla

There were two attachments. The first was a screen shot of a previous email, also sent from an encrypted account, addressed to nicole.soto96@gmail.com, presumably Danny's wife. This one read:

Mrs. Soto,
We need your husband for a short while. Report to no
one and there will be no problems. Otherwise, there will
be consequences. We are watching.

The note was unsigned. I clicked on the next attachment. A video file appeared on my screen. Crisp black-and-white security footage, the camera looked down on an opulent high-ceiled lobby. I watched as elevator doors opened in the back of the frame. Two women emerged, each pushing one arm of a wheelchair. Seated between them was a slumped man dressed in black. His limbs were loose. There was a hood pulled over his head, which lolled forward, his chin to his chest. As they approached the camera, the women stopped and made eye contact with the lens. One of them reached down and removed the hood. The other grabbed the man by the hair and pulled up his head so the camera could capture his face. They posed for a moment, then pulled the hood back on and wheeled him away. It had been a few years since we met, but the face was unmistakable. It was Danny Soto.

The entire video was twenty-seven seconds. I played it again, pausing on the faces, noting the empty lobby desk behind them. The women looked like Tarantino ninjas, as if they were in costume. Tight black fatigues, shoulder holsters, black hair cut in crisp bangs across their foreheads. They were Asian and very tall, both beautiful in a severe and scary way.

They brought to mind my former partner, Cassandra Kimball, sought-after dominatrix when she wasn't assisting my investigations. She had that same look. There had been a time when I considered her my closest friend. She knew more about me than anyone else. She was my confessor, my protector. The one person I trusted above all.

That is, until she lied to me, used me, and let me down. It was Cass who pulled me into that case with Stevie Cohen. Ultimately, it was her fault that the kid would be a haunted, scarred mess for the rest of his boyhood, and perhaps beyond. She wasn't present when he pulled the trigger and saved my ass from a vengeful meth-head white supremacist. In fact, she'd been in prison, suspected of the crimes that hateful psychotic committed. But she set it all in motion—by bringing me into her troubled love life and lying about the true nature of things. I was there when she was released from Rikers, but found I couldn't forgive, not yet anyway. She told me she was resettling in the city, after her ill-fated sojourn upstate in the Catskills. I said welcome home. Then I ignored her requests to get together. That was a little over a year ago. Like the drinking, I knew my ghosting of Cass wouldn't be permanent, but if and when we did reunite, it would be on different terms, my terms. No more mysterious Cass, who consumed the secrets of others but shared none of her own. If she wanted to be a part of my life, I would need to be allowed into hers.

I was staring at these faces, these female ninja-guards, with Danny Soto unconscious between them, and cursing the memories of Cass, when the phone rang. I looked at the screen, a blocked number as the girl indicated.

"Layla?"

"You watch it?"

"I'm looking at it," I said. I checked the time-and-date stamp at the top of the video. Last Thursday, 10:08 p.m. "Where were you when this happened?"

"Out," she said. "I got home around eleven. I figured my dad was asleep. It's not like I checked on him."

"Who were you out with?"

"A friend, not that it's your business."

"It is if you want my help."

"I was at a concert, okay? With my music teacher."

Who could have been paid off to keep her out of the apartment while the abduction took place . . . There'd be time for that later. I examined the two ladies alongside the wheelchair.

"Layla, have you ever seen these women with your father?"

"No."

"Think hard."

"I'm sure," she said. "I'd remember women who looked like that."

"So, this stuff was sent to your mother? Did she forward it to you?"

"She did."

"The email was pretty clear about not sharing it with anyone. Why would she do that?"

I heard her sigh into the phone. "I doubt that even occurred to her, that I might count as 'someone.' My mother doesn't understand boundaries."

"Think she might have told anyone else?" I asked.

"She says no. I believe her. She doesn't really have friends. Maybe her sister, but I doubt it. As for cops, she told me not to consider it."

"Does she know you're talking to me?"

"No."

"Layla, you realize that just by doing this you could be putting your father in further danger?"

"I told you . . ."

"That you think he's already dead, that your grandmother is behind it—yeah, you mentioned that. Now you're going to need to tell me why."

"It's not like I could see that video and not do anything," she said. "Maybe my mom can just go pop some more pills and forget about it, but I can't. I thought about it all weekend. Then I remembered your name."

"Listen, if you want my help, you need to start answering my questions. Also, I'm going to need to meet with your mother."

I heard her huff and then go silent. I thought she was going to hang up, hoped for it in fact. When I heard her breathing, I said, "Sorry, kid, those are my terms. You're still a minor. You want my help on this, then your mom needs to sign off on it."

"How about I double your rate and my mother stays out of it?"

"We haven't discussed my rate yet, and no."

"A hundred grand," she said. "For a month's work, maybe less."

The number caught me up, but for just a moment. I mustered some pride. "I'm not helping you for a million without your parent's permission."

"You realize that will only complicate matters."

"Nevertheless."

"You know how many people would kill for that offer? I mean, literally."

"Then maybe you should ask them. But here you are talking to me."

"I could get it to you in cash, like today, if you want."

"Listen, Layla, I'm busy and this doesn't sound like it will work out."

"Ugh. Fine. I'll try to set up a meeting with my mom, but your fee just went down to fifty."

"Even that's too much."

She let out an arrogant laugh. "My dad's right. Most people don't want money, they just think they do."

"Perhaps."

"So, you'll help?"

"When your mother agrees to my involvement, yes."

"Fiiine," she said. "I'll call you back after I talk to her."

She ended the call without saying goodbye. I sat there sipping my sparkling water, petting the ghost of my hound, trying not to think of the closest bar.

Chapter 3

Nicole Soto agreed to meet the next morning at the Blade Lounge heliport on West 30th Street and the Hudson. Her daughter informed me that she loathed the city in the summer and wouldn't be staying long. The helicopter ride from Southampton was forty minutes. She would give me one hour of her time at the lounge before returning on the next chopper back, in time for her afternoon tennis lesson. I'd try not to exasperate her with too many questions about her abducted husband.

Layla was waiting to meet me by the path along the West Side Highway. She'd traded yesterday's red sundress for a black one. As bikes rushed past, I caught riders gawking at her. She scowled at my approach, turned, and said, "C'mon, you're late, she's landing any second."

I followed her across the street to the helipad as her mother's ride came into view over the river. We watched as it lowered before us, its arms slowing in revolutions until it touched down in a gust. Three passengers departed before her, a trio of harried interchangeable suits, rushing off to meetings in air-conditioned rooms. Then, a pair of toned and tan calves stretched out over the steps, before all of Nicole Soto emerged, carrying a small purse and no luggage. She wore a white woven sundress that ended just below her knees and flat, strappy Grecian sandals.

To call her beautiful would be insufficient. She was a stunning brunette, tall and graceful, with a walk you noticed across every room. She'd been taught from a young age, at some Country Day or another, how to carry herself, how to move with a regal confidence that said: *Keep dreaming* . . . A woman destined to marry wealth. With her daughter a senior-to-be in high school, she must have been at least in her middle forties but she looked a decade younger. My career, such as it was, was spent serving women like Nicole Soto. I didn't presume to be an astute observer of all humans, but there was a certain type I knew with some certainty: unhappy, sophisticated married women in the highest tax bracket. I reminded myself of the first rule in dealing with them: Never get caught staring.

Daughter gave a slight wave as mother approached. I slipped my phone from my pocket and glanced at the time, doing my best bored, I've-seen-better put-on. As she stopped, she frowned, looked from me to Layla and said, "I really can't believe you've done this."

"Mom, this is Duck Darley. He insisted on speaking with you."

She extended a manicured hand. "Nicole," she said as I took it. "Why don't we chat in the lounge?"

I followed mother and daughter inside. I'd been told that the Blade Lounge contained the highest concentration of fuck-wads you'd ever find, and in this city the competition was high. In summers they congregated here at the end of workweeks, talking too loud about too much money, sipping their rosé, before being whisked off to their shingled castles in the Hamptons. But on this midweek morning in July it was just an empty room furnished with ugly leather seating, brand posters as art, and poor lighting. A twenty-something girl dressed in Blade insignia came hurrying over at the sight of us.

"They called ahead," she said. "How are you this morning, Mrs. Soto?"

"I'll be better in an hour," she said. "When does the next flight depart to Southampton?"

"At one p.m., ma'am."

"Is it full?"

"I don't think so, no. There are still a few seats available." The Blade girl glanced at Layla and me. "Will they be joining you on your return trip? I'd be happy to—"

"No, they will not, but please reserve three seats for me. I'd forgotten how uncomfortable your seating is."

"Of course, Mrs. Soto. I'll book you a full row across."

"Thank you." As the girl retreated, Nicole Soto glanced around the room and down at her daughter. "This place is a glorified bus station," she said. "But your father does not like us to use the company helicopter without him. And it's not like I can reach him . . ." At that she turned to me and said, "Shall we sit? I don't have long, and this was an unexpected errand this morning."

The women settled onto a black leather couch. I sat across from them in a low-slung club chair. I waited for Nicole to begin. She took her time, tapping at her phone, sighing, searching over our heads for the Blade girl that greeted us. She came hurrying back and asked if she could get us anything to drink. Nicole said, "A bottle of rosé, please." She glanced at me. I fought off the urge, shook my head. "One glass," she added.

"Thank you for coming in," I said. "I'm very sorry to hear about your husband."

She ignored my comment, kept looking around the space with a frown. Her display of haughtiness would have rendered most women unattractive, but Nicole Soto was used to her behavior having no consequence. She knew how she looked. The hostess returned with a chilled bottle of Whispering Angel and filled her glass.

"Perfectly dreadful," said Nicole with a sip and a smile. She set it down, crossed those tan legs, and took my measure. I straightened up, sucked in my stomach.

"Mom," said Layla. "This is the guy who helped the Cohens. Remember, the kid from school?"

"Oh yes, Juliette's boy," she said, brightening. "I understand you had a . . . relationship . . . with her."

Her pauses were plump.

"Stevie's a great kid," I said.

"I'm sure his mother was very . . . grateful."

"He also met dad," said Layla. "Remember Charlie McKay, the psycho who worked for him? Duck solved that case too."

Nicole Soto took an imperceptible sip. "My daughter is easily infatuated," she said. "I appreciate your being a gentleman and asking to speak with me."

"As I said, I'm sorry to hear about your husband's situation. I doubt I can be of much help, but your daughter is very persuasive. I'll try to look into his disappearance, discreetly, if you'd like, but only with your permission."

"My permission?" she said with a raise of an eyebrow. "You don't look like a man who asks for such things."

I eyed the bottle of wine before me, felt myself salivate. I was plenty stoned, but a drink would help me deal with this flirty baiting.

"Your daughter offered me quite a bit of money to look for him. I couldn't take that in good conscience from a minor without official approval."

"How much did you offer him?" she asked Layla.

"Fifty," shrugged her daughter.

" 'Quite a bit', that's a relative term, isn't it?"

For the first time, mother and daughter shared a look that resembled a genuine bond. Both looked at me and smirked.

"Okay, for that royal sum you have my approval to ask around," said Nicole. "But if anyone—anyone official, a police officer, a federal agent, an attorney, a colleague of my husband's—if this reaches anyone like that, there will be a problem."

"I understand."

Nicole Soto's face went cold. The beauty drained from her eyes. "No, Duck Darley, you don't. By 'a problem' I mean this: I'll have you killed. That is, if the people who took my husband don't kill you first. Is that still worth 'quite a bit of money' to you?"

I put my hands on my knees and pushed myself up. "Nicole, Layla," I said, "it was nice meeting you both."

"Oh please!" cried the mother. "I'm kidding. Quit being so dramatic. No one is killing anyone. Please sit down, Duck."

I did, for the moment.

"I understand you must be used to such violence in your life, but that is not what we are dealing with. I can assure you my husband's crimes, whatever they are, are strictly white collar."

"I saw the video," I told her, "of Danny being wheeled from your lobby with a hood over his head. He looked as if he'd been drugged. Accompanied by a pair of armed women. Some might consider that a violent abduction."

She glanced at her daughter.

"Relax, mom," said Layla. "I emailed it from an encrypted account."

"I never should have sent that to you. I should have known you'd do something irresponsible with it. Didn't their note state clearly that we were not to report it to anyone?"

"So why did you send it to me?"

"I didn't think their instructions applied to immediate family."

"You just forwarded it so that you could have someone else to stress with."

"I am not stressed, darling. I'm sure they . . ."

"Excuse me," I said. "Who is 'they'? Your daughter mentioned . . ."

"Nai-nai," said Layla. "I told him I thought nai-nai was behind it." Then to me, she added, "That's grandma in Chinese. Dad's mom is from Shanghai."

"What? Why did you say that, honey? Why would nai-nai have anything to do with this? She would never hurt her own son."

Nicole took a swallow of her rosé, shook her head as it swished down her throat. She uncrossed, and then re-crossed, her legs. She noticed her heel hammering and tried to slow it. The mention of her mother-in-law agitated her in a way that transcended the general agitation caused by all mothers-in-law. I thought I even caught a tremble of fear in her voice when she uttered the word *hurt*.

"Layla, why do you think that?" I asked.

"Because she's the Dragon Lady."

"Honey, stop," gasped her mom.

"What? That's what you call her."

"Let's back up for a moment," I said. "Have either of you been in touch with her recently?"

Both women shook their heads.

"When was the last time you had contact with her?"

Nicole Soto shrugged. "Not for some time," she said. "Maybe the holidays? She's not one to stay in touch."

"She texted me on my birthday," said Layla. "In May, so like two months ago?"

"If neither of you are in touch with her, then could you

explain why one of you thinks she's responsible for abducting her son?" I turned to Nicole. "And the other seems shaken by the sound of her name."

"I am not *shaken*," said Nicole. "Please. And her name is Eileen—Eileen Chung—*not* the Dragon Lady. I merely don't like the woman. I am not the only wife who does not get along with her mother-in-law."

"Layla, what about you? Do you get along with your . . . nai-nai, was it?"

"She's nice to me, she's just weird."

"Then why . . ."

"Because she's involved in shady shit," said Layla. "I heard dad talking to her on the phone last week. He was pissed. She's married to this really powerful old Chinese guy now. I think she was helping dad make some kind of investments in China, with his help."

"So, your grandfather is . . ."

"Dead for decades," said Nicole. "Eileen is on husband number three now. Each has been richer than the last. Danny's father was thirty years older than her. They met when he was working in Hong Kong and she was a twenty-two-year-old secretary. She broke up his first marriage. Lionel Soto died of a heart attack when my husband was in grade school. I hear he was a good man. We named our son after him. Eileen remarried less than a year later."

"I love how you make her out to be a gold digger," said Layla, "when you're married to a billionaire."

Her mother glowered at her. "You father was nowhere close to that when we married."

"Right, he was only a multimillionaire." She rolled her eyes. "Such a hypocrite," she muttered.

"Please excuse my daughter," said Nicole. "The ages between sixteen and twenty-five—I do think it's the most ignorant time in life, don't you agree, Duck?"

I did. That was right in the sweet spot when I became a weed dealer, got caught, did thirteen months in Rikers.

"What kind of shady shit?" I asked. "Do you have any idea what your dad might have been talking about with her, when you overheard him?"

"I couldn't really catch details," said Layla. "They talk in this sort of broken Chinglish. When he gets really upset, he shouts in Chinese. I've been taking Mandarin forever, but I still don't understand him when he's mad."

"What did you hear?"

"He owns a hedge fund, right? They push their chips anywhere they think they can multiply them. It doesn't matter where, as long as their stack gets bigger. That's how my dad explained it, anyway."

"What did you hear, Layla?" asked her mother.

"He was upset with nai-nai," she said. 'I heard him yell '*ni de xian sheng ben si le*,' which means something like 'your husband is stupid.' "

"What else?" I asked.

"I also heard him say *du fan*. That means 'drug dealer.' That's all I could really understand. I wasn't even in the room. I heard him yelling outside the door."

"When did this conversation take place? How many days before he was taken?"

Layla thought for a moment. "Four," she said. "It was on a Sunday night, and dad was taken last Thursday."

"You overheard this conversation at home, at your apartment in the city?"

"Yeah, he was in his office. It's a pretty big place, so I doubt he thought I could hear him. I was walking from my room and stopped outside the door when I heard the yelling."

I turned to Nicole. "Where were you that night?"

"I've been out east with Lionel since school got out. My

daughter has decided to spend most of this summer in town, for her own reasons."

Mother and daughter exchanged a look.

"I'm a musician," said Layla. "I play piano. My teacher is here. I need to be here to practice with him. This is summer before senior year, I need—"

"Your *teacher*," said her mother. "How is Michael doing?"

"He's fine, mom. How's your tennis? What's your instructor's name again, Ryan? You must be getting plenty of sun with your afternoon lessons."

"Brian. I'll be sure to send him your best. Which reminds me . . ." She looked at her phone and glanced at the doors to the heliport. "I should be getting back shortly."

"Before you go, I'm going to need . . ."

"Money, of course you do."

"That too, but I also need some more information."

"You could start with Danny's first wife," she said.

"And she is?"

Layla rolled her eyes. "Dad wasn't married before. She means his business partner, Peter Lennox. That's what mom always calls him."

"That's the more important marriage in my husband's life," said Nicole. "Peter and Danny started the fund together. He likes to say that Peter's the only person he truly trusts. He makes a point of saying it in my presence."

"I'll get you his contact info," said Layla, "and show you how to send email from an encrypted account, if you don't already know."

I shrugged like I did. "I'm guessing a man in Danny's position has been missed at work. Has anyone from Soto Capital questioned his whereabouts?"

"Not to me," said Nicole, "but that's not so surprising. Ever since that McKay scandal, Danny has become very insular. He used to like hosting parties for the whole staff. Now only Peter is welcome."

"But not even Lennox has been in touch since Danny was taken?"

"No, he hasn't."

"You try to reach him?"

"I did." She took another sip of wine. "I told Peter that my husband was on another of his meditation retreats. Danny thinks it sharpens his instincts. When he's gone, he leaves his partner in charge."

"So, for now, you don't think his staff is wondering?"

"I don't care what his employees think. You'll have to ask the first wife."

"I'll enjoy talking with Mr. Lennox."

"No, you won't," she said. "He's a prick."

"Noted."

"Will there be anything else?"

"You can come back home with me," said Layla. "The building staff will do anything we ask, they're all scared of Dad."

"Not everyone, evidently," I said.

"No, not everyone," said Nicole. She rose, lifted her glass, and drained the rest of her rosé. "They are going to be very sorry they messed with Danny."

"Your daughter mentioned that you have private security for your family?"

"Layla, would you put him in touch with Richard Gross?" Turning to me, she added, "Richard has worked for us for ages. He's a former Recon Marine. If you need help . . ." She paused, considered her daughter seated tense before her. "Honey, why would you seek out Mr. Darley here, someone we don't even know? Why didn't you just go to Richard?"

"Because she's not sure whom you can trust," I informed her. "Abductions are almost always orchestrated from the inside. The absence of any building staff when Danny was wheeled out shows that there was advanced planning. Folks who have been inside your home, who work inside your building—quite a few people must have played a part here, even if it was just accepting a bribe to make himself scarce for a while."

"Richard could not be bought," she said. "We compensate him well, more than anyone in his position . . ."

"Money's only one means of coercion."

Behind us, out the doors of the lounge, the helicopter prepped for takeoff. The Blade girl checked her iPad screen, tapped at it with manicured nails, and approached us. "Mrs. Soto," she said, "your return flight will be departing in—"

"Just a moment," she snapped. She looked at her daughter, seemed to consider how much parenting was required. "You should join me," she said. "Until this is sorted, you need to stay out east."

"No," said her daughter.

"Layla, honey, I know you're trying to help, but what if our building isn't safe? Someone took your father from our apartment and wheeled him right out the front door. If you want this man to ask around, fine, but you cannot stay there while this is happening. This is not a request."

Her daughter let out a laugh so genuine it made her mother wince.

Nicole Soto's crafted confidence, her impenetrable sense of above-it wealth, was being penetrated. The gates of their castle in the sky had been broken, the king taken from his lair. The queen was helpless in exile at her beach house, presented with evidence of the abduction, and she was expected to do nothing but wait. Told to tell no one.

She'd failed at that. Her daughter and I stood before

her, prepared to delve deeper, even if it put her husband—
and her children—at further risk.

"Layla, please . . ."

"I'm not coming with you," she said.

Mother shook her head. A hand clutched her purse. She
glanced out at her waiting ride. "Your brother," she said.
"I need to get back, if only for Lionel. Go home to pack a
bag if you must, but I expect you on the six o'clock. A car
will be waiting."

She turned and strode through the doors and onto the
tarmac as the helicopter blades began to rotate. A few
paces from the open chopper door, she stumbled. She recovered quickly, but in that single misstep Nicole Soto's el-
egance crumbled away from her.

Chapter 4

We shared a cab up the West Side Highway and crosstown to the Soto family apartment in Midtown. In recent years, the central stretch of 57th Street had earned the moniker Billionaires' Row. Each year new *supertalls* soared past one thousand feet, built for foreign wealth, mostly Russian and Chinese and Saudi. It was a safe place for these oligarchs and party members and oil barons to park tens of millions, purchased through anonymous LLC shell corporations. The places invariably sat empty. I found so much of twenty-first-century Manhattan architecture to be offensive, but particular disgust was reserved for these towers. Empty and ugly and obscenely expensive, they offered nothing to the city, nothing at all. The richest irony being that Midtown Manhattan was a loathsome place to live. The views were special, granted, but to live that high above humanity, cloistered atop a tourist-packed pocket of town? Maybe if I were worth a billion, I'd understand.

As we inched east on 57th, I remembered a conversation I once had with Charlie McKay about his boss.

"Didn't you guys live in Greenwich?" I asked.

Layla raised an eyebrow and nodded. "Yeah, how'd you know?"

"I remember Charlie mentioning it. He and his sister visited once, at some kind of company retreat?"

She shuddered at the memory of that unholy pair. "How is she?" she asked. "What was her name again?"

"Madeline," I said. "And I don't know. She disappeared again soon after . . . all that."

"And you were, like, there, weren't you?"

"Front row seat."

"That's so sick. She'll never be okay, will she?"

"Probably not."

We sat through a red light at Eighth Avenue, both of us looking out either window, impatient for a new topic.

"Did my mom seem loopy to you?" she asked.

"Maybe a bit," I said. "Why?"

"Because she's a pill head. She's basically a junkie."

Like her casual insistence that her father was dead, she spoke the words with a matter-of-fact coolness.

"What's she on?" I asked.

"OxyContin and Adderall, mainly. She has lots of other stuff too, but she's heavy into the Oxy and the uppers. A rich lady's version of speedballs, right?"

"More or less."

"She tore her rotator cuff playing tennis two summers ago. I think that's when she started on the opioids. Found herself some doctor without a conscience. She doesn't even bother to hide the bottles. They're all lined up in neat rows in her medicine cabinet. It's pathetic."

Mental note to canvass the master bath at the apartment . . . Just to confirm.

"Layla, do you have any extended family, aunts or uncles, grandparents, besides your nai-nai? You mentioned your mom had a sister?"

"Why?"

"It would seem you could use a bit more adult supervision."

She rolled her eyes. "My mom's parents are dead. Her sister, my aunt Josephine, lives out in L.A., in, like, Bel-Air. And my dad has two half-sisters that we never see. They're in London. Nai-nai's second husband was some kind of English aristocracy. My dad hated him."

"So, that leaves your aunt Josephine. You see her much?"

"Yeah, she and my mom are pretty close. She comes out to stay with us a bunch, especially now that she's between husbands."

"Maybe you should ask her to visit."

"I'm not telling her about dad. Mom would kill me. No way. Besides, she's in Europe for the summer. She's in Croatia now, according to her Instagram."

As we sat gridlocked next to Carnegie Hall, Layla pointed up at the tallest of the supertalls, a bland phallus of cubes that stretched higher than any other. You could see it from the Palisades in Jersey, as you approached the George Washington Bridge, the first glimmer of skyline above the trees. More would soon join it, but for now it held the title, the world's highest residential building. I made a habit of hate-reading such things.

"That's our place," she said. "Up there at the top. Wait till you see the view. I was pissed when dad made us move back from Greenwich, until I saw the apartment. It's like something out of a sci-fi movie."

The rich are not like you and me . . . I'd always scoffed at that celebrated cliché from F. Scott. Having been both rich and poor, I felt confident that the classes were, in fact, exactly alike. Only the rich were worse—because they could get away with their sins. But in talking to the Soto women, Fitzgerald might have been right. They existed on a different plane of reality—in the most literal way, inside an apartment that looked down on the Empire State Building. Mother and daughter might have bickered and mistrusted each other, but they were products of the same rarified environment. They needed each other to temper the solitude. How does one relate to the rest of humanity when money ceases to exist in any real sense?

Nicole Soto I could handle. She was a species I had experience with, a breed whose habits were familiar and predictable, all the more so when you factored in the pill addiction. But this seventeen-year-old ice princess had me off balance. Precociousness was a given for any Manhattan teen, yet even by those warped standards she seemed too independent for her years. She was still a minor, though already worth more than millions of her fellow New Yorkers combined. Her mother may joke about having me killed, but to this sharp young woman beside me, it might seem like a logical notion if things went sideways. I needed help, and without forethought, I blurted it out.

"Do you remember reading about my former partner, Cassandra?"

"The dominatrix?" she asked. "Yeah, she sounds pretty twisted. What about her?"

"What would you think about my calling her . . . for help?"

Layla Soto went silent for the slow passage of an avenue. Without turning, she said, "All right. Ask her."

"I don't even know if she'll answer. We haven't spoken in a while. Things didn't end well between us, after that case with Stevie Cohen."

"You were going out, weren't you?"

"Contrary to popular assumption, no."

"Never?"

"Ever."

"But you wanted to."

"We were friends and business partners. It wasn't romantic. Someday you'll understand."

But she already did, of course, and I wasn't going to admit it.

"Those women who took my dad," said Layla, remembering the video. "They looked like mistresses too. Who do you think they were?"

"I'm not sure, but that's something that Cass might be able to help with. She's talented with that sort of thing."

"Then text her."

I took out my phone; Layla did the same. "Give me her number while you're at it."

"Why?"

"Because if she's going to work for me, I need to be able to contact her too." When I hesitated, she said, "Relax. I won't reach out until you two have talked and smoothed over whatever unrequited crush you have going on."

I shared the contact and ignored her jab. My first text to Cass in months, I typed: **Can we talk? Could use your help . . .** Hit Send.

"Tell me about Richard Gross," I said. "And Peter Lennox."

Layla leaned over the front seat and said, "This is good. We'll get out here."

Our driver shrugged and pulled over on East 57th between Madison and Park. "Cash or card?" he asked.

"Cash," she said, handing a twenty over the seat. She turned to me and added, "You need to use cash for everything, every ride, every meal, whatever. Cards are too easy to track."

"You're the boss."

Outside, the sweltering crush of a midday Midtown sidewalk soured every mood. There might be hotter hellholes on earth, but there is nothing that feels quite as unbearable as a July day in the city when the temperature pushes past one hundred and the humidity is like some satanic joke. The heat collects in the canyons between the buildings, holding it there, circulating it in bus exhaust and cigarette smoke and the endless fumes of slow-moving traffic. It's a miracle we don't all die of lung cancer. It's also a miracle there aren't more raving, sweating lunatics who run amok and shoot up crowds, if for no other reason beyond insanity from the heat. I glanced at Layla. Once again not a drop of perspiration on her; she seemed impervious.

"So, about your bodyguard, Mr. Gross," I said.

"He's, like, a total badass. After the Marines, he worked for Blackwater in Iraq and Afghanistan. Dad said he was a mercenary and did a bunch of private security for high-ranking people over there. Dad was involved in some kind of investments in the Middle East and met Richard on a trip to Dubai. They got along, and he recruited him to come back to the U.S., to work for us. Said it was a lot safer, with better pay. I think Richard was bored at first. I mean, he went from guarding embassies and heads of state to taking me to school, but then I think dad got him more involved with his company and started to make him rich, so Richard started liking it more. Anyway, for a while he was like part of our family."

"For a while?"

"I suspect something happened between him and my mom. I'm not sure, and it's not like dad fired him or anything. He kept working for us, it just got more professional all of a sudden."

"When was this?"

"Last year sometime, in the fall."

"Which is why you sought me out, instead of calling him."

"No, that's not why. I don't care if he screwed my mom. It's not like either of my parents are faithful to each other. I came to you because I needed someone on the outside.

You said it yourself when we were with my mom, when these things happen it's almost always someone on the inside."

"You think Richard Gross was working with whoever took your dad?"

"Put it this way," she said, stopping at the corner. "I think if he was doing his job, it would have been almost impossible for anyone to get to Danny Soto."

"Fair enough. What about your dad's partner, Peter Lennox?"

"What about him?"

"Your mom doesn't seem to like him much."

"How observant."

"Any idea why not?"

"Got me. Uncle Peter's all right. My mom seems to have a problem with most people."

We turned right on Park Avenue and I followed her past tall, vacant spaces of empty storefront. I couldn't fathom which businesses could afford the rent. A luxury brand in need of a new flagship, or yet another bank branch to compete with the half dozen others within eyeshot . . . No cars were parked in the deep circular driveway that wound before her building's entrance. As we approached, a doorman turned at the sight of us and stiffened.

"May I help you?" he asked.

"Who are you?" asked Layla.

The doorman, long and lean, Latino and proud, seemed to soften at the challenge. "Ma'am, my name is Marco. My apologies, you are . . ."

"Where's Sammy?" she asked.

"On vacation, ma'am."

"Since when?"

"I'm not sure. I just started. You are a resident, I presume?"

"My last name's Soto," she said. "Look it up."

She strode past him. I followed in her furious wake, offered an embarrassed nod of apology for the girl's treatment. He scowled at me. Next, Layla approached the front desk.

"And who are you?" she asked of the seated portly man behind it.

He stood and offered a hand. "Miss Soto, it's a pleasure to meet you. I'm Dennis."

She ignored his outstretched arm. "Change of management around here?" she asked.

"That time of year," he said with all forced pleasantry. "Some of the regulars are taking their vacations."

"Right, whatever."

Again, I tried a sympathetic smile on the scolded help, and again he glared at me. I was presumed a rich asshole by association; I would have done the same. As we waited at the elevator, Layla glanced back at the two strangers now watching over the entrance to her home.

"Vacation, my ass," she muttered. "They're cleaning house."

Chapter 5

The apartment was on the top floor, the ninety-sixth. The ride up took about forty seconds. I was informed that it was the fastest elevator on earth. My ears popped about halfway through. I tried to imagine the disorientation of traveling such heights, at such speeds, every time you arrived or left home. Taking a dog out to piss would be a daily adventure in time and space travel. It was like crossing into another realm. Sealed off above the concerns of mortals, whisked into the clouds, onto floors that must have swayed in the wind. I wondered if the Sotos could feel their home shift in severe weather. I doubted it. Life in these parts was engineered to feel as little of the outside world as possible.

The elevator doors opened onto a grand gallery. There was a mix of Asian art and antiques, alongside some masters of the West. I recognized a Singer Sargent, a Rossetti, even a Vermeer. My estimation of Danny Soto rose. I hoped to find him if only to have a conversation about his collection. I walked to the Vermeer and admired it.

"My dad's big into the old stuff," said Layla.

Sometimes even the most advanced teenagers show their age.

"Impressive," I said, and meant it.

There was much to envy about the Sotos' lives—their multiple homes, their means of travel—but the pieces hanging before me, those I coveted. They were timeless and priceless. The exercise of assigning a dollar amount was beside the point. To paraphrase Dylan, they put infinity up on trial. I was shaken from my arty reverie by the music coming from the living room.

I found her seated at a Steinway grand piano in the center of the room, tickling the keys. Her wrists aligned with her forearms as her fingers moved lightly with grace. I listened to the sounds she made, stopped before a cubed window at least ten-feet square and regarded the view below. The combination of sights and sounds felt holy. Beneath us, Uptown Manhattan stretched out with the preserved nature of Central Park unfurled. From this vantage the city looked reduced, humbled. It must have satisfied a billionaire's lust to conquer in a way that few things could.

As she paused, I asked, "Is that . . . ?"

"Rachmaninoff," she said. "Like you knew. He used to play in the concert hall next door, on these same pianos."

"Michael's taught you well. I assume that's who you were with the night your dad was taken?"

Layla dropped her hands from the keys into her lap. "It was, and so what? You shouldn't listen to my mother. She's just jealous of his attention. He's my teacher, but he's not a perv."

"He here often?"

"Usually three days a week, except I canceled on him yesterday. He's probably wondering what's going on."

"He know about your dad?"

She regarded me across the piano's black, winged expanse. "No one knows, and no one will," she said. "Except my mom, you, and maybe your partner, if she agrees to help us."

"You mind if I have a look around?" I asked.

She waved a hand around the space and went back to the keys.

I walked down the gallery, resisted the urge to stop and gawk at more art. The first room I entered was a formal dining room with a long, sleek table assembled for sixteen. A Japanese landscape painting dominated the wall. I moved on to a far-flung kitchen, with its islands of white marble and appliances by Gaggenau, including a steam oven. I remembered Stevie's mom, Juliette Cohen, insisting that they were essential these days. Anyone with any culinary taste had one. There was not a spec on any surface. I reminded myself to ask Layla how often the housekeeper—or keepers—came. I took a peek inside a palatial pantry. Stocked healthy, no junk food or soda in sight. The views from their kitchen looked west, out to the Hudson and Jersey beyond.

Next came a darkly furnished office library. Walls of floor-to-ceiling bookshelves, a wide oak desk, a couple club chairs, another absurd view. Inspecting Danny Soto's bookshelves left me less impressed than his taste in art. He appeared to be incurious of fiction. There were tomes of financial treatises and investment wisdoms, volumes of securities nonsense, the only interesting section being a few shelves devoted to narrative nonfiction, all finance-oriented. Michael Lewis, James B. Stewart, and the like. The drawers beneath his desk were all sealed with good strong locks, not pick-able without time and tools. In the closet, a few dinner jackets, a dry-cleaned tux, a safe secured to the floor. I could spot no small cameras or faint red recording lights, but I had the distinct feeling of being watched. Whoever took him may have planted spyware across the apartment. Someone might be watching me on a closed circuit as I snooped. My face would be run through databases, tracked, and investigated. A positive ID wouldn't take long.

The master quarters took up the southwest corner of the apartment. Off the bedroom, separate his and hers sections branched out. In his, a reading lounge stocked with a full bar; a mahogany walk-in closet; and a dark stoned, manly bath. For her: a dressing area big enough for a wedding party, an even larger walk-in stocked with enough shoes to impress the wife of a Filipino dictator, and a bathroom of richly veined marble. The centerpiece was a freestanding tub placed before the high cubed window. It looked carved from a single slab of quartz. No, the rich were not like you or me. If your daily bathing experience took place inside a tub like that, before that view, one could not possibly remain grounded in any semblance of reality.

I remembered Layla's comment about her mother's pill habit and went to her medicine cabinets. Opened one and was treated to a collection that would make a drugstore cowboy hoot and holler with junkie joy. Along multiple shelves there was a cornucopia of orange pill bottles. I began checking the labels. All the greatest hits, and some I'd never heard of. I listened for the sounds of the piano coming from the living room, not wanting to get caught ogling the stash. She could really play. Rachmaninoff— like I knew.

Back to the orange bottles, with the soundtrack pouring from the Steinway, I hesitated. I realized I wasn't living clean with my regular intake of weed and Xanax, but compared to the Duckman's past appetites, it was progress. Yet now here I was, presented with a virtual pharmacy of a rich woman's pills, ones she would never miss. There must have been an equal stash out east at their beach house.

I stared at the lineup, ran my fingers along the childproof tops. Adderall and Klonopin, Xanax and Ambien. *"One pill makes you larger and one pill makes you small . . ."* Feed your head indeed. She could have all those. What I really lusted after was a few of her tasty pain pills. I discovered a bottle of my old favorites, the Vicodin, and tapped out a handful. The thick white pills felt familiar in my palm. I could already anticipate their warmth as the high came on. But Layla said her mother was into the stronger stuff, the OxyContin. Those were reserved for the top shelf, and they didn't come from any pharmacy. Two orange bottles were listed as alprazolam, aka Xanax, the writing faded with age, the scripts long since filled and taken. Now they held something else. I opened one and peered in, recognized the pink Oxies. Eyeballed about fifty in each bottle. Nicole Soto was falling down a very slick slope. Taking a few, say ten, would almost be a public service.

The addict's brain is a delicate thing. We can learn to stop hunting, or to limit our appetites, but when we happen upon a bounty, well, what's a man to do?

He's supposed to return those pills where he found them. Close the medicine cabinet. Walk away. Save those mind-melters for someone else's issues.

Did I do that? Like hell.

I didn't swallow any though. Not yet. I was still telling myself I'd just hang on to them, for . . . whenever. It wasn't the first time I'd looted pain pills on a case, and the previous time ended rather badly. I was the old definition of insanity—doing the same damn thing and somehow expecting a different result. I pushed away such rationality, resumed my search of the apartment.

The kids' bedrooms were down another long hall lined with Venetian wallpaper and antique sconces. Not much family photography on display in chez Soto, or maybe it was off in some other wing. The apartment, like its windows, was a very large cube, about one hundred feet per side. I tried to imagine what it would look like on land, a sprawling square ranch house, with windows tall as trees, a big white aquarium of wealth. But up here they were high enough for no one to peer in. Perhaps when the other supertalls were completed, other rarified neighbors would be able to spy on one another across the clouds, though most of these apartments were used so infrequently I doubted peeping would be a problem. Aside from drones, and perhaps a rather conspicuous hovering helicopter, the top-floor Soto apartment appeared to be the most private glass house on earth.

Both Layla and her brother's rooms were immaculate, both bigger than my apartment, with their own foyers and full baths and dressing rooms. Between their bedrooms was another family room, a lounge for the young folks, stocked with every gadget and video game a kid could desire. Two more guest bedrooms completed the lap, and then the sounds of the piano grew louder once more. I estimated the apartment was somewhere close to ten thousand square feet, but it felt well laid out for family. As much as I wanted to rant at its tackiness and over-the-top displays of poor rich taste, I had to acknowledge its style. Danny and Nicole Soto had built a home up here in the clouds.

Returning to the living room, I spotted a red canvas bag on the coffee table. It hadn't been there when we entered, and I didn't think I heard Layla stop playing, but somehow it had appeared. I went to it, picked it up, and peered in. I felt Layla watching as she played a concerto. Inside the bag were a half dozen cell phones, cheap flip ones. Beneath them, bound stacks of hundred-dollar bills. I thumbed through one, guessed about fifty in each. I counted a dozen total, sixty grand. The music paused, and I glanced up.

"I added another ten for expenses," said Layla. "Remember, pay for everything in cash."

"Thanks," I said.

"From now on we only use those burners to talk. No more calls or texts from your cell, okay?"

"You watch too much TV."

"I watch none at all," she said. "But I know smart-phones are super easy to hack. My dad told me always to act like every email, call, and text is public. There's no pri-vacy on those things, didn't you know that?"

"Sure, Big Brother's always watching, I got it."

"I don't think you do. If you're a nobody, nobody's gonna be watching, but if you live like this"—she waved her hand around her home—"you can bet people are try-ing to listen in on everything you say."

"Like father, like daughter," I said.

She liked that. Her spine seemed to straighten at the comparison.

"Have a good look around?" she asked.

"Beautiful home you've got here."

"You check out my mom's bathroom?"

"That's quite a tub."

She made a face. "I meant the medicine cabinet. See what I told you?"

I resisted a glance down at my bulging pocket. Tried to meet her gaze without guilt.

"Appears your mom has a few ailments," I offered.

"Ha. You're funny, Duck." She stood, placed her hands on her hips, and tilted her head like a curious pup. "You wouldn't take any, would you?" she asked.

"I'm living clean these days," I lied.

She laughed. "I don't believe you. But I don't care either. C'mon, I'll show you the rest of the building. The ameni-ties and common areas are awesome, better than any hotel in the world, and we've stayed in pretty much all the great ones."

The elevator whisked us back down. I wanted to try the boyhood move of jumping as it descended to feel that extra sensation of falling, but at these speeds I figured I might break an ankle on the landing. We got off on the fourth floor, which contained private meeting rooms, a screening room, a billiards and bar room, along with a restaurant-sized kitchen and a formal dining room.

"This floor is for, like, when you want to entertain but don't want people in your own space, you know?"

I nodded like I did.

"There's a full-time chef and bartender and assistants to reserve the movie room and the meeting rooms," she said, walking me through the space like a hotel concierge. She stopped in front of the theater, big enough to screen a film for twenty of your closest friends. "I had my b-day here last year. We got the latest Christopher Nolan movie before it came out." She shrugged like this was a standard seventeen-year-old's birthday. "It's weird, I think we're the only people in the building who even use this floor. I've never seen anyone else down here."

"I've read that most apartments in these places aren't occupied. Most owners are foreign, right?"

"Yeah, we have no idea who our neighbors are. Maybe my dad does, but we don't. Nobody's ever around. It's like our own private palace. Except this one time, when I saw a bunch of women getting out of cars and rushing through the lobby. They looked like prostitutes, super skinny, tons of makeup, and barely wearing anything. A few older Middle Eastern guys were making them hurry and pressing the elevator button over and over. It was classic. I took a seat in the lobby and laughed with Sammy, the doorman. He was cool. I wonder what happened to him. Do you think he could have been involved?"

"Was he working the night your dad was taken?" I asked. "I mean, did you see him when you got home later?"

She thought about it for a moment. "No, now that I

think of it, there was nobody at the desk. I was . . . I had a little bit to drink . . . so I wasn't really paying attention, I guess."

"He might have been paid to make himself scarce for a while," I said. "I'd like to talk to him, if you can help me reach him?"

"Sure, I can ask."

"Anything else in the building you'd like to show me?"

"Want to see the pool?" she asked. "It's pretty sick."

It was indeed. One floor below the meeting rooms and the theater and bar and dining room, there was the health center, complete with massage rooms, hair and nail salon, gym, and across the entire southern exposure, a twenty-five–yard three-lane lap pool. Like the rest of the shared spaces, it was empty. I knew there had to be staff on call at all times, but we had yet to run into anyone.

"I assume people work here?" I asked. "Even when no one is using this stuff?"

"Oh, they're around. They're always watching, waiting to see if you need help with anything, but you're not supposed to see them." She slipped her foot from her sandal and dipped her toes in the water and swirled them around. I watched the ripples, longing to leap in and disrupt the vacant tranquility.

"It's gotta be the easiest job on earth, working here," I said.

"So boring though, right? I'd be so bored. And none of the building staff is allowed to look at their phones. That's a rule. They have to turn them in when they get to work."

"Says who?"

"The building manager, this guy Bill Willis. You don't see him much either, but he's the main guy in charge, I think."

"You mind introducing me?"

"Sure," she said, shaking off a wet foot. "C'mon. His office is off the lobby. Let's see if he's there."

I followed her back to the elevators, scanning around every corner, peering into every room, wondering if I could catch sight of another human soul. Layla seemed unconcerned by the gaping emptiness. The entire building must have been almost a million square feet, the size of a village, one with schools and churches and homes full of life. Yet here, in the center of Manhattan, at the center of the world, it seemed Layla Soto was the sole inhabitant, at the top of this soaring tower.

Chapter 6

On our way to find Bill Willis, we stopped by the front desk. The new concierge smiled at Layla and avoided my eyes. He was a rotund little guy so used to plastering on fake cheer that there was no longer any way to distinguish the sincere.

"That was a quick visit home," he said. "Headed back out into this heat?"

"My comings and goings aren't any of your business," she said.

"I only meant . . . that it's so uncomfortable out there today."

Layla crossed her arms. Her eyes narrowed; her mouth tightened. I recalled those children's books about the bratty Eloise in the Plaza Hotel. Dennis averted his eyes.

"I need Sammy's number," she said. "I know he's on vacation, but I need to talk to him."

"I'm afraid I don't . . . I'll have to ask Mr. Willis."

"You do that. Actually, never mind, I'll ask him myself."

She strode off, leaving Dennis stammering and me trying to catch up. As we turned the corner, out of sight, she glanced back at me and grinned.

"I'm not usually such a bitch," she said. "I'm actually

friends with some of the staff. I just want these new guys to be scared of me." She stopped at an unmarked door and knocked. "Let me talk," she said.

After a moment of shuffling inside, the door opened, and in the frame stood a large ruddy-faced man in a sloppy suit. He emanated that unmistakable cop stench. He frowned at me and beamed at Layla in one seamless expression.

"Miss Soto," he said, "how nice to see you! What can I do for you?"

He looked early fifties, with the years starting to reel. Found a safer, more lucrative career after serving his twenty with the NYPD. He looked back at me, tried and failed to maintain his smile.

"Bill Willis," he said, extending a meaty hand. "And you are?"

"Duck Darley," I said, shaking it. I kept hold while he tried to place the name. I was notorious enough within the department; it didn't take long.

"Death Darley," he said, "I'll be damned. What brings you to our beautiful building?"

"Doing a bit of work for this young lady," I said.

"My mom hired him, technically," said Layla.

"Doing what, may I ask?"

We stood at the threshold, not being invited in. Over his shoulder there was a high panel of screens recording every common area in the building. Each glowed with empty images from different corners. Folks may have valued their privacy inside their apartments, but beyond their front doors, security was the priority. Big Brother was welcome. I thought of the video of Danny Soto being wheeled out. Bill Willis, or whoever worked the night shift, would have seen it, or would have been paid not to. Someone had hacked into the system. Perhaps they had help on the inside.

"That's quite a setup you've got there," I said, peering past him.

"Our residents are important people," he said. "Safety is paramount."

"I'll bet."

He held my eyes for a beat, then looked down at Soto's daughter. "So, Layla, what can I do for you?"

"There's this guy . . . at school," she said, "who won't, like, leave me alone? And our dads sort of work together, which makes it kind of awkward. Duck's helping the problem go away."

"He has been known to do that," said Willis. "He's been known to cause a few problems too, I hear." He looked to me. "I used to work with Detective Lea Miller, years ago. Friend of yours, right?"

"She is," I said. "Might be the only cop with nice things to say about me."

"No accounting for a lady's taste."

I waited for Layla to continue her lie.

"So, this boy, Kyle," she said, "he's been hanging out by the building, waiting for me. I wanted to ask Sammy to keep an eye out, but he's not here today. Do you think I could get his number from you?"

"A boy giving you problems? I'm sure we can help you with that."

"So, give me Sammy's contact, okay?"

"Layla," said Willis like a cringing uncle. "I'm sorry to be the one to tell you this, but Sammy no longer works with our building. I know you two were buddies, but it just didn't work out."

"How did it not work out?" she asked.

"It was an internal matter."

"What if my dad wants to hire him back?"

"Then I'll be happy to speak with your father about it," he said. "I'm confident he'll understand our decision."

"Your new guy out there told us he was on vacation," I said.

They both glanced at me, neither welcoming the intrusion.

"Layla, do you have a picture of this boy—Kyle, was his name? I'll be happy to share it with our staff and make sure he stays away. I assume Richard Gross is also helping you with this matter?"

"Richard has better things to do," she said. "He works for my father. That's why I got the B-team." She raised her chin in my direction, gave a smirk.

Willis returned it. It was the first time he seemed to relax since opening the door. Layla was quick to seize the advantage.

"And what about that dude behind the desk?" she asked. "He was pretty rude. I don't think my mom's gonna like that."

"A recent hire too. I'm sure you'll like him."

"What's with the housecleaning? Anyone else I should know about? As you know, my brother's pretty sensitive to change. He might get upset when he sees all these new faces."

"I'll be in touch with your mother about it. We'll make sure Lionel is comfortable when he returns."

"Right. Anyway, what's Sammy's number?"

"I'm sorry, Layla, I can't give it to you."

I thought she might lose it in a self-righteous tantrum. I couldn't be sure how much was an act and how much was authentic spoiled-rich-girl. The bit about Kyle at school— that was inspired. The line about my being the B-team— that must have been part of the show too.

Layla turned and stormed off, leaving Bill Willis frowning at me.

"Good luck with your case," he said. He stepped back and closed the door in my face.

*   *   *

I found her pacing the wide circular drive in front of the tower. She was swearing under her breath and kicking the pavement like a scolded child. The humidity was cracking, the sky darkening. The barometer plunged, the wind picked up. Storm clouds moved in from the east. We needed a good fierce soaking to sweep away this heat. It would return stickier than ever by evening, but a summer storm is always welcome.

"Kyle?" I asked. "You might have prepped me on your little ruse."

"Whatever, it was the first thing to come to mind."

"What happens when Willis gives your mother a ring and follows up?"

"Like I care."

"Layla . . ."

"What? It's true. There *is* a kid named Kyle in my class and he won't leave me alone. If Bill Willis wants to pretend he's still a cop he can go ahead. At a party last month Kyle grabbed my hand and shoved it down his pants. I hope Willis sends over some off-duty buddies to kick his ass."

If you must lie, always base it in a foundation of truth. The girl had that part down.

"Any idea who works nights in that surveillance room?" I asked.

"No clue."

"Whoever it was would have seen your father being rolled out," I said. "Your building's security must have been hacked. Maybe they had help. Maybe staff was paid to make themselves scarce. I'd like to learn more about this Willis."

"Do what you gotta do," she said. "If he's involved, we'll ruin his life."

I felt a heavy drop hit my head. We looked up together

as the sky went black. The top floors of her building disappeared in storm clouds. A gust of wind swept through
the street, her dark hair whipped across her face. She
wiped it away, moved back toward the awning over the
entrance. Thunder rolled overhead, lightning crackled.

"It's gonna pour," she said. "You wanna come back inside?"

I tapped the red canvas bag over my shoulder. "Gotta
get to work," I said. "You're not paying me to wait out the
rain."

That earned a smile. "Check in later, okay?"

I nodded, moved to go.

"On one of the phones in the bag," she called. "Don't
forget!"

I tapped the bag, offered a thumbs-up and a wink, felt
like a hopeless tool as she rolled her eyes and ran back in.
The rain arrived like a passing plague. I raced across 56th
Street for the cover of scaffolding. Twenty feet in ten seconds and I was soaked. Umbrellas popped open across
sidewalks. Those without cursed and sought cover. Traffic
slowed to a stop as visibility was washed to zero. Anything
that slows the pace of this place is met with virulent agitation. I was joined beneath the scaffolding by fellow panting,
wet souls. No one made eye contact or cared to connect in
this sudden forced pause to our mad lives. Everyone jostled
for space and slipped out phones, cursing the disruption.

I felt a poke in the back as someone tried to lower a
large golf umbrella under the cover. Others grumbled as he
pressed through the crowd, hurrying past, more concerned
with his destination than respecting any personal space. A
woman next to me snarled *Watch it, asshole*, but the suit
didn't turn or offer any apology. There was money to be
made in some tower nearby. The markets did not wait for
the weather.

After fifteen minutes I thought about running back across the street and taking that bullet elevator back up to the Sotos'. I wondered what the view was like from the ninety-sixth floor during a storm like this. Was it all darkness? Was it high enough that she could look down on the rain, above the clouds? What happened when a tower like that was struck by lightning? It must happen.

I might have gone over to ask if not for the arm that was suddenly around my shoulders and the hard barrel I felt pressed against my ribs. When I resisted, the arm squeezed tighter; the gun probed. I turned to meet the eyes of an unsmiling gentleman. I took his measure, didn't like what I found. Never trust a man who chooses to keep his hair buzzed in a crew cut. It's a look for prison wardens and drill sergeants, a sign of sadists, or men with political ambitions.

"Don't make a move," he said.

"In this weather? Don't worry about it."

The nose of his gun found its way between two ribs, about six inches from my heart. One nervous jerk and I was a dead man. I reminded my body to relax, let my shoulders deflate. Remember the aikido, especially in moments of certain defeat. Show the aggressor that further aggression is pointless. I glanced around, but no one in the crowd appeared to notice this holdup in close quarters. They were all too immersed in their phones.

He was a big guy, iron-pumping strong, with wide feet in running shoes; wide thighs in cargo shorts; wide chest in a stretched black t-shirt. There was a barbed-wire tattoo around his right forearm, about a foot from the gun. He had the kind of intense face that did not process doubt. Yep, Marines all the way . . .

"Relax, Richie," I said. "No need to be a dick."

My casual ID caught him up. His position shifted, rattled by surprise. I was lucky he didn't squeeze the trigger. Before he could stammer, I said, "I get it. Your boss is missing. You saw me with the daughter. You're worried you've lost control of the situation. And you have, Richard Gross."

"Okay, smart guy, who the fuck are you?"

"I'm Duck," I said. "Before you shoot me, maybe you can buy me a cup of coffee?"

He led me to a diner over on Lex, walked behind me as I found a booth in the back. The rain let up a bit on our walk, but we were still drenched. The waitress came over with menus and a giant stack of napkins, laughed, and said, "I'll give you boys a minute to dry off. Know what you'd like to drink?"

"Coffee," I said. "Black. And a water."

Richard ignored her. As she walked away I took silent pride in not calling *And a Beck's too!*

"You know," I said, "they say spots like this are endangered."

His arm shifted beneath the table. His biceps flexed. I could sense the gun pointed at my crotch. I crossed my legs.

"Seriously," I said. "You should check out this book, *Vanishing New York?* It's like an elegy for places like this. The real Manhattan, you know? Greasy spoons, bodegas, all the little mom-and-pop businesses that give this city character, they're all—"

"Shut up," he said. "Shut the fuck up."

I did. Waited for his speech.

"What's your name?" he asked.

"I told you, Duck—"

"Your actual name, fuck head."

"Darley."

"First name?"

"D . . . Lawrence. Lawrence Darley Jr. Now what can I do for you, Mr. Richard Gross, Recon Marine, employee of Daniel Soto?"

Again, the fidget at the imbalance of knowledge. He didn't look too bright, but his time as a high-performance solider had taught him that intel was everything. Always have more data than your adversary. Process that and you just might survive.

"Okay, Darley, now you can tell me what you were doing with Layla Soto."

"Sorry, Richie, need-to-know basis, and you don't have clearance."

"You want me to shoot you in the balls right here?"

"Not really. But I know you won't, so I'm not gonna worry about it."

I heard the gun cock beneath the table. Rolled my eyes.

"Shoot an unarmed man in a diner? Please. There's not even a silencer on that thing, and even if there was, silencers are a lot louder than in the movies. You touch that trigger and you're not getting out of here without a murder charge. Maybe attempted murder, if I'm lucky and you only turn me into a eunuch."

"Listen, you—"

"No, you listen, Richie. I'm told you were quite the warrior—before you took the money and became a glorified rent-a-cop. I'll assume you haven't gone that soft, but your boss has disappeared on your watch, and that makes you either a failure, or complicit in the crime. Either way, you can piss off."

I gave him my smuggest smile and crossed my arms.

"Where's Danny?" he asked.

"You tell me."

"You want me to take you somewhere else and torture it out of you?"

"Sure," I said. "I know a good dungeon. Want me to make an appointment?"

"What were you doing with Layla Soto?"

"I work for her. But like I said, you don't have clearance."

He pounded the table with his free fist just as the waitress returned with my coffee and water. She frowned at him. "Can't have any scenes here, big boy," she said. "Any more outbursts and I'm gonna have to ask you to leave."

"He's just having a bad day," I offered.

She eyed me, pulled out her pad, asked what we'd like to eat.

"A tuna melt would be lovely," I said. "How about you, Richie?"

He gave her a hard look and said, "Some privacy."

She retreated with a shaking head, went over to another server to gripe about the rude bastard in the back.

"Sure you're not hungry?" I asked. "You don't look so good."

"Listen, asshole . . ."

But before he could complete his insult his face went pale. Sweat leapt from his skin. His shoulders hunched like he was about to puke. His arm began to shake and rattle the tabletop. His body seized in on itself as a wave of pain coursed through him.

"Stay here," he gasped.

Then he lurched out of the booth and raced toward the bathroom.

As soon as the men's room door closed, I tossed a twenty on the table, slid from my seat, and got out of there.

I didn't look back as I weaved past pedestrians on Lexington. The rain was light now and the sidewalks steamed. The humidity was about to be horrific. There were no lit cabs in sight, but the 59th Street subway was close. If I could get down there and board a train in any direction, I'd be clear. For a hardcore Recon Marine, that was a weak display. He couldn't control a little bout of stomach flu in the midst of an interrogation? Maybe he had gone soft working for the Sotos. Something felt off, but as I swiped my card and pushed through the turnstile I was feeling pretty proud of my escape.

As I hit the platform I heard the rumbling of an approaching train. I boarded an express 4 headed south, moved to the center of a crowded car, and kept my head down. The doors closed; the train moved out and picked up speed in the dark tunnel beneath the streets. I took out my phone, discovered a waiting text. It was from Cass.

Chapter 7

Good to hear from you, it read. **Can you come to the Beekman? Working there now . . .**

It took me a moment to place it. The Beekman—one of the newer, hipper hotels in the increasingly cool canyons of lower Manhattan. I had cocktails at the bar once with Juliette Cohen. A stylish place, in one of the city's original skyscrapers, I remembered a towering atrium and plush seating and high levels of attractiveness. The martinis were something like thirty bucks apiece. My ex had picked up the bill. What was Cass doing working at a spot like that?

I composed my reply with care. Where to begin? *Let's forget all your lies and betrayal . . . I have a new case, need your help . . . Carrying sixty grand cash and a few burner phones . . . Our boss is a seventeen-year-old ice princess . . . Her billionaire dad is missing . . . Oh, and I just escaped a Recon Marine who was holding me at gunpoint in a diner . . . Can't wait to see you too!*

Better to save all that for the in-person reunion. I fired off a short reply: **See you soon.**

At the Union Square station, the subway car filled to capacity with damp, sweaty New Yorkers, pressed and resigned together like cattle. Somewhere between 14th Street and City Hall the train stalled, "due to train traffic ahead of us." Riders groaned, tapped at their phones, wiped at their brows. The AC in the car was hopeless, too many agitated, perspiring bodies. I looked into the annoyed faces, looked away anytime someone caught my eye. I wondered what made me mention that book, *Vanishing New York*, during my encounter with Richie Gross. I'd picked it up recently but found it too depressing to complete. It was a blog-turned-tome that detailed all the ways that Manhattan was no longer what it had been. As if that didn't happen every decade for the last, oh, four hundred years . . . But evidently this time was different. The author claimed that the soul of the city had been stripped away in the early years of the twenty-first century—and he was there to document every small business or old-school restaurant that closed, only to be replaced by bank branches or pharmacies or Starbucks.

Fair enough, it was a tragic condition of the city in recent years. For all the safety and wealth and grand ideals that defined Mayor Bloomberg's term, he failed to consider how the great majority of Manhattanites could afford to remain here. It wasn't just the businesses that lined the avenues. We were all being priced out. I was lucky enough to be clinging to a rent-controlled apartment in a nice part of town, but how long would that last?

Perhaps that explained the flood of television shows and books that glorified the seventies in the city. It was a time when things were dirty and dangerous, cheap and cool. The human desperation for the old ways and days when things were more authentic . . . Everyone's forever looking back over his shoulder, convinced that back then, things were different. Everyone wants to close the door the moment he gets in, and then bitch about the price of drinks when he finally gets to the bar. Alas, complaining was sport in this city, naïve nostalgia a form of therapy. That would never vanish.

The train rumbled back into gear. I got off at City Hall and climbed the steps to Centre Street, not sure what was sweat and what part of me was still wet from the rain. I took a moment to appreciate the tall tiled arches. It was well established that the New York subway system was a disgrace when compared to any other major metropolis, but this station—the first ever in the city—was still something to behold. I admired the Woolworth Building across the way, still the single greatest piece of American architecture, and walked south along the edge of the park.

This place—sweaty and crowded and depressingly expensive, but where else were we supposed to live?

The Beekman was a short walk down Park Row, at the bottom of City Hall Park. In the nineteenth century, this stretch housed every major newspaper in town, back when there were dozens of dailies. An entire district for print media—vanishing New York, indeed.

I moved through the lobby doors and was greeted by an attractive hostess behind a stand. She looked at my small red tote bag, didn't take me for a hotel guest.

"Welcome to Temple Bar," she said.

"Does Cassandra Kimball work here?" I asked.

She gave me a confused look. "I'm not sure, I just started. Does she . . ."

I scanned past her to the bar. Cass was standing behind it wielding a stainless-steel martini shaker. She didn't see me as I approached. There was a row of empty green bar chairs; I took the one farthest from her. I'd wait for her to notice me. Overpriced or not, the space was impressive. Period perfect, the bar floor was bathed in light beneath the high atrium. Wrought-iron railings circled the floors above. A few couches were filled with creative types, dressed expensively casual, permitting themselves a cocktail during business hours. A few sat solo, tapping at laptops. Not a bad office.

I watched as Cass poured out a martini and served it to a bearded guy at the opposite end of the bar. He stared at her without shame. She pretended not to notice, offered a professional smile before she retreated. Then she turned to face me. Hands clasped, I smiled, gave her a nod. I tried to quiet the thundering in my chest.

"Well, well," she said as she arrived.

"Hello there."

We leaned over the bar, gave each other a tentative hug, a brushed kiss on the cheek. She smelled just like I remembered, like bottled sex.

"What can I get you?" she asked.

"Just a sparkling water, if you please."

She gave me a questioning look.

"That's right, on the wagon. Weed-only wagon, but still."

Her eyes went wide. "I'm impressed. Good for you, Duck."

"Been a few months now. Feeling good."

"You look great. Really. I can tell."

"We'll see how long it lasts." I waved a hand around the room. "How long you been doing . . . this?"

She shrugged. "Couple months? I couldn't go back to the dungeon. Not after all that. A friend helped me get this gig. It's been okay."

"The tips must be good."

"Yeah, well, not like before." She tried a laugh, glanced away. "Though, I guess the work was a little more . . . challenging."

"Were you surprised to hear from me?"

"Not really."

"Oh?"

"I knew you'd be back in touch at some point, when you were ready." She made eye contact. Her mouth turned down. "Listen, Duck, I'm sorry. About all—"

"I wouldn't be here if I didn't forgive you."

Her shoulders relaxed a bit. She straightened up, wiped a strand of black hair behind her ear. Her cheekbones were high as ever; her wide dark eyes looked weary. The hotel bar uniform didn't suit her—black slacks, black vest, white button-down—but Cass could pull off any look, except perhaps an orange prison jumpsuit.

"So, if I can't get you a drink, what can I do for you?"

"Feel like getting back to work?" I asked. "I'm on a case. I could use your help."

She peered over her shoulder. Another bartender was eyeing her, wondering when she'd get back to pouring drinks. "I don't know, Duck . . ."

"Don't tell me you don't miss it."

"It's not that . . ."

"I mean, I know how stimulating this must be."

"Stimulating is exactly what I'm trying to get away from."

"For how long?" I asked.

"Don't do this."

I looked around. There was no one seated close. We were out of earshot, but I still lowered my voice and leaned in. "A name—Danny Soto. Remember him? He was Charlie McKay's boss. A billionaire. He was abducted, taken from his home on Billionaires' Row in Midtown. Wait till you see the place, I just came from there. It's his daughter we're working for. I just shook their head of security, this ex-Marine Richard Gross, total wuss, but anyway . . ."

"You mean *you're* working for."

"C'mon, Cass." I almost added *You owe me*, but let that hang unspoken.

"I need to get back to work," she said. "I'll be back with your sparkling water. Want anything to eat?"

"I'll take a look at a menu."

She reached beneath her and produced one. "Try the steak tartar."

"If you say so."

She retreated, went and said something to her fellow bartender, a tatted-up hipster who clearly had the hots for her. He spoke too close, placed an unnecessary hand on her shoulder. I still felt some absurd sense of protectiveness. *Get your hands off my partner, tough guy. You have any idea what we've been through together?* Yep, still as pathetically possessive as ever. The platonic sap never stops pining.

I flipped through the menu, read the cocktail list with a lust like it was dirty talk. They were named after New Yorkers long dead, *Architects & Builders* read the top of the page. Never heard of them, but they must have haunted these parts. The Eugene Kelly and the John Frazee—they must have liked their aged rum. The James M. Farnsworth and the Sir Marc Isambard Brunel— whiskey men; the John McComb—must have been a cognac connoisseur. Ah, gentlemen, how I would like to join you right now.

And I almost did. The salivating booze-longing was too intense, the weight of the moment, my reunion with Cass, it demanded a drink—I even looked forward to her disappointed, pitying look when I succumbed and started swallowing them down. But before she could bring my tartar, before I could choose my first of many cocktails to come and rejoice in my old habits, I was subjected to the most vicious and terrifying feeling of my life. I've been shot and tortured and beaten unconscious, but in the moments that followed I have never been more certain of death.

I felt my face break out in icy sweat, my heart raced, my limbs went heavy, my stomach turned. Pain coursed through my back, up my spine, and into my organs unlike anything I've ever experienced. I gripped the bar, tried to stand and move toward the men's room. I remembered Richard Gross had the same symptoms not an hour earlier. I got to my feet, didn't make it three paces until I was projectile vomiting all over the tiled floor. I heard Cass cry out. I tried to swing around and beg her for help. My vision blurred. The pain intensified. It felt as though my insides were seizing and shriveling. My brain was sending out unanswered distress signals. I collapsed in a puddle of my own puke. From the ground, in what I was sure was my last sight, I saw Cass as she rushed toward me.

Chapter 8

Memories from a coma ... Visions and sensations of helpless terror. Nightmare seascapes, tossing beneath black ocean, sinking deeper. The feeling of endless free fall, like a roller coaster without end. I wish I could report some comforting light, but alas, there was only darkness and paralyzed panic.

And then, surfacing. Emerging from a coma is like swimming up from the depths. Those lunatics who practice "free diving," the ones who dive straight down into holes in the ocean, hundreds of feet on a single breath, perhaps they experience a similar edge-of-life delirium on the way up.

With a groggy gasp, I came back to the land of the living. My first bewildered response: I started to weep. It was involuntary. My eyes filled with salty tears and they poured down my face. That black sea I was under came pouring out of my core.

Nurses came rushing in as my vital signs sparked. The room was a blur of antiseptic whiteness, and at the foot of the bed, there she was. Looking at me with that detached expectant gaze, like she knew I'd wake any moment. She stood, went to my bedside, and took my hand.

"Duck. Do you hear me? I'm here."

"Cass."

"My God, you're awake."

Her voice cracked. I tried to turn, tried to squeeze her hand tighter. I couldn't tell if my head was still connected to the rest of my body.

More medical staff appeared. A commotion of relief, expressions of faith, doctors were summoned. I tried to muster some clarity. Tried to see through the tears. The effort left me feeling like I was about to fall back into coma. I stopped trying and let go. Remembered the aikido. Reminded myself to accept the energy, not to fight it. After minutes or hours, I was blinking myself into something resembling conscious thought.

"Are you there?" they kept asking. "Stay with me." As if I had anywhere else I could go . . .

Through it all Cass held my hand and anchored me back to life. It was some time before I learned what happened—a hypothesis of what happened, in any case. No one knew the details. It had been a week.

I'd been poisoned.

Richard Gross was dead.

Someone infected us. They reached him first. Inside the diner restroom, while I ran away, the response wasn't as quick. He died inside that dirty little room, undiscovered until another diner tired of pounding on the door and sought out the waitress. The poison reached my system at a more opportune moment, with Cass nearby, and the staff of a swank hotel on hand. NewYork-Presbyterian on William Street was nearby. I was a best-case scenario.

But that didn't mean I was going to make it. I learned I had received massive blood transfusions. My brain swelled. My kidneys failed. My limbs turned blue. Inspecting them, they were still a faint bruised color. For a few days the doctors weren't sure if I'd regain brain activity. I was almost declared a vegetable. Since I had no one to determine whether it was my wish to turn off the machines, I was doomed to languish in that falling state forevermore. Cass knew I wouldn't want that, but she had no say in the matter. No family either—it's not like my father could make the call while he rotted away in prison, not having seen his son in a couple decades.

Somehow, for some reason, my body kept fighting. *Is he a fighter?* So went the cliché. Well yes, based on prior life experience, he is. But he's also been known to contemplate suicidal tendencies. He's been diagnosed with PTSD. He's a convicted felon. His life hasn't been . . . easy. No shame in his subconscious deciding that it was time to shut things down. Closed for business, on to the next realm, but not yet. When the apocalypse comes they say there'll be the cockroaches and Keith Richards left. Don't forget the Duckman.

When they were convinced my eyes would stay open, the nurses left me alone with Cass. She eyed me with a look I didn't quite recognize. Unsure if it was too soon to lay it on me. Then she smiled to herself, reached out her arm, and opened her palm. There were a handful of pills. I didn't recognize them at first.

"So much for the weed-only wagon," she said.

"Whose are those?"

Then I remembered—Nicole Soto's medicine cabinet. Not the first time Cass had busted me for pilfering pills on a case.

"Cass . . ."

"Relax, it doesn't matter. I'm just glad I found them and not someone else."

"It does matter. I never took any. I grabbed them from . . ."

"Duck, stop."

"I need you to believe me. I haven't done anything but weed, and Xanax, in months. I saw those things while I was searching Nicole Soto's bathroom. I kept some, but I didn't . . ."

She shook her head, glanced down at her other hand. It held the red tote bag. "There's also this," she said.

Sixty-grand in cash and a batch of burner phones . . .

"Who else has seen that?" I asked.

"No one."

"Really?"

"I thought you were OD'ing," she said. "I couldn't believe you were sober when you came to see me. So, while you were unconscious on the floor and someone was calling the ambulance, I searched your pockets. I found these pills. Then I grabbed your bag, thinking there'd be more drugs in there. I was trying to protect you. I thought you'd get a shot of naloxone and recover. I didn't want to see you arrested when you came out of it."

"Thank you," I said.

"Don't mention it."

"I swear I never took any of those pills."

"Duck . . ."

I looked down at the red bag. "That was my fee, plus expenses, and the phones—a clever teenager's idea of precaution. You mind looking after it for me?"

"That's what I've been doing."

"Thanks. Do the Sotos know what happened?"

"I talked to Nicole Soto. They send their best."

"I'll bet."

"Want me to tell them you're awake?"

"Think I'd rather surprise them," I said.

"I'm sure they'll be thrilled."

"Any sign of Danny Soto?"

"None. At least not when Nicole and I talked a couple

days ago. Layla, the poor girl, is terrified. Nicole insisted on paying your hospital bill when I told her you didn't have health insurance."

"How generous."

"Show some thanks—the bill will be a lot higher than what's in this bag here."

"Do I get to keep that too?"

"You'll have to ask."

"And Gross is gone?"

She nodded. "Whoever got to you found him first. Any idea when that might have been?"

"No clue. I'll need to think about it."

"What did you have to eat that day? Where did you go before?"

I shook my head, felt dizzied by the effort. "Nothing. I didn't have anything to eat that day. Just coffee."

"Where?"

"At home."

"Okay, don't force it. You need to rest." Her eyes peered down into the red bag. She reached into it for something. "Oh," she said. "I also found this."

My vape pen, bless her. I activated it at once, held it to my lips and inhaled until the light blinked, and exhaled the vapor across the room. My head sank deeper into the pillow.

Cass scanned the space, looked at the machines, the sterile setting of sickness, at the IV plunged into the top of my hand, feeding me Lord knows what. *Stimulating*—wasn't that what she was trying to get away from? I wondered what compelled me to bring her into this. An easy answer, I suppose. I felt out of my depth, and what did I do when that happened? I sought out my smarter, more competent partner.

A doctor appeared in the doorway. He cleared his throat, waited for my trance to break. I realized I'd been staring. I blinked, smiled, slipped my pen beneath the covers. He was a lean, intense guy with a crown of tight curls and a clean-shaved face.

"How's our patient?" he asked, full of doc cheer.

"Alive and kicking," I said.

"Hell of a thing. Most humans, and I mean like 99.9 percent of them, would have been goners. You've got a hell of a constitution, Mr. Darley."

"I'm well trained."

He looked to Cass. "Ma'am, you mind if I talk to your . . ."

"Business partner," she said.

"She can stay," I added.

That sealed it. Sealed something, anyway. It was enough for Dr. Horowitz. He approached my bed.

"So, as mentioned, we're fairly certain you were poisoned. With what, is the question, and of course, by whom."

"What did you find?"

"Not much, I'm afraid. There were heavy metals in your blood, but so far, we've been unable to determine any specific substance. The fact that you received such significant blood transfusions makes it more difficult. Frankly, the fact that you're alive and have use of your arms and legs—not to mention your brain—is something of a miracle."

"As opposed to Richard Gross," I said.

"Yes, him. We should be able to determine a good deal more from his autopsy. Whoever was trying to kill you did a better job with him. You were meeting with Mr. Gross prior to falling ill, correct?"

"About an hour before, yeah."

"Did you two have anything to eat? Anything you might have ingested together?"

"We were at a diner," I said, neglecting to mention the gun pointed at my crotch. "In Midtown. Neither of us was served. The waitress brought me coffee and water. I don't think I had a sip of either."

"And before that?"

"I'll need to think about it."

"Mr. Darley, I'm not a cop. I'm a doctor. I'm sure the police will have more questions for you. My priority is in seeing that you recover, and that we might identify what made you sick."

"Like you said, I was poisoned. I have the constitution of a mammoth, and I'm expected to make a full recovery."

He laughed. "I didn't go that far. There could be nerve damage. We won't know the extent until you're up and about."

"When will that be?"

"Soon as you're able." He turned to Cass. "How does he seem to you?"

"Like a hardheaded fool," she said. "Which would be normal."

The doctor rubbed at his aftershaved cheek, avoided her eyes, and gazed down at me. *Lucky bastard,* his look seemed to say. I held her hand tighter. He lingered for a moment.

"Well, I'll leave you two," he said. "You're a very lucky man, Mr. Darley."

Told you. Though he may have been referring to my survival.

Chapter 9

I couldn't allow myself to sleep that night. Anytime I closed my eyes I feared I'd fall back into coma. I convinced Cass to go home and get a decent night's rest. It appeared she spent much of the last week curled in the chair, bedside. The weariness was ground deep in her eyes. If I hadn't come striding into the Beekman with that bag of cash, pills stuffed in my pocket, a bloodstream full of poison, she'd still be living her un-stimulating life behind the bar. Death Darley, ever the bad influence . . . Yet at that moment, insane as it sounded, there was nowhere else I wanted to be.

I felt a sense of invincibility that I knew wasn't healthy. But I also felt . . . dare I say . . . loved? It had been a long time since that sensation coursed through me. There had been sex, sure, but were any of those lovely women ever tempted to utter the L-word? I think not. Nor was I. But to have someone holed up in an uncomfortable hospital chair while you languished at the borderlands of life? The knowledge of that felt awfully good.

In any case, as the doc said, it would take more than an assassin's poison to bring Duck down. I wondered where it might have happened. I tried to retrace that day, a week before.

I'd started the day with coffee from the French press at home, lazed about, reading the latest Bruen, until it was time to meet Nicole Soto with Layla at the Blade Lounge over by the river. Was there anything consumed there? Any contact with strangers? I'd declined a glass of the rosé. Couldn't remember if there was water. Then Layla and I were in a cab to her tower. A new doorman and concierge were there, the girl's suspicions were raised, but we'd had no direct contact with anyone. Inside that apartment in the clouds—did I eat or drink anything? No, nothing. Did I touch any surfaces? Sure, I'd scanned every room in the apartment, opened Nicole Soto's medicine cabinet and helped myself, but if I was a target—Richard Gross and I—poisoning the Soto home wasn't realistic. And after that, then what? Layla showed me around that gaping building—those floors of meeting rooms, theater, salon, health club, pool—where we'd encountered not another living soul. Then our brief meeting with the building manager, Bill Willis . . . My heart sped. I remembered the wall of security monitors. I considered his supercilious smirk. He could have called someone after we left. And then . . . Outside in the rain, leaving Layla, racing across the street under the scaffolding . . . Richard Gross approaching and pressing his gun into my ribs, and then over to that diner where he . . .

Wait.

Back up, before that.

That rude suit with the golf umbrella, pushing through the crowd, poking me with the tip. I reached my arm around, felt my lower back. Over my right kidney I felt a slight bump, like the scab of a bee sting. It was where he'd jabbed me, as he rushed past beneath the cover. Before and after that, there was nothing. Not even a sip of water or a brush of contact that could explain it.

What else could it be?

More importantly—who could it be, and what could I do about it?

I never saw his face, only the back of a navy-blue suit, the precise trim of a professional hairline along the back of his neck. The lady next to me calling him an asshole. What else? Average height and weight, no distinguishing characteristics, nothing helpful. Moments later there was Richard Gross sidling up to me with his sneer and his gun, already infected with less than thirty minutes to live.

We like to pretend that there's a linear narrative to our lives, but that's only a past tense construct. Gross was already dead when he saw me. I was already in a coma. Danny Soto, wherever he was, dead or alive, had set it all in motion. His daughter Layla was the innocent courier between abduction and murder.

Only the spirits hovering above us could make sense of such things. Or maybe the capital-G word, if you believed in the Big Man . . .

There was nothing to do but try to piece together what came before. I suspected that Nicole and Layla Soto got the message. My case, such as it was, would be over. I planned to seek them out soon enough, but whatever they said wouldn't deter me. What was I supposed to do? Limp home and take another divorce case, count myself lucky to be living? Well, yes, poor fool. Even the dumbest dogs learned not to race into traffic after being hit. But, no, I needed to chase my obsessions to the end. And the end is always near, especially for hard cases like me.

I could start with Bill Willis and that umbrella-wielding fucker who poked me. An ID was impossible, though who hired assassins that worked not with long-range rifles but poison-tipped rain gear on crowded Manhattan sidewalks? The forces that controlled such men were finite and specific.

I thought of the cases of Russian poisonings that popped up with some regularity in the press under Putin's reign. They were journalists mostly, or loud-mouthed opposition that needed silencing.

I was neither. I was just a snoop hired by a teenage daughter to search for her kidnapped billionaire father. I posed no threat to the social order of any nation. But perhaps Danny Soto did. Perhaps his well-connected, thrice-married Chinese mother did—the one that her granddaughter thought was behind it.

I looked out my hospital room window at a sliver of moon, whitewashed by the lights of lower Manhattan. Windows were lit in the office buildings that crowded the sky. The bedside clock read two a.m. Cleaning crews at work, or abused junior investment bankers being hazed in that formal, sadistic way required of new recruits out of college. The real action was happening down at street level, on the smoking sidewalks and inside the bars that hummed with drunken laughter and lust, mad searches for connection, someone to get you through the night, a little less alone than the morning before.

Goddamn, I wanted a drink. It was safe to say my earnest booze fast was coming to an end. I'd earned some amber and I wasn't going to apologize for it when I took a sip.

I tested my limbs. My knees still bent, the ankles turned. I swung my legs to the side and set my feet on the floor. Nerve damage? Nothing to report yet, Doc. I pushed myself upright for the first time since I staggered from the bar in front of Cass last week. I swayed, steadied myself. Checked the IV in my hand. Tried a step, then another. I guided the tower and tubes connected to me over to the window. Looked out and down at my city—born here, lived here, would die here, sooner than later.

I thought of my old hound, Elvis. Among the spirits that hovered, I missed him. He never judged, never doubted, only loved. And ate—the hound would lurk like a shark in chummy water and steal food from any plate he could reach. Aside from Cass, he was the only being I cared for much. When he died, I did not cope well. Many drug-fueled nights followed, a desperate attempt to whiteout memory and grief. Perhaps I'd been close to joining him this past week. That wouldn't have been so bad. My mother was out there too, somewhere. Faith always felt like a foreign country, but as they say—there are no atheists in the foxhole.

Climbing back into bed, I considered a prayer. But sent where? That's when I always stumbled back toward disbelief. Where do you expect those prayers to land, into Jesus's punctured palm? Into the lap of the Father, who sits like some smug Santa in the clouds, gathering goodness and tracking sin? I wished I had it in me to believe such things. It would make life so much more bearable. To be a happy clapper, a confessor, to have a conscience cleansed weekly with muttered holy poems—it must settle the soul. Take the leap. He will catch you. Don't forget the capital H. But goddamn it, I just couldn't.

I lay there on top of the covers. I looked again at the IV plugged into the top of my hand, the tubes I was tethered to. I considered the tough-guy routine, those badasses in bad crime stories that rip out the needle, leap from bed, and stalk from the hospital without looking back, as a comely nurse calls out concern. Based on my bio it would seem I had little regard for my own mortality. I couldn't deny it—sometimes the wish for death thundered in my ears like a screeching morning subway on a hangover. But when I was presented with it on the proverbial platter, I always clung to life. It was that way with plenty of junkies.

Every time they tie off a vein and plunge a spike into their arm they're courting the big one. Yet faced with a true holy-shit-that-was-close OD, some will step back from the edge, kiss the ground, and praise life. Until they itched and inched back toward the stuff that made life just a bit more . . . okay, a lot more . . . *interesting*.

I'd managed to swear off plenty of bad habits in recent months, but there was one addiction I knew I could never kick—that adrenaline surge that comes when I'm on a scent. When I accept a challenge, when someone more helpless than I comes asking for help—someone who knows that she or he lacks my resolve—these are the times that will get me killed, because I'll never be able to resist.

Dying on the job—there was honor in that, licensed or not.

But dying of a swollen brain at home, post-coma, because I'd been too impatient or dumb macho to wait for a doctor's hospital release? There was no dignity there. I needed to stay put until it was medically permissible to walk out. That comely nurse and wise doctor could still watch my departure with concern, but I wanted their blessing first. I needed them to tell me my brain would continue to function. My limbs would still work. Tell me it was going to be okay. Actually, don't. Liars made me want to blot out reality with booze and drugs. But at least tell me I would survive this time, for now. The haunted mind-rumblings after near-death experience . . .

I hit my pen again, held in a hit, breathed it out, and did it again. I probably didn't need to hide it from the doctor. How could any medical professional deny me this proven treatment at a time like this? A drink would be even better, but for now, the weed would do.

I found my iPhone charged bedside, courtesy of Cass. I opened a browser and Googled: *poisoning with umbrella*.

The first hit—a four-decades-old murder of a dissident writer from Bulgaria. Poor bastard's name was Georgi Markov. He defected from the East in the sixties and settled in the UK, where he worked for the BBC and Radio Free Europe, ranting on air about the crookedness of his abandoned homeland. His trash-talking must have reached his intended audience. One damp September day in London, someone stabbed him on the sidewalk with an umbrella. It fired a pellet into his leg, containing a poison called ricin, a lethal, natural substance that came from the seeds of the castor bean. The former Soviet Union was said to have weaponized it; the KGB was assumed to be behind Markov's hit, yet no one was ever arrested. A British documentary was made about the case—*The Umbrella Assassin*. The primary suspect was reportedly known and continued to move freely across Europe. There was mention of copycat attempts using poison-tipped umbrellas, but with less success.

So, a proven means of attack among the powerful and murderous versed in such things, with the innovator still at large. A starting point, perhaps, though if Danny Soto's troubles were connected to his mother, as his daughter believed, then that would point toward China, not Russia.

I spent some more time Googling past poisonings. According to a recent article in the *Washington Post*, "the ancient art of poisoning is making a killer comeback." Clever. Putin, that old KGB operator, was a fan. He was probably nostalgic for the days when he was able to carry out hits himself. There was a long roll call of dead dissidents he'd eliminated. But none of that really resonated.

My eyes opened a bit wider when I came across a 2011 case involving a Chinese billionaire named Long Liyuan. He was poisoned while ingesting a bowl of cat meat stew. Cat meat, that wasn't even the offending part of his meal. It was laced with a substance called *Gelsemium elegans*, a rare plant toxin that only grows in Asia—where its moniker is "heartbreak grass." I wondered if leaves of that grass were coursing through my system. The autopsy of Richard Gross would help shed some light.

Whatever it was, it hadn't been enough to take me down.

Chapter 10

I must have dozed sometime after dawn. When I woke I found Cass seated back in the bedside chair. She smiled up from her phone, looked down and kept reading. A sharp painted nail scrolled her screen. Her dark eyes burned at whatever she was reading. I let her continue in silence. I checked for feeling in my limbs, clarity in my head. Had to admit, I was feeling rather normal, cured even.

Cass set her phone in her lap and glanced up. "Vladimir Kara-Murza," she said.

"Should that name mean something to me?"

"A Russian activist, he's survived multiple poisonings."

"Lucky man."

"The two of you. Seems to be pretty rare to survive something like this."

"Yet here I am."

"You give any more thought to how you might have ingested it?"

"I have."

"And?"

I turned over on my side, pulled the bedsheet down, my hospital gown aside. "Take a look at my lower back," I said. "See anything there?"

She came over to inspect. I felt her nails on my flesh. An

involuntary shudder passed through me. She peered close. "What am I supposed to be looking for?"

"See anything that looks like a sting or a puncture?" I asked. "I could feel it last night, and I think I know how it got there."

Her nails glided along my lower back, her nose almost touching skin. "I don't . . . wait, there's a little bump here, almost like an ingrown hair, is that what you mean?" She scratched at the spot.

"That's it."

"That's what?"

"Where I was infected," I said. "I think it was with an umbrella, shortly before Richard Gross approached me. It was raining, and I was crowded under scaffolding with a bunch of people. Someone poked me with the tip of his umbrella, some suit in a hurry. I didn't think anything of it then, but I don't know what else it could have been. That's gotta be it."

"Jesus."

"You weren't the only one doing your homework. I was up half the night Googling. Umbrella as weapon—it's happened before."

"Wait, I think I came across that too. While you were in the coma I was poring over all these poisoning cases. They always seem to involve Russia. What was the umbrella guy's name? He was a journalist, right, from Belarus?"

"Bulgaria. A guy named Georgi Markov."

"That's the one. I read about that guy."

"His case seems to have been an inspiration to assassins everywhere."

A nurse came in pushing a cart with vials and a syringe. She ignored Cass, wished me a good morning, and checked my IV. I watched as she stabbed needle into vial, went to the port in my arm, and began to administer my morning meds.

"A double dose, please," I said. When she arched her eyebrows, I added, "I've got a high tolerance."

"Sleep well?" she asked.

"Horribly."

"At least you're awake."

Couldn't argue with that. I gazed up at the bag of fluids, awaiting the hit of new drugs. I felt them fast. "Ahh, that's *bet-ter*," I said, savoring the warmth and fuzziness seeping through my veins.

The nurse wasn't in the mood. She had the look of someone too used to seeing last days and the void that came next. She glanced down, gave a tight smile, and turned for the door. "The doctor will be in soon," she said.

When she was gone Cass set her phone down and regarded me like a pet at the vet. She lifted a hand and ran her fingers through her ink-black hair; let it linger on the back of her neck. I wished I could eliminate my physical attraction to her. Here was my one true friend, the only person in the world who would care if that poison killed me. Here was the person I sought out for the competence that I lacked. It wasn't sexual, never would be; she made that clear. I needed to shut down those other feelings.

"So, while I was comatose, what else did you learn about my case?" I asked. "What can you tell me about Danny Soto?"

She sighed, said, "Very little, I'm afraid."

"A guy that rich, there must be a ton online about him."

"Not necessarily. Plenty of rich people pay to have the Internet scrubbed of all presence. There's next to nothing on the guy. Aside from his Forbes rankings, and assorted society pictures of him and his wife, at benefits and whatnot."

"What about his company?"

"Soto Capital? Same deal. A multibillion-dollar hedge fund with almost zero web presence. The company has a homepage, with a picture of the Manhattan skyline and a few sentences of financial jargon. That's it."

"No profiles, no stories in the *Wall Street Journal*?"

"Nope. The most I could find about Soto Capital involved *us*—and our dealings with Charlie McKay."

Danny Soto's dead wunderkind trader, a former teammate of mine . . . A case that would haunt me forevermore.

"That's the most press they've ever received," she continued. "Big wealth can be super secretive, and they're no different. They have the ability to move world markets, yet their Internet presence is almost nonexistent. That press with Charlie McKay and his sister must have made them crazy."

They weren't the only ones.

"Nicole Soto mentioned her husband's partner, a guy named Peter Lennox. She referred to him as his first wife. Apparently, that's where Danny's true loyalty lies. Find anything about him?"

"I can check again, but that whole company seems to take discretion to a new level."

"What about the Sotos' building?" I asked. "I told you where they lived, right? Before I started puking all over your bar . . ."

"You did. It was one of the last things you said. There was something on that website Curbed, saying Soto was the rumored owner of the top floor. The post also mentioned their place in Southampton: 2200 Meadow Lane, it set some kind of price record out there. Aside from the trophy real estate, that's it. Appears all those Billionaires' Row apartments are owned by anonymous LLCs."

"Most are foreign, Saudi, Chinese, Russian. When I was there the entire building felt vacant. Layla Soto says there's almost never anyone around."

"Sounds like it's money laundering in plain sight."

"Fanciest laundromat on earth," I said. "A bunch of empty palaces stacked on top of each other, all paid with cash, with connections hidden behind shell corporations."

"How is that legal?"

"You think the law applies to that kind of wealth?" I asked.

"Touché."

"So, what's the media been like on this? Did I make another *Post* cover?"

"There hasn't been any, Duck. Like, none. No mention of you collapsing at the Beekman, your coma, nothing on Richard Gross dying in that diner—not one story that I could find."

"How is that possible?" Perhaps I thought too much of my notoriety in the tabloids. "I'm 'Death' Darley, the *Post* loves writing about me. You're telling me Roy Perry hasn't reported anything on this?"

"Nothing. I even reached out to that bloated buddy of yours. He says he heard you had a heart attack and wishes you well."

"You tell him I was poisoned and in a coma?"

"Of course."

"And that's all he said?"

"He made clear that he didn't want to touch whatever was going on. He said he'd buy you a beer when you got better."

"He's on the wagon."

"Him too?"

"We were both on the weed cure," I said. "Soon as I get out of here, I'm having a goddamn drink."

"I'd advise against that."

"Noted." I hit my vape, hoped it could soothe my growing agitation. "Roy, some fucking friend," I said. "He didn't even care about the story? That guy's a hound for gossip."

"There are some powers at work here, Duck."

"No shit."

"Whoever tried to kill you, it came from a high place. The guy you were hired to look for is one of the wealthiest men in the world, and he's taken great pains to protect his privacy. The media is not touching this. It's a non-story. I'd be surprised if these doctors were even allowed to follow up with your blood work, or Gross's autopsy for that matter."

"What if I start making some noise? I'm good at that."

"You start banging around the china shop and next time you won't wake up. You realize that just by sitting here with you, I'm probably putting myself at risk too?"

"Yet here you are."

She sighed, gave me a look that was worth dying for. "Here I am," she said.

When Dr. Horowitz appeared back in the doorway he was not alone. His omnipotent doctor's bearing was replaced by a submissive discomfort. The reasons for that stepped into the room behind him. They were a pair of bland white men in blue suits, wearing interchangeable expressions of vacant authority. They looked as though they were engineered to be as forgettable as possible, not a single defining characteristic between them.

The doctor stopped at the foot of my bed, tried, and failed, at a smile. "You're looking well," he said. "Good night's rest?"

"Who're your friends?" I asked.

He grimaced, stepped aside. The pair moved past him and did not extend their hands. "I'm John," said one. "This is my associate, Jack." The other nodded. "We'd like a few moments of your time, Mr. Darley."

"John and Jack," I said. "You have last names, or badges, or anything that would entice me to talk to you?"

One of them looked at Cass, the other at Dr. Horowitz. "If you'll excuse us, please," they said in unison.

The doctor turned to go.

"She stays," I said, looking to Cass.

"No, she doesn't," said John or Jack.

"Or what?"

They glanced at each other, communicating with empty eyes, trying to determine how little it would take to clear the room without drama. I helped them along.

"Look, you're obviously a couple of government clowns. What are you, CIA, FBI, NSA? Whatever you've got to say, I'm just going to repeat it to my friend here, so you may as well say it in front of her."

John or Jack cleared his throat, looked at Cass, then down at his feet.

"I should go," said Cass. She leaned down and kissed my cheek, gave me a wink. "I'll be right outside."

I watched her follow Dr. Horowitz out of the room and shut the door behind her. Noticed the effort it took for them not to eye her as she moved past. When we were alone, they surrounded me on either side of the bed. Both crossed their arms and looked down. Despite appearing mediocre and forgettable in every way, they now carried an air of backroom menace.

"We are indeed with a federal agency," said one. "The particular organization is not important."

"We're here about a matter of sensitive national security," said the other.

"You are very lucky to be alive," continued his partner. "As you know, a decorated member of our armed services was not so fortunate."

"Richard Gross," I said. "He introduced himself by shoving a handgun into my ribs."

"He had reason to believe you were involved."

"With what?" I asked. I couldn't be sure how much they knew, but it had to be more than I did, and if they weren't even giving their last names, I wasn't offering much.

"We understand you were at the home of Mr. Daniel Soto," said John or Jack. "May we ask in what capacity?"

"I'm a friend of the family," I said.

"Whose friend—Mr. Soto's or, maybe, his wife's?"

"We understand your primary means of employment is infidelity investigations," said Jack-John.

"And that you have a history of becoming close to wives after proving they've been wronged by their husbands."

"How did you come to *understand* all this?" I asked.

They both smiled. "On Google, of course. You've generated some press in the past, Mr. Darley, not all of it complimentary."

"Not to worry," added John-Jack. "There is no government file on you, if that's what you're thinking."

"All due respect, but you hardly warrant one."

"I do now," I said. "Or you wouldn't be standing here."

"Were you in the employ of Nicole Soto, Mr. Darley?"

I looked back and forth at them. "Listen—John, Jack, I can't tell you apart, whichever's which—I've met Nicole Soto exactly once, for about twenty minutes, and no, I was not 'in her employ,' and no, I was not sleeping with her, as you're implying."

"What brought you to the Soto apartment the day you fell ill?"

"The word is *poisoned*," I said. "How about I tell you that after you tell me why—and who's behind it?"

"We're investigating the matter," said Jack-John.

"Which means you haven't got a clue."

"When did you last see Daniel Soto?" asked John-Jack.

"Let's see—about three, four years ago? I worked a case involving a former employee of his. Maybe you're familiar with it."

"Charlie McKay—we are, yes, a terrible situation. How's the PTSD?"

"A joy."

"And you've had no dealings with Mr. Soto since that time?"

"None."

"Yet, you've been inside his home. Who accompanied you?"

"Let me guess—you guys both have law degrees? Never ask a question you don't already know the answer to, right? You tell me who I was with."

They looked at each other. John nodded to Jack, or maybe the other way around. "Layla Soto, their seventeen-year-old daughter, is refusing to speak to us."

"Smart girl."

"We know she has been living primarily in the city this summer with her father, while Nicole Soto and her younger child, Lionel, are settled in Southampton. Did Layla ask for your help with something?"

"Ask her parents."

"The mother is not talking either, and Daniel Soto is not . . ."

"Available?"

"Layla asked you to search for her father, didn't she, Mr. Darley?"

"Something happen to him?" I asked.

John-Jack reached into his pocket and slipped out a pen. He began to click it open and shut. He tapped it against his weak chin and smirked down at me. "Something happen to yours?" he asked.

"Rich criminal father disappears from a kid's life—that must have really resonated with you, Darley. You sure you want to take a case that hits so close to home?"

"Might be hard to stay objective. With a personal connection like that, no way they'd let a cop stay on the case."

I sat up in bed with a jolt of rage. "I'm no cop," I said,

"but maybe we should call some. NYPD know you're here?"

I grabbed my phone from the bedside, pressed nine and one, but before I could reach the second *one*, it was taken from my hand. I grasped after it like a child losing his toy. John-Jack slid it inside a blazer pocket.

"No need for dramatics," he said.

"We're trying to help you," said his partner.

Both men leaned in close. I could feel their breath on either cheek, smelled it mingle at close range. Altoids failed to cover the scent of stale coffee.

"Listen," said John-Jack. "There's a reason this case hasn't made the papers. There's a reason the NYPD is not involved. There's a reason none of this exists in any public capacity."

"That reason is called national security," said his partner.

"You OD'd. You have a history of drug abuse. Richard Gross suffered a fatal heart attack. That's what happened. Understood?"

"You keep pursuing this, they'll hit you again."

"And next time they'll be successful."

"Are we clear?"

I looked from John to Jack, or maybe the other way around.

"Who are *they*?" I asked.

Chapter 11

They left without returning my phone. I was given a new one, the latest vintage. I discovered all of my contacts had been uploaded. My music library was restored too. How thoughtful, so much for privacy. I wondered if everyone's password-protected iCloud was open source for anyone with the right level of government clearance.

"Use this, and only this," I was told. "For your own safety."

My movements would be monitored—as security or surveillance, depending on how I wished to view it. If I returned to my regular routine of divorce cases, investigating standard variety city sin, then that would be that. Whoever tried to poison me might determine that I was no longer a threat, that the message was received. I would be allowed to live after another brush with death.

I'd been given a glimpse of the big-ticket tectonic evil that operated beneath our feet. Nothing to see here; please disperse. Yet again I was reminded that there were multiple realities, depending on perspective. It existed outside of ourselves, isn't that what Nietzsche said? Or maybe it was Kant, one of those inscrutable, quotable German philosophers. What was the more likely reality: heart attack and overdose, or poisoning and conspiracy? Facts were subjective; the word itself was a self-contained five-letter oxymoron. The attempt on my life, the murder of Richard Gross, and my week in a coma—these things *existed* in a certain sense, but did they really? The official version, the one for the permanent record, would be something else. Gross suffered a heart attack at a Midtown diner, after a history of high blood pressure. Lawrence Darley suffered an overdose, fell into a coma, and somehow survived. Would the doctors and nurses dispute this? Not if they were forced to sign nondisclosure agreements by order of the federal government. Any American blind enough to believe this kind of misinformation only went on in other countries was a fool.

If I persisted in pursuing this, or felt inclined to speak "the truth," I would soon succumb to another "overdose," this one more final than the last.

When Dr. Horowitz returned to my hospital room, he had trouble making eye contact. With fake cheer he said that I would be released in a few hours. He told me "the authorities" were speaking with my partner, and that she would be briefed on these sensitive matters. A nurse, one I had never seen, joined him and presented me with a clipboard of documents needing my signature. I needed to sign them if I wanted to go home. I asked if I could read them first. She stood over me with pen outstretched. Her bland look was about as memorable as those agents out there. Dr. Horowitz turned and left. I asked her again if I could read the docs before signing. She sighed.

"Your country is doing its best to help you right now," she said. "Please don't make this more difficult than it needs to be."

"Tell my *country* that I'm not signing anything without being allowed to read it."

I snatched the clipboard from her hands and flung it like a Frisbee at the window. It dropped to the floor in a splash of papers. This new "nurse" did not react. She walked to the forms, bent down, and gathered them. Then she straightened the stack and fastened them back beneath the board and walked from the room.

A moment later she returned with John and Jack. There was not a kind look among the trio. The door was shut behind them; the nurse stood before it, blocking anyone from entering. John grabbed at my right arm. I yanked it away and swung at him from bed. The response they expected. Jack delivered the shot to my other arm. The room filled with dark spots and disks and spinning, unsmiling figures. I was out in seconds.

It was late afternoon when I regained consciousness. The sun spilled through the blinds in parallel lines of orange light. I was dressed in my own clothes and lay atop the bed sheets. I sat up and rubbed at my eyes. Discovered I'd been freed from the IV and the tower of fluids. Cass was at the foot of the bed, pulling on my shoes.

"What the fuck?" I asked.

She didn't look up. "Let's just get out of here," she said.

The clipboard of bogus release forms, the shot in the arm, the agents who drugged me . . . It came back in bits and blurs.

"I'm free to go?" I asked.

"Yes," she said, still without eye contact.

"Where's the doctor, what's his name? Horowitz?"

"There's a car waiting for us downstairs," she said.

"I didn't sign those papers," I said. "I refused, and then . . ."

"And then you did."

My shoes on, Cass stood, exhaled, and walked to the door. She slipped out her phone, tapped at it. "Let's go," she said. "Seriously, we can't stay here."

* * *

There was a black Town Car waiting curbside in front of the hospital entrance. No sign of John or Jack or that mystery nurse. There was no sign of anyone familiar as we left the hospital ward. Those on duty kept their eyes averted, buried in whatever medical necessities, until we were past them and waiting for the elevator. Neither of us spoke. And we knew better than to break the silence in the back seat on the car ride home. The driver was a young crew-cut, wearing a fixed frown. An early assignment for a new recruit, his job was to keep quiet and get this bit of collateral damage out of the way. I glanced out the back window, searched for tails. I knew there had to be folks following us, but I failed to recognize them.

We were deposited at my doorstep on East 17th Street, thankfully with no sign of Mr. Petit's heir, Kent, lurking about. I was in a state of considerable irritation. An act of rash violence could have been imminent. We exited the back seat without thanking the driver, shut the door, and went down the steps to my garden flat. Cass joined me. Once inside with the door bolted, we still did not speak or look at each other for long.

The apartment was neat and tidied, the living space of a semi-clean, almost-responsible citizen. There were no bottles, empty or otherwise, anywhere. The sink was empty, dishes put away, countertops wiped. Books were lined with order on the shelves. Even the throw pillows were plumped and positioned at the corners of the couch. My sole vices—the weed and the Xanax—were stashed away in a cedar cigar box on a high shelf.

Cass scanned the surroundings, moved back to the bedroom for further inspection. She returned rather impressed.

"Seems you've become a respectable civilian," she said.

"A temporary condition," I said. "Want to get a drink?"

She arched a thin manicured eyebrow. "I don't want to be your enabler, Duck. You've clearly been doing well. Don't let this throw you off."

"An attempted poisoning, a coma, and a government cover-up? Why would I let little things like that rattle me? I didn't suggest a bender, Cass. I just know I've earned a drink. You can join me or not."

She considered me, sweating in front of her. I went to the AC unit in the window and blasted it. The apartment may have been clean, but after a week away during the dead of summer, the space was stifling. I set my new government-bugged iPhone on the coffee table. "You comin'?" I asked. "I won't be reachable without this thing."

"Can we walk a while first?" She reached in her bag and set her phone next to mine. "Let's walk and talk, out in the open without anyone listening. If you still decide you want to drink after that, we can stop somewhere later."

"Fair enough," I said.

"But, Duck, if you want to get drunk, I'm leaving, okay? I can't be around you like that, not anymore."

I almost balked at her conditions, then remembered the way she'd kept vigil bedside in the hospital. It was the kindest gesture I could recall. No one else would have even considered it. Someday maybe I'd express how much it meant to me, but not yet. We were both allergic to earnest displays of affection.

I popped a Xanax before leaving, retrieved a fresh vape pen, and opened the door.

Outside, sweet Jesus, it was hot. The sky was low, a colorless blanket of polluted humidity. Sweat leapt from every crevice before we reached the corner. This city is not suitable for habitation in July or August. Anyone with any dollars and sense flees to beaches or mountains. Layla Soto would now be ensconced at her family's Southampton estate with her mother and brother, awaiting their father's return, or at least news that he might be alive. I doubted I'd be welcome, but I intended to see them as soon as possible. Let the federal agents try to stop me. Let Danny Soto's enemies try to poison me again.

Cass and I moved slowly south down Second Avenue into the East Village. The heat prevented rapid movement. We passed any number of bars with blasting AC and strong drink. I felt a pull to enter each one. I tried not to look too long into any of them. Cass paused at the corner of 12th Street and lit a Parliament. She sucked down a drag, exhaled a plume from the corner of her mouth as we crossed.

"So, what did those agents tell you?" I asked.

"John and Jack? Very little. They said this was a matter of national security and that I was expected to forget about 'this little episode.' Those were their words—*this little episode*—a kidnapping, a murder, and an attempted murder that put my partner in a coma for a week. The fucking arrogance."

"Does that mean we're partners again?"

She smoked and searched my face. "I suppose I'm not wired for un-stimulating work."

"Told you."

"Don't push it, mister."

"What about your gig at the Beekman?"

"I quit, last week when you were comatose. It was never meant to be a long-term thing. I was just doing it until I figured out what to do next."

"You done with dungeons?"

"I don't know. We'll see. If you ever get your shit to-gether, I was thinking that maybe we could make this an actual business."

We walked another block, my chest bursting with silent joy. "Like, partners in an agency?" I asked. "You know I can't get an investigator's license, right?"

"But I can. And convicted felons *can* start a company. There's nothing to stop you from incorporating."

I'd never considered making it official, or doing any-thing official for that matter. It had always been a part of my nihilistic pose. Never seek work, never pretend that it matters, never do anything that could be construed as join-ing the straight world. But then, no one had ever wanted to join me.

This bright shiny future was sounding just a bit too good to believe. I stopped. She walked a few more paces before she noticed and turned back.

"What?" she asked.

"Why?"

"You don't trust me anymore, do you?"

"Should I?"

"Can we sit somewhere and talk?"

Cass scanned past me, her eyes skipping past bars and bank branches and closed restaurants. They settled on a small coffee shop on East 10th Street, a few doors west of Second Avenue. In a wide plate-glass window, it read THE THIRD RAIL.

"There," she said.

I followed her inside. Found us a seat in an empty cor-ner by the window. She went to the counter, said the cof-fees were on her. I shrugged, regarded the other patrons. Each one was seated solo, entranced in front of a laptop. Pods were plugged into each set of ears. Cass's physical presence usually breaks every trance in each room she enters, but not this one.

She returned, balancing two steaming cups. I reached for mine. The heavy calm of the Xanax was starting to settle into my limbs and I needed the counter-effect of the caffeine. The hot black liquid splashed over the edge onto her fingers. She didn't flinch.

"Thanks, but when I said I wanted a drink . . ."

"I told you, if you want to get drunk later, suit yourself. I just can't be around for it."

I raised the mug, took a searing sip. She didn't touch hers.

"Why, Cass? Why now?"

"Duck, when you were in that coma, when I didn't think you'd come out of it, all I did was think. I was sitting there hour after hour by myself, just sitting there. Every time I looked at you it broke my heart. I felt responsible for you lying there unconscious like that."

"Unless you know the suit who stabbed me with a poisoned umbrella tip, you're not guilty of that."

She gave a sad smile, lifted her cup to shield it, and took an imperceptible sip.

"I betrayed you," she said. "I lied to you and used you. The last time, when I asked for your help . . . I'm so sorry."

"In the past," I said. "We make our own beds."

"I messed up."

"And you almost went away for a murder you didn't commit. You've done your penance."

"Can you quit being so fucking forgiving?" she asked. "Seriously. Tell me I'm an evil bitch. Tell me to go to hell."

"After you feel sufficiently punished, then I should grant forgiveness and accept your offer?"

"Yeah, something like that. You know I have issues with pain and punishment."

"I thought your job was to offer the cure for those issues."

"You know what they say about shrinks? How they're their own first patients? Same goes for the kink community."

"You still haven't answered my question—why? I have a near-death experience and now you want to partner up and become an official private eye? Out of what, guilt? Sorry, but I know you better than that. What else?"

She averted her eyes, looked over at the laptop-tappers nearby, immersed and ignoring us. Raised her cup, blew on it, and took a drink.

"Maybe, like, fifty percent of it?" she asked. Her dark eyes lit with the truth of the statement. A smile played on her painted lips.

"I'll buy that. Maybe like forty-nine percent, but I'll give you the over-under."

"Gee thanks."

"And the other half?"

"It's complicated."

"Shocking."

She fixed me with that stare, the one I'd fallen for too many times to count. The one she'd leveled on countless slaves before they scampered to do her bidding. But I had the upper hand now, and I wasn't inclined to submit so easily. Maybe if she'd allowed me to gulp down a few bourbons first. But I was just out of a coma, clean and sober, and she knew it.

"Doesn't it bother you?" she asked. "The way another world can exist right above our heads, another reality with different rules and so much more at stake? It sickens me."

"Then don't think about it."

She grabbed a napkin and swiped at her lipstick, rubbing it off in angry, absent strokes. She crushed the stained tissue in her fist. "I can't help it. The curtain parts an inch and I need to know what's behind it."

"Whiskey helps," I said.

"Don't be trite. I fucking hate clichés."

"I'm serious. Helps more than anything else I've found, sadly."

"So, you'd rather numb your brain with alcohol, pretend none of it matters?"

"I didn't say that. I told you, I've been sober for months. Weed only. And Xanax. But whatever, that's as clean as someone like me can get without hanging myself."

"Now that you've somehow survived a professional hit and a coma, you want to drink yourself stupid again?"

"I'd say I've earned a round or two."

"Let's work together, Duck. Let's do this right. We can form an LLC, maybe get an office, make a real go of it. How many cases have I solved for you?"

"*For* me?"

"Okay, *with* you."

She winked. I couldn't deny it. Our loose operating arrangement in the past went something like this: I brought in the clients, with my damaged though relatable pedigree, a former rich kid with sins and secrets of his own, while Cass handled the technical expertise, the investigative work that involved real smarts. I'd pay her a cut. Whatever I thought was fair, which was always generous, and she never asked for more.

"Fifty-fifty?" I asked.

"Of course."

"Because you feel guilty about using me last time, and, oh, because you're obsessed with that powerful otherworld that operates in its own unfair reality."

"That about covers it."

"And now you want to start—officially—with a case that could get us both killed in short order?"

"Yes."

She stuck out a hand over the table. Her nails were long and sharp, painted crimson, like a cat's paw after a kill.

I took it.

Chapter 12

Of course it bothered me too, that ruling world beyond us. I was a product of it, or perhaps a forgotten piece of shrapnel tossed from it. My father, Lawrence Darley Sr., once considered himself a part of that reality, the one that emerges like the parting of clouds after you earn your first billion or so, the one that eliminates laws of the land and is governed by something else. At a certain level of wealth and power, no one goes to jail. No one pays for his crimes.

Never confuse the weather for the sky.

My father learned that one the hard way. He fell from the clouds and landed with a century-long prison sentence. If the death penalty were an option for white-collar crime, he would have received it. There was still a sizeable population of the Upper East Side that cursed my last name every time it was uttered. Not that I blamed them; my dad evaporated many a life savings.

Which should have made me bitter toward a man like Danny Soto, who was evidently a high-level financial criminal. Whatever he'd done to get himself abducted, whatever was drawing the interest of government agencies, it showed Soto was anything but innocent. You'd think, given my childhood trauma and resultant daddy issues, that I'd want to see a man like that burn. And maybe I did. But more than anything, I was like Cass. I was curious. I wanted to find out *why*.

After our coffees we continued to walk south with no particular destination declared. Despite the heat there was a spring in our steps. There was always that surge of endorphins at the start of any case, but this time it was a matter of magnitude. With a handshake, Cass and I were now actual partners, and we were going to start that partnership with a possible death sentence. If we had any sense between the two of us and wanted to join in a going concern, we should have put this Soto business behind us and accepted the next divorce case that came our way.

Like she'd go for that.

"So, who do you think is behind this?" she asked.

"I told you, that guy with the umbrella. It had to be him."

"No, I mean Soto's disappearance."

"His mother," I said. "At least that's what his daughter thinks."

"Why would Layla say that? What's the deal with the grandma?"

"She overheard her dad talking to her on the phone, yelling in Chinese. Soto's mother is Chinese. His American father died when he was a kid. Danny may have been doing business with her latest husband, some billionaire from Beijing."

"What else did you learn about her?"

"Not much. I was on the case less than a day before they hit me. I know the grandmother's name is Eileen Chung. Layla's mother, Nicole, refers to her as the Dragon Lady. She's not a fan of the mother-in-law."

"Where is she now?"

"Nicole? In the Hamptons, I assume, along with her kids."

"No, Eileen, the grandmother."

"China? I'm not sure. Like I said, I barely got started."

"I'll see what I can find. It would help to know the name

of her latest husband. The ruling class in China doesn't exactly have much of a presence on Google."

"Maybe they placed a wedding announcement in the *Times* Style section."

She ignored the comment, quickened her pace. "We also need to learn more about that building of theirs. The resident of the highest floor doesn't just get taken out the front door without collusion."

"Did I show you the video?"

"What video?"

"Sorry, I can't remember how much I told you before I started puking and dying on your bar's floor."

"Very little. You just mentioned Danny Soto, that he was Charlie McKay's old boss, that he lived on Billionaires' Row, and that you'd just seen their now-dead security guy."

"Poor Richie Gross," I said. "He was pointing a gun at my crotch in that diner when the poison kicked in."

"And you were up at the Sotos' place before that?"

"Yeah, wait till you see it," I said. "It's the highest apartment on earth."

Cass snorted, shook her head. "It would just piss me off, seeing how those types live, looking down on the rest of us."

"The art alone is worth the trip."

She didn't share my appreciation for the old masters.

"Those places are monuments to international corruption," she said. "A bunch of goddamn middle fingers spread across the skyline."

"And our client lives at the top of the highest one."

She lit another smoke. I thought she was going to inhale it in one go. We were standing at the corner of Second and Second. I remembered a Russian bar a few steps away called Rosie's. It was a comfortable little vodka spot where I once got wasted with an attractive Ukrainian lady who would later try to kill us. I wasn't sure if I wanted to run from it or go inside. I wondered if Rosie would remember me. She'd been quite a host once my date started speaking her language.

"It's incredible that those Occupy Wall Street folks aren't protesting every day in front of these buildings, you know?"

I knew what? I reached for my pen, took a healthy hit.

"Duck? Are you listening to me? Those places are fortresses, guarded with total secrecy. Whoever took Danny Soto had to have access inside the tower."

She followed my eyes to the placard set before Rosie's. HAPPY HOUR VODKA, it read. ALL CARAFES HALF OFF.

"Fine," she said. "If you're salivating that much, go have a drink and I'll wait for you here. Will that help you pay attention?"

I shook myself out of the boozy murderous memory. Gave a shudder, turned, and crossed the street.

"I'm listening," I said, striding ahead of her. "It was obviously an inside job. Wait till you see the video."

"What is this video?" she called.

I told her about it. The encrypted email to Nicole Soto, which mother then forwarded to daughter, and daughter forwarded to me. The short note informing Nicole that her husband had been taken, to keep quiet and all would be fine. But who keeps quiet? No one. Attached—that lobby security video. The twenty-seven-second clip of Danny Soto being rolled from the elevator in a wheelchair flanked by a pair of severe Asian ninja women, a hood pulled over his head. The way they paused in front of the camera, looked into it, removed Danny's hood, and held his unconscious head upright for a clear visual. With identification confirmed, they dropped the hood and wheeled him off.

"They were sending a message," said Cass.

"To whom?"

"Did Nicole recognize the women with her husband?"

"She claimed she didn't. I think I believe her."

"You think?"

"She never should have sent that video to her daughter. It was a weak thing to do. When I refused to investigate without an adult's consent, Layla had no choice but to bring her mother to meet me. She wasn't happy about it. Nicole couldn't wait to get on the next helicopter back to the Hamptons. Her concern for her husband wasn't exactly palpable. Layla told me her mom's a pill addict, which I seemed to confirm when I searched her medicine cabinet."

"And helped yourself," said Cass.

"But I didn't pop any," I reminded her.

I ignored her eye-roll.

"If she didn't know those women, why send it to her? What were they posing for?"

"Maybe she wasn't the only recipient," I said.

"Perhaps not."

"Right before I was poisoned, Layla and I met her building's head of security," I said. "Guy named Bill Willis. You should see the bank of screens he monitors, total Big Brother style. I assume the system was hacked, for the kidnappers to send that video, but he could have been involved—or at least was paid to look the other way."

"I'll look into him," she said.

We were standing at the light on Houston, construction pounding as usual. Over three decades in this town, I couldn't remember a time when this crosstown artery wasn't a mess of jackhammers, orange barriers, and gaping potholes. I overheard a group next to us pronouncing the street name like the city in Texas. Goddamn tourists. I wanted to lean in and explain—*it's pronounced like the sound you'll make when I slap you upside the head: Owwww ... HOW-ston.* As opposed to the place in the flyover zone where oil-drunk Republicans live.

"Where are we going?" I asked as the light changed.

"Home," she said, and raised a hand for a passing yellow cab.

But we weren't going to mine. Cass informed me that it wasn't safe. It wasn't just my bugged phone; she said there were probably hidden cameras as well. It sounded like paranoid nonsense, but I've learned more than once that there's no such thing as paranoia. If you think someone is coming for you, if you think they're listening to your conversations and moving in for the kill, they are. There are pharmaceuticals for this condition, but they don't erase the truth of the madness.

We went to her place instead. It was just my second visit. The first time was without her, while Cass was locked away in Rikers on a murder charge. I didn't like to think of that prior visit. It whipped up too many painful memories. The apartment was in Chinatown, on Orchard Street, just north of Canal. The sign reading SUCCESS: HOSIERY FOR MENS-LADIES-KIDS was still affixed over the storefront. Another defunct neighborhood business replaced by an art gallery inside; the cycle was always the same throughout the city. Ethnic founders are replaced by the arts and the gays and the broke creative class; hip restaurants and bars follow; real estate begins to turn over; tenements are transformed; rents go up; leases expire; it wouldn't be long until the banks and the drugstores took over. New York was vanishing indeed.

Cass lived on the first floor in the back. The hall smelled of stale smoke and stalled ambition. It was a skinny railroad apartment with kitchenette and bath on one side, a postage-stamp-sized living area, and a bedroom in the back that looked out on alley rats. The last time I'd been in there it had been converted into a small, though well-equipped S and M dungeon.

I peeked my head inside the bedroom door and saw it transformed back into more traditional sleeping quarters. A queen bed, a dresser, a framed print by Bosch—*The Garden of Earthly Delights*—it was a normal pad for a decidedly abnormal friend.

"What's become of us?" I asked.

"What?"

"We've both become far too respectable. No booze in my place, no sex toys in yours."

"I haven't been doing much entertaining," she said. "I decided to put all that stuff in storage."

"Too much built-up scar tissue?"

She shrugged, sparked a smoke, and cranked the AC unit in the living room window. "Something like that," she said.

Cass settled onto her futon, curled her legs beneath her in that feminine way. I sat across from her in the only available chair. Crossed my legs and regarded her. She paired her phone with the black Bluetooth speaker on the coffee table, scrolled through her music, tapped at the screen, and sat back. A gorgeous female voice filled the room for a verse. Another joined in harmony. I didn't recognize them.

"First Aid Kit," said Cass. "They're Swedish sisters. Like 'em?"

I did.

The song was "Heaven Knows." It lifted my spirits. We didn't speak until it ended. I could've sat in silence and listened away the rest of the day. I watched as Cass leaned over the side of the futon and picked up a laptop from an end table. She opened it and began to type with concentration.

"Come here," she said, scooting over a bit. "I want to show you something."

I joined her. Our thighs brushed as I peered down at the

screen. The contact sent a rush through me that I resented. It was Pavlovian. If we were going to be partners—and Lord knows that was the best thing I could have hoped for—I needed to extinguish my attraction to her once and for all. It certainly wasn't reciprocated.

You never knew what was going to be waiting when Cassandra Kimball said she wanted to show you something. More often than not it was something that shocked and disturbed, outraged and disgusted, something that forced one into righteous action. This time it was merely the homepage to Gmail.

"This is how we'll communicate," she said. "We need to take precautions. We have to assume they have access to your email, along with your phone."

She clicked on Create an Account beneath the log-in window.

"What should our name be?" she asked.

"For what?"

"Our shared anonymous account," she said. "Which will neither send, nor receive emails."

"Then what's the point?"

"The Drafts folder—that's the point. When we have information to share, we log on to this new email, and type it up as a draft, but we don't hit Send. Then, the other person logs on—from random computers, not your own, say at the Apple store or something. You read the contents of the Drafts folder there, and then delete them. When emails are sent, the transmission is recorded on both accounts, along with the IP addresses. But this way, there's no transmission, nothing to be tracked from either side."

I considered that, had to acknowledge the brilliant simplicity of it.

"How'd you think of that?" I asked.

"I didn't," she said. "It's from General Petraeus."

The name rang a distant bell, but I couldn't quite place it.

"That decorated general who torpedoed his career by having an affair with his biographer," she said.

"Oh yeah, David Petraeus, right? I remember that dude. They said he could have been president."

"Would have been better than the current clown," said Cass. "Anyway, I read that's how he used to communicate with his mistress—through the Drafts folder on Gmail. Apparently, it's a well-used tactic by terrorist networks too. When you're worried someone might be looking in on you, this is a go-to trick."

"You sure all this shit is necessary?" I asked. "What about just setting up encryption software? That's what Soto's abductors did. That's what Layla Soto did too, when she forwarded the video to me. Then I deleted it and emptied Trash."

"But there's still a record of the transmission, and you have to figure there are ways to break through any software, especially when we're talking about the government, or whatever powerful folks took Soto."

"But there's nothing to hack if we're just writing unsent emails and then deleting them from the Drafts folder."

"Exactly."

"The genius simplifies," I said.

Chapter 13

We entered the account-holder name as "Warren Zevon"—the dead L.A. singer-songwriter best known for "Werewolves of London." Cass and I were fans. Ask me, it doesn't get more underrated than Mr. Z. He was especially popular with literary types, as his songs tended to be filled with beautiful, hard-bitten turns of phrase. Even Ross Macdonald was a fan. When I suggested that as the name, Cass reached for her iPhone, switched the music from First Aid Kit to *Excitable Boy*, his best-known album, and smiled.

"Perfect," she said, as "Johnny Strikes Up the Band" came on. "We'll call the email 'lawyersgunsandmoney@ gmail.com.'"

It was a reference to the last song on the LP. Like the werewolf's hair in his hit song, it was perfect. Our password would be ExcitableBoy1978.

I watched as Cass completed the registration for our new email. Our partnership was feeling more and more official with each step. When she was finished, she hit Compose and a new email window popped up. Then she tapped her fingers at random across the keyboard, placed the cursor over the X in the top right corner, and closed it. The number (1) appeared next to the Drafts folder in the left-side toolbar.

"When either of us logs on and sees that, we click on it, read the details, take as few notes as possible, and then delete. Make sure always to hit that Delete Forever icon when it prompts you."

"Easy enough," I said. "So, where you headed next?"

She shut the laptop and set it aside. "I realized I might have a use for the Chamber, after all," she said. "I'm not too keen on working sessions any longer, but it's a perfect spot to work in private. If anyone's watching, no one will think twice about my going back there. On our walk, I remembered an old regular of mine who might be able to help."

"Who's that? What's he do?"

"Guy's name is Harold Lester. He's a hotshot real estate broker. He used to come see me once a week for years. Loved to brag about his latest deals. I remember him saying he never brokered any property worth less than ten million."

"Nice commissions."

"Seriously. He'll be familiar with the apartments on Billionaires' Row. These folks don't trust just any broker, and if Harold wasn't full of shit, he'll know better than most what's going on in that tower. Maybe he'll know something about the building's security too. I'll see if he can find out who this Bill Willis works for."

"So, what, you're gonna reach out, tell the guy his former mistress is ready to start whipping him again? And then you'll grill him for insider real estate details during the session?"

"It will be more elegant than that," she said. "But yes, something like that. You don't know how much these guys love to share, especially after. Successful men love nothing more than to talk about their jobs."

"Let's see what he knows."

"When you were comatose, I looked into those LLC fronts buying the apartments. It's still hard as hell to find out who's behind them, but there's been some changes in regulation recently, efforts to spot money laundering, sketchy owners, et cetera. Now all title insurance companies are required to disclose the identities of anyone purchasing real estate through LLCs. I don't entirely understand it, but the idea is to close loopholes on a lot of these shadowy transactions."

"So, we just have to ask the insurance companies? What are we going to do, claim the Freedom of Information Act?"

"Not exactly. They're required to disclose the names to the Treasury, if they ask. The Treasury doesn't need to share that info with anyone, and it's not like they can follow up on every purchase."

"But the big ones in flashy new towers on Billionaires' Row . . ."

"Are on the radar, yes."

"How's your slave broker supposed to help?"

"Look, everyone needs title insurance—it's supposed to confirm that the buyer *and* the property is legit. It protects both sides if there are any future legal problems. The broker works with the title company to get the deals done."

"So, the broker finds out the identities behind the LLCs too, when deals close?"

"Not necessarily. A lot of times they don't want to know. Neither do the developers. Secrecy is part of the business model. There are only so many people on earth able to afford places worth tens of millions of dollars. A lot of them don't want you to know where their money comes from, for various reasons, whether it's oil or drugs, crooked regimes or dirty politics, whatever. Say the dictator of a third-world nation wants to buy his daughter a pied-à-terre, but most of his country lacks running water.

You gotta keep that shit quiet. Sometimes it's just bad optics, like a fat cat hedge-funder who doesn't want to publicize a nine-figure bonus, even if the money's made legally."

"It's like the health club model," I said. "If everyone who bought a membership actually showed up and went to the gym, the business would fall apart."

"How is that remotely similar, Duck?"

"They just want your money, they don't want to know who you are. The whole thing *depends* on them not knowing."

"Okay, if that helps you understand, then yes."

"But you think connected brokers like your slave might be able to find out these secret identities, through this title process?"

"Not asking questions is not the same as not knowing. You don't think these guys get curious? It's another form of ego currency—'Guess who's behind that purchase, you'll never believe it.' "

"Well, if whipping and grilling an old slave can produce some leads, then back to the dungeon you go."

Cass rolled her eyes, lit another Parliament. As she exhaled I watched the plume rise and disperse across the room. We sat beneath the suspended, cancerous air, looking off in opposite directions. The smoke broke apart and seemed to disappear into the surfaces.

"What's your next move?" she asked.

"The Sotos," I said. "I'm heading out east."

"To Southampton?"

"That's where Nicole and the kids are holed up, isn't it?"

"You sure that's a good idea?"

"It's my *only* idea. Layla Soto brought us into this. She almost got me killed. They owe me an update, at the least."

"Paying your hospital bill and letting you keep that cash isn't enough?"

"Nope."

"You know how many people will be watching that place? The ones who poisoned you, those government agents, they're all gonna have a close eye on the Soto family."

"Precisely. If I'm with them, I'm less likely to be stabbed with any more umbrellas."

"Not necessarily."

"You think Danny's captors *want* to get caught?"

"I think anyone who uses that kind of creativity with a hit wants to be noticed. There are easier ways to kill someone and make it look like an accident. But a poison-tipped umbrella? That sounds like a statement, a calling card."

"So, you think those agents know who's behind it, and they're trying to keep a lid on it?"

"Perhaps, or maybe they're more concerned with the public's perception and want to contain it. Think about it, Duck. A double poisoning on a busy Midtown sidewalk? It could be construed as a chemical attack. That's the kind of thing that provokes panic and chaos. Why wouldn't they try to suppress that stuff, especially if they know who did it?"

"Then who was it, fucking Putin? Did Russia kidnap Danny Soto?"

Before she could answer, a loud knock rattled her front door. We looked at each other, tensed.

"Who is it?" called Cass.

No answer.

We waited, breath held. The silence stretched. The slim space beneath the doorjamb darkened with whatever presence stood on the other side.

Another knock, this one louder and longer than before.

"Who's there?" she called again.

I put a finger to my lips, I'm not sure why. She'd already announced our presence. Cass stood and began to tiptoe toward the door. I grabbed her arm, pulled her back. I stuck out my index finger, raised my thumb, in the mime of a gun.

Pointed like I was the one standing in the hall. She understood, moved away from the entry.

There were maybe two inches of cheap wood, a deadbolt, and ten feet separating us from the visitor. I told myself it could have been the landlord or the super, there to complain about the cigarette smoke. Then I remembered the stench of her hallway, realized that burning tobacco in this building was not an issue. I watched the door, imagined I could hear heavy breathing behind it. We waited for the visitor to pound again. Perhaps no more than a minute passed, but it felt longer.

We heard the sound of footsteps retreating back down the hall. Cass leapt up and went to her bedroom. I found her kneeling alongside the bed, reaching under it. She brought out a black backpack and a large shoebox, opened the lid, and revealed a black Beretta 9mm. Cass removed it with care.

"What's that?" I asked.

"Your cash, and the burner phones. I transferred it to my backpack."

"Since when did you become a gun owner?"

"Since I got shot."

She stood, checked the chamber. Seemed to know what she was doing. Yet another layer of Cassandra Kimball revealed. I loathed guns. I'd been shot before too, trying to protect Cass from a stalker years ago, but that didn't make me want to go out and buy a firearm. It did the opposite, in fact. I knew that in my line of work handguns were de rigueur, but I wanted no part of them. Besides, as a convicted felon, I would never be licensed to carry. My black-belted aikido abilities would have to suffice. Though I recognized the relief I felt in looking at it in her hands as rather hypocritical.

"Loaded?" I asked.

She responded by raising the piece and moving toward the front door.

"Cass, wait." For what, I didn't know.

She ignored me. Two paces from the doorknob the knocking erupted again. I thought she'd fire the damn thing just out of surprise. I stood behind her, watching her toned shoulders flex as she leveled the Beretta, holding it steady with two hands like she must have learned at the firing range.

"Anyone who comes through that door gets a bullet!" she shouted.

We heard the sounds of another language on the other side. Two voices, both female, speaking Chinese, I think. Which wouldn't be so unusual, this being Chinatown, but before I could exhale at some almost-tragic, wrong-address mistake, I remembered the women on that security video, posing alongside Danny Soto and then wheeling him away.

"If you can't understand, find someone to translate," called Cass. "I'm armed. You've got the wrong place. Get out of here."

More hushed Chinese came from the hall. Again, the sound of retreating feet. I knew they wouldn't be going far.

Cass lowered the gun, turned back to face me.

"Let's go," she said. She moved into the bedroom and pushed open a window. Her body folded over the ledge. She stuck one leg through and stepped out onto the fire escape. I grabbed the backpack of cash, strapped it over both shoulders, and followed.

We were on the first floor, a few feet above the broken glass and debris in the alley, but Cass did not descend. She reached up, pulled down the iron ladder, and started to climb. I was close behind, didn't bother to ask where we were headed. She never looked back. At each floor, I glanced over my shoulder, waiting to see someone in pursuit, and followed her up another level.

The tenement was five stories. At the top, the fire escape ended with a low spiked iron gate that blocked roof access. Cass reached up, grabbed it, and hoisted herself over in one effortless motion. I hesitated, made the mistake of looking down. She'd made it look easy, but one slip and I'd be falling fifty feet to my death—or impaling myself on the spikes. She looked at me through the barrier.

"C'mon," she said. "You need a hand?"

"I got it," I said.

But I almost didn't. In my pride to do it myself, my front leg didn't clear the spikes. I fell back, my hands clinging to the iron. My heart pounded in panic. Then her hands were on me and she was helping me to safety on the roof.

Chapter 14

"You recognize them?" she asked.

I nodded.

We were lying prone on the tar rooftop, our eyes peering over the front of the building down at the street. Parked below us was a new model black Range Rover with smoked glass. Standing before it were two tall Asian women. They were impossible to mistake—the same ones from the security video with Danny Soto. Both were still dressed in their form-fitting combat wear, like they'd walked off the set of an action movie. Fitted black fatigues, gun holsters visible across each chest. There was a driver behind the wheel, but only his hands were visible. The back-seat curbside window lowered. The women turned to it, their backs blocking the identity of whoever spoke to them from inside. When he—or she—was finished, the window went up and one of the ladies opened the front passenger door and climbed in. The Range Rover pulled out, driving north up Orchard.

The other woman scanned the sidewalks, then crossed the street and took a seat on the third step of a stoop. She reached into a pocket and produced a pack of smokes. Slipped one between her lips, lit it with a match, and inhaled. Her eyes never left the entrance to Cass's building.

Looked like she'd drawn the short straw for a stakeout—
and perhaps a planned murder when we emerged.

"Damn," whispered Cass. "We don't have our iPhones.
I can't get a pic."

"How do you suggest we get out of here?" I asked. "Back
down the fire escape and out the alley?"

"I couldn't see the license on the car either," she said to
herself. Looking down at our would-be assailant, she
added, "Who are you, girl? Who you working for?"

"Cass, did you hear me? Can we get out the back?"

"Would you shut up? I'm thinking."

I considered possible points of egress. We could go back
down the way we came, search for gaps in the alley and a
climbable chain-link fence that led to the street behind us.
To the south, on Canal, there would be storefronts lining
the block, the same if we tried to go north up to Hester.
Maybe there would be an open back door—or one easily
kicked in—that led to another tenement where we could
get in and get out unnoticed. I was going to suggest these
options when Cass pointed down to the corner. The black
Rover was back.

"They must be circling," she said. "Probably looking
for ways we could get away."

"We can find one before they do," I said. "There has to
be a restaurant or bar behind us. We can go through the
kitchen."

"True." She pushed herself up and moved low across
the roof toward the fire escape. "C'mon," she called. "I
think I know a spot we can try."

I followed her, reminding myself to take care climbing
back over that spiked gate. Cass reached the ledge and
prepared to hoist herself over and onto the fire escape. She
glanced down, then flung her head back out of sight and
moved away from our exit.

"Fuck!" she said. "They're down there."

"Who?"

"The other woman, the one who drove off. A guy's with her."

Without thought I stepped to the edge and peeked over to see for myself. As I looked down, they looked up. Our eyes met. I didn't recognize the guy. Perhaps he was my umbrella-wielding assassin, there was no way to tell. But the woman was unmistakable. It was like they were in costume, dressed not to blend but to leave an impression. She and her partner had us cornered from the front and the back. I'd forgotten about Cass's Beretta until I heard it lock and load behind me.

She'd removed it from the back of her jeans and was holding it upright, with her right hand raised at forty-five degrees.

"We have the higher ground," she said. "Let them try to come up."

"You prepared for a shootout?" I asked. "You kill ' em all and then what?"

"Then we both might live. How's that?"

"Not for long," I said. "You shoot anyone right now and we're fucked."

Cass looked at me. Her finger flexed around the trigger of the weapon. There was a vacant glaze to her dark eyes, an inward, almost inhuman focus on self-preservation. In dogs they refer to it as rage syndrome. It's a rare condition, but present in all breeds. Sometimes animals just turn. Threatened and panicked, rational choices can be swept behind the soul's curtain. When it's *kill or be killed*, don't try to talk sense to someone. Instead I grabbed her by the other arm and pulled her away from the edge.

"Over there," I said, pointing at a protruding roof-access doorway atop a neighboring tenement.

We ran across the tar, leapt over the low divisions that separated the connected buildings at the top, and tried the door. Locked. Fucking hell. I scanned in all directions, running out of options, beyond the bullets Cass was prepared to fire. I wondered if they were on their way up the fire escape. If the women spoke English, they would have understood that Cass was armed. It would be a foolish move to approach blind from below. Perhaps they also understood the reality that few are able to aim and fire at someone first. I didn't want to wait and see if Cass would hesitate.

Across a few more rooftops, there was a corner that almost touched the building behind it, on Ludlow. It was the only other spot where I could see rooftop access from an interior stairwell.

"This way," I said. "Let's go!"

It was a couple feet, no more than three, that separated the two structures. Not a long jump, but a precarious one. We'd die faster falling to our deaths than waiting for the folks scaling that fire escape. I banished the thought, didn't break stride. This time I landed without a stumble on the other side. Cass landed clean next to me. She reached the door before I did. Her hand turned on the knob. This one opened.

We closed it behind us. Someone had neglected to latch it from the inside. I fastened the lock, gave thanks, and raced after Cass. Down three flights we reached a landing. We swung open the first door we saw and stepped into a dark, cavernous room lit with noise and light across one wall. I was aware of the eyes upon us in the darkness. We turned and looked up. Bruce Willis was twenty feet tall. He was standing wild-eyed holding a samurai sword. We'd stumbled into a goddamn screening of *Pulp Fiction*.

"The Metrograph," I gasped. "The theater on Ludlow. C'mon."

We raced up the aisle, avoiding the confused looks, and burst out into a quiet lobby. Behind us, I heard Marsellus Wallace talking to Bruce. Things were about to get medieval on some ass.

No one paid us any mind as we speed-walked past the theater's bar and low-lit common areas. It was one of those hipster theaters that showed classic films in a well-curated space with cocktails, a spot made for third dates and sex after.

Out in the open on Ludlow Street, we kept moving, running south, then went left on Canal and reached the F-train's East Broadway stop at the bottom of Seward Park. A train was pulling in, northbound, as we leapt the turnstile. The doors opened onto a mostly empty car. Panting, we lowered ourselves onto a bench with our backs to the windows and bent down. Neither of us exhaled until the doors closed and pulled into the tunnel. We didn't speak until we were three stops away, in Soho, at the Broadway-Lafayette station. Cass stood, moved for the sliding doors.

"Let's change here," she said. "We can switch to the 4."

I didn't bother asking why.

Ten minutes later we were walking among the herds through the majesty of Grand Central Station. Above us the celestial recreations of the emerald cathedral ceiling glittered. Spectral late-afternoon light streamed through the massive windows. It was one of those moments in Manhattan when you realize that parallel universes are not the stuff of science fiction; they are always just a subway ride away.

I followed Cass down the wide marble steps at the end of the soaring space. She seemed to know where she was going. She didn't look back as we passed the rows of tracks, the kiosks of food and beverages and newsstands, then through the low-arched atriums where sound traveled up and over from corner to corner in some charmed trick of acoustics. It was one of those minor marvels of the city that always impressed dates still new to town.

Cass strode into the famed Oyster Bar and headed for the saloon in the back.

"You thirsty?" she asked, as she pushed through the swinging doors. "I fucking am."

I didn't disagree. What better way to fall off a wagon?

We saddled up, taking a pair of stools at the elbow crook of the curved bar. We'd barely spoken since Cass had been ready to shoot our pursuers. Now she did not appear concerned about my streak of sobriety.

"Two double Jameson," she said to the white-aproned bartender. "Neat."

He nodded, turned and reached for the green, crimson-capped bottle. He grabbed a couple tumblers in his other hand. I salivated just watching him pour. I've read that for abusers of various vices, whatever they may be, the brain's dopamine spikes just before, not during the actual ingestion of the fix. The high is in the anticipation. I was living, lusting evidence of that. The Irish called it "taking the cure" for a reason.

The whiskey appeared before us. We raised it. The glass hovered beneath my chin, so close I could smell the sweet burn. I set it back down. I watched as she shot hers and shivered as it coursed through her. Setting it down, she looked over at my full glass.

"Can't do it," I said. "Not like this, not after that."

She reached for my hand and squeezed. Then she grabbed my glass and flung its contents on the barroom floor, erasing the roaring temptation before it could overwhelm.

The bartender returned. He crossed his arms, appeared

to consider asking about my waste of a perfectly good glass of Jamie. He was a bull-chested ruin with a bulk made to absorb hard living. A gray-speckled mustache and sideburns helped disguise his bloat. When he smiled his cheeks puffed wide and his eyes squinted.

"Been a while," he said to Cass.

"No longer working in the neighborhood," she said.

"Shame."

He said it without a note of flirt, just a statement of fact. It was indeed a shame for any bartender to lose the privilege of serving her. When she made no move to introduce me or further the small talk, he tapped the bar and retreated toward the raised arms of thirsty commuters.

"The Chamber's a few blocks away," she said without looking over. "I used to unwind here sometimes after sessions."

"Did the bartender know your line of work?"

"Tony? God no. I told him I worked in marketing."

"Whatever that is."

"Got me."

We managed a laugh. She knocked my knee with hers beneath the bar.

"I'm proud of you," she said.

"Don't be. It won't last."

Truth was, I wanted to swallow down a bottle of the stuff. The thought of *never again* was too much to bear. But perhaps I was a little proud of myself too. In lieu of the drink, I slipped the vape from my pocket and took a pull.

Cass shifted in her seat, reached around to her lower back and adjusted something. I remembered the Beretta tucked back there. A private citizen carrying a loaded handgun in a heavily patrolled area like Grand Central was unwise. There was a higher concentration of law enforcement in this building than perhaps anywhere else in America.

"At least tell me that thing is licensed," I said.

"Does it matter?"

"It does when a NYPD German shepherd starts barking at you on the way out."

"Relax," she said. "It's legit. And no one's gonna see it."

"We hope."

"We've got bigger problems than my legal firearm, Duck. What do you suggest we do next? Neither of us can go home."

"No, probably not, but we've got enough cash to fund our time on the run." I tapped the backpack that was now nestled on my lap beneath the bar. "How much you need?" I asked, unzipping the top.

The glow of green bills made me feel almost safe. Funny, the illusions that cash can create.

"Here," I said, "take this bundle. You want two?"

Each stack was wrapped with fifty hundred-dollar bills. I slipped her ten grand, which she stuffed to the bottom of her handbag. In our racing across Lower East Side rooftops, it was a goddamn miracle that neither of us had lost our baggage.

"I'm gonna go by the Chamber," she said. "Rebecca's got an apartment in the back, for visiting mistresses. It's usually unoccupied in the summer, when the city's dead."

Rebecca was the owner of the dungeon. Until Cass left I knew that she was Rebecca's favorite employee—or at least her highest grossing. She'd welcome her back with open leather-clad arms.

"You sure an anonymous hotel wouldn't be safer?" I asked.

"No way. Rebecca's security is badass. The place is like a

fortress. Security cameras, soundproof doors, thick locks—
it's a dungeon. We take that shit seriously. Plus, there's a
landline and Internet on a secure network."

"Sounds like that's our command center," I said. "You
hole up there while I go see the Sotos out east."

"You sure that's a good idea?"

"Nope."

Chapter 15

Reemerging among the masses in the main terminal, I scanned the faces around us. We may have managed to shake that black Range Rover and the pair of female warriors, but the sense of being hunted was palpable. I felt like a primitive man, exposed in the jungle, knowing at the stem of an underdeveloped brain that danger lurked. Our genes were programmed to fight or take flight in such situations.

While Cass hunkered in at the Chamber, I was about to flee to one of the wealthiest neighborhoods on the planet—Southampton, Long Island. Specifically, I was headed to Billionaires' Beach, aka Meadow Lane. Danny Soto clearly liked his signifiers. For a hedge-funder who guarded his online presence with intense privacy, his chosen addresses could not be more conspicuous. I remembered Nicole Soto moaning about being unable to utilize her husband's company helicopter, instead having to take the plebeian Blade service to whisk her back to Manhattan. According to a real estate blog, the Sotos' home was at the end of Meadow, number 2200. Their neighbors included Calvin Klein, an evil Koch brother, and other assorted rulers of industry.

To get there I would be eschewing helicopters, and even

the Jitney bus service. Instead, I'd be riding the rails, switching trains multiple times, first the purple 7-train to Times Square. There I would change to the 1-2-3 red line and take it one stop down to Penn. Then it would be the Long Island Railroad out to Jamaica, Queens, where I'd switch to the Montauk line bound for the Hamptons. It had been some time since I made the journey, but it was easy enough. The Hamptons, I liked to tell people, was much like the English said of France: beautiful country, a pity about the people.

In the atrium outside the Oyster Bar, Cass surprised me with open arms. I stepped into her embrace.

"Take care of yourself," she said in my ear.

"You too."

When she let me go, I could have sworn her eyes were damp, but before I could confirm, she walked off without looking back. I watched until she disappeared in the crowd. Rush hour was beginning and Grand Central swarmed. I stood there for a beat, savoring the moment. I had a bag full of cash, a partner who cared about me, and something to solve. If I died in this particular line of duty, I could live with that. Now there was a riddle for the Buddha.

I kept my head down and moved with intent, like the rest of the self-obsessed citizens in my midst. Get from point A to point B, wherever that might be, and please stay out of my way. In public spaces, that was the New York mantra. A reasonable request for anyone who's spent any time here, which was why those dawdling, gawking tourists were always so infuriating. The rep that New Yorkers were rude was erroneous. We were only rude to those who disrupted the natural current. Those were often visitors, so our bouts of brusque impatience were often directed their way. With each other we were a live-and-let-live lot. Do what you want to do, go where you want to go, just please stay out of my way while I do the same. It was easy to slip into that stream, among my people, as I boarded the subway holding tight to my bag of cash.

The underground station beneath Times Square was even worse than Grand Central, or better for my purposes. It was packed with countless fast-moving bodies all headed in different directions, toward the web of subway connections that converged under this self-proclaimed "crossroads of the world." I even relaxed a bit, knowing that no one could keep track of me amid this controlled chaos.

There was a 2-train arriving in the station as I reached the platform. I squeezed myself in, raised my arm to the ceiling of the subway car to steady myself as it pulled out. I glanced over at my exposed armpit. A foul insult to humanity, there was a wide, wet stain the size of a football beneath it. In our racing-across-rooftops, switching-trains getaway, I'd worked up a vicious sweat. It was ninety degrees outside; on this sardine-packed subway car, even with the AC pumping it had to be over a hundred, with a sickening humidity. I lowered my arm as soon as I could steady myself with the train's movements. Made the mistake of glancing at a pretty college-aged girl wedged onto the bench beneath me. We made eye contact for a beat. She looked on the verge of a claustrophobic panic-attack, and my sweating bulk was the thing that might push her over the edge to hysteria. She had no music or book to occupy her. Her revolted expression announced that this town was not for her. Alas, it's not for everyone.

The doors opened at Penn Station. The subway car expelled us as the hordes pushed their way in new directions. I stayed in the fast-flowing current, followed the signs for the Long Island Railroad. On Fridays in the summer there would have been mayhem around the LIRR, with workaday summer renters already half drunk, racing off to their shares of crowded beach houses. Fortunately, it was midweek and the crowd was mostly composed of sweaty commuters trudging home to the interior stretches of the island.

While I waited in line, I slipped a few bills from my bag, with discretion. It would be bad form to whip out a wad at the window. I paid for my ticket in cash, apologized for not having anything smaller than a hundred. The ticket clerk yawned. I bought a round trip, wondered when the return might be, or if I'd be returning at all.

For the ride I bought the daily papers at Hudson News, but when I boarded and found a seat and started to read, it was no good. I couldn't focus on the words. My mind kept returning to my meeting with Richard Gross, when we both sat unknowing with poison working its way through our systems. I'd been with him for his last minutes alive. I didn't hold the gun he pointed at me against him. He was panicked. He'd lost his boss, lost control of a situation. For a solider as highly trained as he was, this constituted a major failure. I wondered if he had a family, a wife or girlfriend, any children, a mother who loved him. What would they be told? That he had a heart attack on the toilet in the back of a dirty New York diner? He didn't deserve that final insult. I doubted his loved ones would believe it. Big strong Recon Marines don't die that way. Though death seldom comes in the ways we envision. It always steals your dignity first. In everyone's final moments, I suspect any proud notions are exposed as illusion. Would hearing the truth make things easier or harder for his family? The knowledge that he was poisoned, by an unknown assassin, a piece of collateral damage in a wider plot they would never know—that would be the opposite of closure. Better to believe that he suffered a sad fate due to a bad ticker. I hoped the Gross family wouldn't make noise. No good could come of it.

If only I could take my own advice.

The train rumbled out of the tunnels beneath Manhattan and the East River and emerged in the blight of Queens. The journey would be a little over two hours, passing through tiers of urban and suburban and then pastoral realities. I gave up on reading, folded up the papers, and stared out the window at the hot asphalt communities sweeping by. Sunnyside and Woodside, Elmhurst and Rego Park, the train rumbled by the gridlock of the Long Island Expressway, passed alongside the more upmarket oasis of Forest Hills, and then it was time to disembark at Jamaica. The Hamptons-bound packs changing to the Montauk line were easy to spot. They were mostly young and loud and dressed expensively casual. Guys in designer t-shirts and shorts and flip-flops, careless outfits that still clocked in at a couple hundred bucks. Girls in short-shorts and form-fitting tank tops, or sundresses, lots of blond ponytails or brunettes with bangs, all feeling rather smug to be taking this midweek jaunt, able for one reason or another to super-size a summer weekend. Older second-home owners and seasoned summer renters tended to bypass the train, preferring the more genteel jitney bus service or the comforts of their own cars. At the upper echelons, they relied on helicopters and services like Blade.

I chose the first empty pair of seats I saw, settled onto the aisle, and set my bag on the vacant window seat. A group of three girls and a guy settled into the facing four-seater next to me. An Igloo cooler was set between their feet. The guy helped himself first, then opened another for what appeared to be his girlfriend, based on the familiar way his hand landed on her bare thigh. He toasted her, took a gulp, breathed out a burp from the side of his mouth.

"Ahh, the champagne of beers," he said to his bottle of Miller High Life.

"Such a gentleman," said his girl. "Serves himself first and doesn't even offer one to my friends."

"My bad," he said with a smirk. He reached back into

the cooler, produced two more, twisted off the caps, and handed them over. "Ladies, my apologies. Cheers."

They touched bottles, with three eye-rolls and one clue-less grin. The girl on the aisle must have noticed me gazing with longing—not at her but the beer in hand. I guessed her to be late twenties. Tall, short brown hair, toned arms, she wore no makeup, and didn't need any. She turned to face me. Her blue eyes were crisp, with the alertness of an athlete, the sort who went for pre-work runs, without a hangover.

"Want one?" she asked, taking a sip.

"Hey," protested the guy. "I only got a twelve-pack, that's like . . . three each."

"I'm good, thanks," I said, though I'd be a lot better after gulping down a few of those.

I brought out my vape, took a hit, and offered it to her. She accepted, handed it back without offering any to her friends.

"Where you headed?" she asked.

"Southampton," I told her.

"Nice."

"How 'bout you?"

"Montauk," she said. "We're renting a place in Ditch Plains."

"Hipster-ville by the beach."

"I know, it's a total scene, but whatever, I like the waves."

"You surf?"

"A little. I'm not good or anything, but when it's not too crowded it's fun. Do you surf?"

"Not me," I said. "I'm a swimmer, prefer the chlorine to salt water."

"You should try it. Paddling's the hardest part, and if you're a swimmer that won't be hard for you."

"Perhaps."

She extended an arm across the aisle. "I'm Sara."

"Duck," I said, taking her hand.

She held it. We regarded each other for a not uncomfortable silence. Her friends grinned at each other. One elbowed her. Sara turned back to the group. "This is Nikki and Erin," she said. "And Erin's boyfriend, Mike."

I offered a wave to the foursome, kept my eyes on Sara.

"So, is Duck your real name?" asked Erin, the girlfriend.

"Yeah," I lied. "My mom's name was Mallard."

Sara giggled; the other three didn't seem to get it.

"What's your last name?" she asked.

"Darley."

She blinked, the name registered.

"Duck Darley? Are you that investigator guy?"

Here we go. A *Post* reader, someone with a morbid fascination for tabloid scandal. I'd made some appearances in certain media, gained some notoriety among folks who read or watched such things.

"That would be me."

"Oh my God," said Sara. "I was obsessed with that case, the one with the twisted Olympic swimmer guy and his sister?"

"Charlie McKay," I said. Just saying the name produced a rush of post-traumatic stress. I felt myself start to sweat again.

"That was so messed up," she said. "I used to work on this show, *Inside Edition*? We covered that story a lot. We also did a piece on your other case, with the little boy and the neo-Nazi?"

"Stevie Cohen," I reminded her. "Always nice to meet a fan of my work."

"I'm a total news junkie," she said. "Now I'm a producer at Vice Media."

Hard-hitting journalism for the cool kids, complete with offices in Williamsburg. I checked out their HBO show on occasion. It was better than anything on the network news.

Sara sampled her beer, considered the best way to phrase what I knew was coming next. I let her think it through.

"Would you ever . . . like, want to do a story with us?" she asked. "You'd be ideal. My boss, Shane, he would totally go for it."

"I'd have to think about it," I said.

"Of course." She reached into a purse and slid out a business card. "Here," she said. "Just let me know. My cell's on there. Text me if you'd like to surf sometime too."

I slipped it in a pocket as we held eyes. "I will indeed."

"So, why are you headed to Southampton?" she asked. "For work or just to relax?"

"Seeing some friends," I said.

My stated destination broke the spell of our flirtation. My thoughts returned to the Soto family, and whatever was awaiting me at their beachfront castle on Meadow Lane. Sara's expectant eyes awaited more banter. I was fresh out. I excused myself, grabbed my backpack of cash, and weaved down the aisle to another train car for the rest of the ride.

Chapter 16

The name on her card read SARA MOYNIHAN. I wondered if there was any relation to Daniel Patrick, our former New York senator, and namesake of the long-delayed replacement to Penn—Moynihan Station—that would move across Eighth Avenue to the transformed Post Office, creating a proper, grand hub, as opposed to the current low-rent disgrace that was New York's Penn Station. It would explain her not having to work on a summer Wednesday, being able to zip out to Montauk with her fellow summer renters, many of whom had means of support that extended beyond salaries to well-off fathers.

The title below her name read SEGMENT PRODUCER. A cool-sounding gig at a cool company, but one that paid maybe sixty, seventy grand, tops. Not enough to afford rent on a decent apartment, much less a summer share in the Hamptons. Her lifestyle had to be funded elsewhere, not that it was any of my business. That's what it took to live in Manhattan in this century. Either work in finance or have someone supporting your endeavors in something more enriching and less, well, enriching.

I looked at the number listed next to *mobile* on her business card, reached for the iPhone that wasn't in my pocket. Remembered the burner phones stacked atop the cash in the backpack. I wanted to apologize for ditching her, wanted to continue our flirting from the proverbial arm's reach of text, as opposed to our literal one across the aisle. I wasn't sure at first what made me retreat. I told myself that it was some protective, noble instinct, not wanting to put her in harm's way, should she be the reporter type who always searched for some seam in a possible story. But the fact was I fled because the beer was looking too good. I knew how it went. You think you can manage a few. You convince yourself that you can settle into a new controlled rhythm of moderation. What I really wanted was an unbridled, around-the-bend drunk. It would feel so good, even as I knew the wreckage that would come later.

I reminded myself now was not the time to lose control.

I wondered how Cass was faring, if she was safe and ensconced at the flat in back of the Chamber. Wondered what she would learn online, or from that slave real estate broker she mentioned. If anyone was capable of unearthing secrets, either from diligent research or indelicate, kinky torture, it was Cass Kimball. How would I reach her next? Our planned communication through the Drafts folder on Gmail was genius, but whose computer would I use? There had to be assorted laptops and iPads scattered about the Soto residence, but would those be safe? What was my alternative, ordering a Lyft to the public library? Where else could I go to check email in private, on an anonymous device?

I spent the rest of the ride staring out the window at the south fork of Long Island scrolling by. I thought of Gatsby and Fitzgerald's rich descriptions of West and East Egg, where wealth, nouveau and old, collided with tragedy, setting the template for tales of the lost American Dream. I knew that F. Scott's "Eggs," geographically, were nowhere near the Hamptons; they were just past Flushing on the north side of the Island facing Westchester, in Great Neck and Manhasset, but every trip out east conjured those images. I suspect I wasn't alone. The Hamptons seemed to be the ultimate manifestation of Fitzgerald's vision, surpassing even his wildest projections of decadent wealth and the accompanying demons.

Each time the train passed close to the water I felt a surge of calming energy. There was a reason waterfront real estate would forever be the most prized. No matter the climate change and the inevitability of being washed away by rising sea levels, there was something about gazing out onto the sea that quieted the soul. The privilege to do so from one's own home . . . it couldn't be called priceless, since the prices were set by the world's richest. Let's just say it was an exorbitant asset deemed worth the risks.

The wealth began to announce itself around Westhampton and Quogue. The houses visible from the tracks seemed to inflate across a more tamed landscape. At the Hampton Bays station, the conductor called out, "Next stop, Southampton, next stop, Southhhhampton!" As we rolled across the narrow slip separating the Peconic River and Shinnecock Bay, I grabbed my bag and queued up by the closest exit. There weren't many of us disembarking. A few stiff older ladies looking irritated by their mode of transport, a couple out-of-work banker types wearing folded baseball caps advertising ACC colleges. And me—a scruffy-bearded, limping, pseudo P.I., recently poisoned, now monitored by government agents, and hunted by some unknown foreign foe that wanted me dead, or at very least to cease my search for Danny Soto.

Stepping out into the fading sunshine of Southampton station, I scanned for any suspicious characters or cars in the parking lot. Not that I'd be able to recognize them even if they were staked out right in front of me. More likely, they'd be sitting on or near the Soto estate on Meadow Lane. I wondered about government drones, if this case warranted such measures. Human eyes were redundant compared to those all-seeing eyes in the sky. I wondered if I'd be seeing that black Range Rover, carrying those female ninjas.

I thought about my few friends on the NYPD, about Detective Lea Miller, who'd become immersed in a few of my past cases. We had a brief pity-bound romance, and then developed something like a friendship, despite my instinctual lies and omissions whenever I found myself in a police station. What would Detective Miller think of all this? Had the death of Richard Gross and my "overdose" at the Beekman reached her desk? It seemed unlikely. If it had, and she made inquiries, they would have been silenced by the feds in the name of national security. A good suspicious cop like Miller would tread with caution.

I considered those I could trust. Came up empty. Cass, I supposed, despite her past betrayal. Miller would do what she could, though I couldn't expect her to risk her career and life for me. She was too sensible for that. She would counsel me to stay away from all this. *Don't be a fool, Duck, this is way above your pay grade . . . The kidnapping of a billionaire, a cover-up by government agents, a poisoning for Christ sake . . . Walk away before your death wish comes true.*

I could hear her voice. Envisioned her petite figure before me. Her ever-practical attire, her efforts to look unattractive failing, she was earnest and true, and she would be right. What was I supposed to do? Count myself lucky that an attempt on my life had failed? Close the curtain and slink away? Cass and I were partners now, real ones, and our firm would be setting its sights a bit higher than the bad-marriage dramas from which I'd managed to carve out a living.

It was more than that. Like soldiers who return from combat, with horrors seared in their memories, there was difficulty in reentering a life with the volume turned way down. That dull sense of safety couldn't be trusted. You longed for those technicolor moments of fear and violence despite yourself, knowing it was the only time you could still feel alive. When you found yourself immersed in a new situation that made the blood surge with the old intensity, you almost wanted to run toward the threat.

There was a line of cabs waiting in front of the station. I hailed one, climbed in back, gave the address. The driver was a young surfer dude with a deep tan and salt-crusted hair. He gave a knowing nod when he heard *Meadow Lane*, glanced back and sized me for someone not typical to such rarified locales.

"Friends out here?" he asked.

"Going to my house," I said.

"Oh, 2200—that's the Sotos' place, right?"

"You know Danny?" I asked, playing along.

"Yeah, man. I see him in the waves sometimes. Seems okay, you know, for one of them rich douches."

"How do you know I'm not one?"

He laughed. "Different smell, dude. No offense. Also, guys like Danny Soto don't hail cabs at the train station."

So much for never losing the rich kid's scent . . . It stayed with me throughout high school, after my mother and I fell from the Upper to Lower East Side following my father's conviction, and then through my stretch in prison for dealing weed. It didn't help in either spot. Now, when I could use it, it seemed to have washed off. Alas, the cabbie had me pegged. I might have started life in the orbit of families like the Sotos, but now I was closer to the level of drivers hustling for summer tips.

I rolled down the back window, breathed in the ocean breeze. My driver appeared to object.

"You don't want the AC?" he asked with a side eye.

"Like the fresh air, if you don't mind."

"That's cool," he said. "Guess you don't get much of it in the city."

That I did not. I made a habit of seldom leaving Manhattan, even in the most frigid winter and the worst of summer. It wasn't healthy. I should have escaped the asphalt more often. Yet as much as I grumbled about the madness of Gotham, I never felt comfortable anywhere else. Forty-eight hours elsewhere and I was anxious to return. Still, I couldn't deny the smells of the sea. The temperature had to be about the same as the city; we were less than a hundred miles east, but here, surrounded by water and green it was a different climate. There was a reason that families fled their urban confines each summer, and it wasn't just for the views and the beach and the extra space for the kids. It was a readjustment of the central nervous system, despite the many assholes that infested this land.

I reminded myself that artists and writers like Jackson Pollock and James Salter and Peter Matthiessen got here before the wagons of cash started rolling in. Like every conquered neighborhood, the cool kids got there first, before it was overrun.

Of course, they all loved it here. The light was spectacular. The sun was beginning to set, the sky azure, streaked with a palette of purples and pinks. It was easy to picture couples and families and lone figures pausing at the caramel edge of the tide, regarding nature's latest masterpiece, exhaling, and padding back across the sand as darkness fell.

"Just be a couple minutes," said my driver. "We'll take the back roads around this crazy-ass summer traffic."

"You here year-round?" I asked.

"How could you tell?"

"Same way you knew I didn't own anything on Meadow Lane."

He laughed. "Most summers I try to get out of here,

avoid all the city d-bags. But my ma's sick, so I stuck around this year. It hasn't been so bad. I'm making decent money driving, but I can't wait till it clears out again in the fall."

"What do you do in the off-season?"

"Construction, mostly, some landscaping. I got a friend who's a builder out here. It's cool, get to be outside, it's nice and quiet, and the waves are usually decent."

I wished I could be satisfied with a still life of solitude like that. A couple hours outside the city, there were many second-home communities that were virtually deserted for ten months a year. Multimillion-dollar houses shuttered and maintained by local staff, visited on occasional weekends, on holidays or school breaks, but vacant for the better part of three seasons. For those left behind there wasn't much to do but enjoy the cold ocean and empty beaches. I'd lose my mind. Without the endless buzzing energy of the city I'm not sure I could function. Or maybe it was just what I needed—a healthy low-stress life of good honest labor.

I was pretty sure I'd drink myself to death after one mind-numbing winter.

On either side of the road, homes were shielded by high green hedges. Driveway entrances afforded a gawking glimpse. Aging couples pedaled beach cruisers down the middle of the street without acknowledgment of the headlights behind them. The cab slowed. The Atlantic came into view between beachfront estates. We turned right onto Meadow Lane.

It was a thin finger of land between bay and ocean. An inevitable future hurricane would swallow it whole. Yet the combined value of the homes across this narrow peninsula reached into the billions. Perhaps they had joined rich forces and found some way to beat back the sea's inexorable rise. Maybe there were secret trenches that would divert the water to less valuable surrounding areas. One of the homes on this street belonged to a Koch brother, one of the world's foremost climate-change deniers. It would be a fine bit of karmic justice for his house to be washed away thanks to science he refused to believe.

We passed a long modern structure of steel and smoked glass. It recalled a medium-sized city's museum.

"That's Calvin Klein's pad," said the driver.

He might have sartorial sense, but he had shit taste in architecture.

Construction dominated acres of beach and dunes down the lane. Fortresses in progress, each impossible to comprehend in size and scope. Seeing the steel frames, maybe these new castles needn't worry about hurricanes. They looked built to withstand the apocalypse. I remembered a piece in the *Post* about the trend of luxury basement panic rooms in the Hamptons—except now they were more underground mansion-bunkers than "rooms."

A little farther on, my driver pointed out one familiar to anyone with a subscription to Showtime. It was a shingled Hamptons archetype, overdosed on steroids. It stretched about the length of a block, maybe an avenue. Every window was lit. I considered their electricity bill.

"That's the place on—"

"*Billions*," I said. "Good show."

"That chick, the blonde who lived there, what's her name?"

"Not sure."

"Whatever it is, chick is fine."

"Houses like that," I said, "tend to come with trophy wives."

"Along with pool boys to service them."

I thought of my time with Juliette Cohen. I tried not to relate. I was her son's swim teacher before I joined her in the bedroom. That wasn't the same as *pool boy*, was it?

My few prior trips to these parts had involved visits to clients. Burned divorcées eager to exact a measure of carnal revenge before draining the soon-to-be ex's coffers. On more than one occasion, I had been that measure.

This would be a different sort of house call. There wouldn't be happiness to see me, despite the fact that I carried a bag full of their cash. It appeared my hiring had made a bad situation considerably worse. If I had a stronger sense of pride and a deeper grasp of my mortality, I'd leave the money on their doorstep, turn around, and have the cab take me back to town. There would be plenty of bars hopping on this summer night, full of tanned lonely ladies. I leaned between the seats.

"What's your name, buddy?"

"Andy."

"I'm Duck."

He didn't reply with something stupid like *quack, quack* as most did. I liked him better for it. He turned up the radio a touch. It was Dylan's "Series of Dreams." Another point in his favor.

"So, Andy, if things go sideways out here, where would you suggest I crash nearby?"

"You mean, if the Sotos' guesthouse isn't to your liking?"

"Something like that."

"Anywhere near the beach or town and you'll get ass-raped. Even the shitholes are, like, five hundred bucks a night this time of year." He shrugged. "Got me. I'd just crash on the beach if I was you."

We passed a high hedge with a white mailbox perched at an opening. The number read 2180. The Soto house would be coming up. Andy flipped on his blinker. Before he could turn into the drive, we were blinded by high beams behind us.

"Who the fuck . . ." he muttered.

Another car came out of the shadows on the bay side and sped onto the road in our path. Andy slammed on the brakes. I was thrown against the back of the front seat. The car behind stopped inches from rear-ending us. They left the brights on. Moments ago, the road had been empty. Now we were pinned between two vehicles a few feet from our destination. The one in front of us was a black Crown Vic. I turned and looked out the back. Same color, same make, the go-to sedans of law enforcement everywhere.

Car doors opened. Men in suits stepped out. The high beams went off behind us. The men in front approached the cab. One walked to the driver's side, the other hung back. His right elbow was cocked, his hand at the butt of a gun, ready to draw as needed. I recognized their inter-changeable features.

"I don't need this shit," said Andy. "Whatever you got going on . . ."

He spoke in a neutral tone, more irritated than scared, like a man who'd been hassled by cops before and knew the score.

The agent named John or Jack tapped on his window. Andy lowered it. A flashlight clicked on and shone in his eyes.

"Was I speeding, Officer?" he asked.

"No."

"Whatever it is, I guess you need to see my license and registration."

"Shut up," said the agent. He leaned forward, peered through the window, and shined the light in the back seat.

We made eye contact. He frowned. I asked, "What the fuck do you guys want?"

Andy shot me a look, startled but with a note of thrilled approval.

"Darley, would you get out of the car?"

"No," I said.

"We'll give you a hand if necessary."

I unzipped my backpack, took out a burner phone, turned it on, and showed it to him.

"I'm calling 911," I said. "You can explain your assault on a private citizen to the actual cops."

Hearing that, Andy locked the doors. He started to roll up his window. John-Jack removed his head before it pinned his neck. When the car was locked and sealed, Andy looked back at me.

"Start talking, cowboy," he said.

"Federal agents," I told him. "Don't know what agency. We met while I was in the hospital."

"Hospital?"

"Someone tried to poison me."

"Jesus Christ, man. I really don't need this."

"I'm helping the Soto family with something. You don't want the details."

"No shit I don't. I just want to go home and get high."

We looked out the windows at the agents surrounding our car. Two more had appeared in back. John-Jack was standing in front of the driver's-side window, arms crossed, looking like the impatient father of a toddler. His partner, Jack-John, still had a hand positioned at the butt of his gun, but he didn't look quite as eager.

"Well?" asked Andy.

"I'm thinking."

"Quit yer thinkin' and call 911 like you said!"

"Good thinking," I said.

I punched in the three digits on the burner. Put it to my ear. The feds saw me doing it and tensed. I thought for a moment one of them might bash in the back-seat window and take me by force.

"Nine-one-one, what's your emergency?" asked the voice.

"I'm blocked between two cars, in front of 2200 Meadow Lane," I said. "They came out of nowhere. I'm worried this is a carjacking. Please hurry."

Less than two minutes later, a fleet of cop cars came roaring and blaring down Meadow Lane.

Chapter 17

We kept the windows up and the doors locked as they came screeching to a stop. Guns were drawn, lots of hysterical shouting. The agents looked pissed, but they knew enough to get down on their knees as instructed. These Hamptons cops had little opportunity for such action. A carjacking on Meadow would be big news, a highlight of the summer. Local cops might feign disdain for the loaded citizens on blocks like this, but they knew that some lives were more valuable than others. Think of the rewards for saving one of these fortunate sons or daughters. Stuff like that got new station houses built. It accelerated careers, whether it was admitted in cold winter pubs or not.

The chaos increased when their firearms were discovered. I heard shouts of "Gun! Gun!" followed by the agents being forced from their knees to their bellies on the road. Cuffs were produced, wrists were sealed behind backs. They tried to explain with cheeks pressed in gravel. In the cops' excitement they'd failed to profile the Crown Vics as fellow law enforcement. When they took a moment to listen to the steady voices beneath them, they became less zealous. Two cops went to either Vic, opened the doors and had a look through the glove box. What they found deflated the moment.

I saw one cop mouth to another *Oh shit*.

Handcuffs were removed. Guns were holstered. Apologies made. The agents stood, brushed themselves off. The whole just-doing-our-jobs routine. Reluctant handshakes were offered and not taken. Then, with a collective pivot, everyone seemed to turn at once toward me.

I gave them a smile and a wave.

When John-Jack knocked on Andy's window, he lowered it.

"Sir," said the agent, "I'm going to ask that you unlock your car, so your passenger can step out. Then you'll be free to go."

Andy looked back at me as he clicked the locks. "Sorry, dude . . ."

"No worries, buddy," I said. "You did good."

I opened the back door and climbed out. Waited to be braced, treated like a criminal. No one touched me. The local cops mumbled that they should be going. They gave me a few withering looks. The Crown Vic in back reversed to give Andy enough berth for a three-point turn. He offered a nod of commiseration as he drove off. The fleet of local squad cars followed. Then it was just me and four unhappy feds on this fancy beach road.

"That was cute," said John-Jack.

"So was your ambush," I said.

"We're here to protect the Soto family," said Jack-John.

"From me?" I asked.

"What are you doing here, Darley?"

"I came out to return their cash. Have a look." I motioned to the backpack over my shoulder. "Layla Soto paid me fifty grand to help find her father. As you know, that didn't work out so well. It didn't seem right to keep the money for a job not done."

I heard one of the anonymous agents behind me snicker. John-Jack smiled, then snorted. "A noble knight errant," he said.

His partner came forward and tried to take it from me. I resisted. He pulled harder at the strap. Without forethought, I grabbed his wrist, turned it, and swept his legs out from under him. A simple aikido progression, no pain involved, just humiliation. He landed on his back on the side of the road. I heard guns drawn and cocked behind me.

"Assaulting a federal agent is a felony," said John-Jack.

"So is grand theft," I said. "He just tried to steal fifty grand from me. I merely subdued my assailant."

Jack-John rolled over and came up on his hands and knees. I thought he would rush me, that or reach for his piece and fire one at my chest. There's no faster way to make an enemy than to embarrass a man in front of his peers, especially when you're talking about figures of authority.

"How do you think this is going to play out?" asked John-Jack, all calm reason. "Think, Darley. Turn around, walk away. Keep the money, okay? After what you went through, you've earned it. But do not come near the Sotos again." He stepped a little closer, lowered his voice, leaned in. "If you do, one way or another, you're gonna wind up dead."

"What's going on out here?" asked a female voice behind us.

All of us turned. Layla Soto was standing by wrought-iron gates, hands on hips, wearing a floral kaftan and Birkenstocks. She saw me through the group of suits.

"Duck?" she asked.

"Evening, Layla."

"What are you doing here?"

I showed her my backpack. "I was coming to return your money," I said.

She looked to the agents, regarding each with a glare. "And what are you all doing here?"

"Ms. Soto, as discussed, we're keeping an eye on you and your family."

"An eye?" she asked with a raise of an eyebrow. "You said we wouldn't even see you."

"Yes, but when Mr. Darley approached . . ."

"You're not here to protect us from *him*, are you?"

"Ms. Soto . . ."

"This guy almost died while working for us. For me, actually. My family owes him, and you're out here harassing him on the street?"

"Is your mother home?" asked John-Jack. His face was flushed. His patience was evaporating. "May we speak to her?"

"She is, and no, you may not." Layla fixed her eyes on me. "Duck, would you like to come in?"

"Love to," I said.

I stepped between the agents, waited for an outstretched arm to block me. None appeared. Jack-John was on his feet now. His jaw clenched. It was taking every ounce of handbook discipline to restrain himself. Layla punched in a code on a keypad by the gate. It swung open. I nodded my thanks as we walked through and turned back to the agents. "Will there be anything else, gentlemen?" I asked.

"Remember what I said," called John-Jack. "One way or another, Darley."

"Noted," I said.

"C'mon," said Layla.

The gate shut behind her. I followed onto a lit gravel driveway. Across an expanse of impeccable lawn, the great house rose up. It was a rambling French Tudor restored from another age. Unlike the newer obnoxious constructions nearby, which announced themselves with such over-compensating pretension, this one looked like a rebuke to all fortunes made in the last half century. It was no less large. Indeed, it seemed to stretch even longer end-to-end than the *Billions* house down the road. But this one didn't offend. It could have been an entire French village on the sea. It was so unlike the Sotos' sky-high Manhattan residence that the disparity was disconcerting. Layla sensed my line of thinking.

"This is really my mom's place," she said. "It was dad's compromise when we moved back to the city from Greenwich. She's always hated that apartment. She calls it 'the cloud cube.' So, he bought her this."

"This is . . . better," I said.

"Better views too." She looked up at her home, one of her homes, and appeared to regard it with an objective eye. "My parents have totally different tastes," she said. "I have no idea why they stay married."

I took in the place, wondering which residence was more valuable—their highest-of-high penthouse on Billionaires' Row, or this manor on the sand. Both might carry price tags over nine figures. Such sums were difficult to grasp. I considered the cash I was holding. It was nothing to these people, nothing at all.

"Welcome to Chateau de Soto," she called over a shoulder. "Let's go, keep up."

I trailed after her across the circular drive, up wide plank steps, to a double-height arched front door. She pushed it open with some effort and closed it behind us. I stepped into the high center hall. The ceiling was vaulted, crisscrossed by dark beams, with a heavy antique chandelier hanging over us. On either side, grand staircases swept around the foyer to the rooms above. The walls and floors were beach-house bright, but the accents—the steps and the beams and the railings—were in a mahogany that lent the place a solemn air. And of course, there was the art. Nicole Soto appeared to be a fan of seascapes. I noticed works by Winslow Homer, J. M. W. Turner, masterpieces I could have sworn were in museums.

"Layla?" called a voice from somewhere deep in the house.

"Yeah!" she called back.

"What was all that outside?"

"Hang on!"

"What?"

The perils of mansion living—it required voices to project across wide expanses.

"I said hang on!" called Layla again. "We're coming!"

I followed her beneath the staircases, through an ocean-facing formal living room. Past our reflections in the glass, the beach and the dark sea. A crescent moon and stars lit the waves. Perhaps not as unique as the one from their apartment, but a better view indeed. We found them in a den off the living room. A wraparound sectional sofa faced a large flat-screen TV mounted within a wall of bookshelves. It flickered with a video game.

Nicole Soto was curled on the couch with her legs tucked beneath her. She peered at us over the top of a trade paperback. I recognized the cover—*Asylum*, by Patrick McGrath. A story of sexual obsession and madness . . . I had Nicole Soto all wrong. In our brief encounter at the Blade heliport, I'd figured her for another frivolous Hamptons housewife. A tennis-playing, pill-popping, Botox-smoothed beauty without much depth. Not the sort who would be drawn to McGrath's gothic visions. Before her, seated with legs crossed on the floor and holding a game console, was Layla's brother, Lionel Soto. He looked about twelve. His eyes were transfixed on the screen. His thumbs worked the controller. He did not turn his head or seem to register our entrance.

"It's you," said Nicole from her sofa.

"I'm sorry to disturb you," I said.

"What was all that outside?" she asked.

I started to answer, then realized she was speaking to her daughter.

"They were hassling Duck," said Layla.

"Who was?"

"Those feds, I forget their names."

"They assured us that we would not see them," said Nicole.

"That's what I said."

"Why were they bothering you?"

It took a moment; this one was directed at me.

"I was coming to give you this," I said, holding out the bag. "It's the cash that Layla gave me, or most of it. I didn't earn it."

Even as I spoke I was telling myself to shut up. I came with no intention of returning my payment. That was just something I told the agents to leave me alone. Wasn't it? I wanted answers. I was no generous martyr.

To my relief, Nicole Soto scoffed. "Please," she said. "You certainly earned it. My daughter almost got you killed."

"I'm sorry about Richard Gross," I said. "I understand he was a good friend of the family."

Mother and daughter eyed each other. Silent accusations shot between them. Layla broke the staring contest and turned to me.

"Are you feeling better?" she asked.

"I'm not dead," I said.

"We see that," said Nicole.

"You're, like, fine?" asked Layla. "The doctor said you might have brain damage."

"No more than I did before," I said.

"I trust your hospital bills were settled?" asked Nicole.

"They were, thank you. I'm sure it wasn't cheap."

She closed her book, set it in her lap, and swept a strand of hair behind an ear. "It was more than you'll find in that bag of yours."

"Again, my thanks." I stepped forward and set the backpack on the coffee table. Lionel still did not appear to register my presence.

"Enough with your pride," she said. "Keep the money, Duck."

I picked it up again, tossed it over my shoulder. Fuck my pride. I didn't need to be told twice.

The three of us waited for the other to speak. Suddenly, Lionel burst from his trance. He flung the controller across the room and let out an anguished cry.

Nicole did not flinch. She looked toward a doorway and called, "Ida!"

A nanny materialized at once. She was a short, stocky Filipino woman of indeterminate age. She kept her head down, went to Lionel, and set a delicate hand on his shoulder. Lionel recoiled at the touch, then seeing who it belonged to, softened. His eyes had that highway stare, gazing at something invisible on the horizon. His lower lip hung slack. He rose and shuffled off with his nanny. He did not turn to give his mother a kiss goodnight, and she did not ask for one.

"What would I do without Ida?" Nicole asked no one in particular. She reached over to the coffee table and picked up a glass of rosé. I watched her take a sip. Told myself to decline if she offered.

"Would you like a glass?" she asked.

"No, thank you," I said.

She gave a vague smile as she unfurled herself from the couch. Drinkers recognized each other. She stretched her arms over her head, gave a feline yawn. Like her daughter she was wearing a kaftan, hers white and sheer, with a black bikini visible beneath. Her body looked tennis-toned but comfortable in its life of leisure. She moved in a distant way, like a ghost unconcerned with being seen. I remembered her collection of pills.

"Come with me," she said, drifting past.

We were seated in a screened breakfast room off the kitchen. A half-empty bottle of rosé was being chilled in a silver ice bucket between us. Outside I could hear the waves rolling and crashing nearby. A light breeze carried the soothing salty smells of ocean. The temperature had dipped just so. I was neither sweating nor chilled, a rare equilibrium. Sheets of far-off lightning lit the horizon at irregular intervals. I wondered who might be monitoring us. A screened, lit room facing a dark empty beach left us more exposed than I cared to consider.

A trained gunman with a scope could take us out with ease. A small craft could be waiting on the sand. He—or she—could make an escape by water and be off into the starry night. I tried to suppress this scenario. If they wanted to take out the rest of the Soto family, they would have done it by now. I told myself I was safe in their presence.

"Do you think we're being watched by drones?" asked Layla from an open refrigerator.

"Probably," I said.

The notion made me feel better. Layla removed a roll of string cheese, peeled it open, and began tearing off strands with the door still open. She examined the stocked shelves in the way of oblivious teenagers.

"Layla, I thought we agreed," said her mother. "No snacking after eight."

Daughter shut the fridge, turned to her mom. She tore off a large chunk of cheese. Popped it in her mouth with a smirk and rejoined us at the table.

"That glass of wine has more calories than this string cheese," she said as she sat.

Nicole reached for her glass and took a drink. "I'm too tired to argue with you. Just be mindful of what you put in your body, okay?"

"You do the same, mom."

I sat through another standoff. This time mother was the one to relent. She looked to me, set down her glass a little closer. "Layla, would you mind if I spoke to Duck in private?"

"Yes," said the teen. "I would mind."

"Let me rephrase that—I need to speak to Mr. Darley alone. Please go up to your room. Or go to the den, or the theater. Put on a movie. Go for a night swim in the pool. Do whatever you like, I don't care. But please leave the grown-ups to talk."

"The *grown-ups*." She eye-rolled.

I gazed at the cold, sweating bottle of rosé, could almost taste it on my lips. My defenses were crumbling. Why was I torturing myself like this? What was I trying to prove? And while I was at it, I wondered where she kept her little orange bottles of pharmaceuticals.

"Now," said Nicole.

Layla glared at her mother, then at me, expecting my support. When I kept quiet she stood and stalked from the room. We watched her fling open the fridge and grab another string cheese, then slam the door and disappear into the endless empty rooms of the house.

"You have no idea what it's like to have a teenager," she said.

No, I did not. But I did know what it was like to search for a rich, destructive one with demons too dark to consider. Layla seemed far more adjusted than the doomed Madeline McKay, whose disappearance I'd investigated some years back. Ever since, I'd been uncomfortable around the age group. They looked so close to being adults, and most thought they were, but they failed to see the dangers around them, the leering men with bad intentions, the true ugliness of life that awaited. Even Layla Soto, with her preternatural poise, was not as wise as she thought.

I doubted I'd ever become a father, but I wanted to protect these kids. I wanted to beseech them to cling to their innocence for as long as possible. Because it wouldn't last.

Nicole eyed my water glass. "Are you certain I can't get you anything stronger?" she asked.

"I'm not certain at all," I said. "I've been taking a break from the booze for a while."

She frowned, lifted the bottle from the bucket, and drained the rest into her empty glass. "Let me know if you change your mind," she said.

She stood and went to a nearby wine fridge. I watched her lean forward at the waist as she pulled another cooled bottle from a shelf. She gazed at the label in her hand with an incurious pause. "We're well stocked with the summer water out here. Sometimes I swear it contains no alcohol at all."

I watched her open it. She watched me watching her. The way her hand gripped the neck of the bottle was rather hard to confuse. She pressed down on the screw, lifted it, and popped out the cork. Returning to the table, she set it in the bucket and let it breathe. Then she leaned back in her wicker chair, folded her arms beneath her chest, and regarded me.

"I don't think I've apologized properly for bringing you into this mess," she said. "I should have refused, when you insisted on getting my blessing that day at the Blade lounge."

I thought of it less a blessing than a matter of covering my ass before going to work for a minor. But why press the semantics?

"No apologies," I said. "I accept a certain degree of risk anytime I take a case."

"This one almost got you killed."

"Not my first rodeo."

Nicole crossed her legs. She drank her wine. Her kaftan slid up and exposed bare thigh. She sought my eyes. I offered them. "Why did you really come out here?" she asked. "Please tell me it wasn't to return your fee. I know you're smarter than that."

"No," I said. "It wasn't. I don't know why I insisted on that."

"Then what?" she asked. "You don't still expect to work on this case, do you?"

"I couldn't just walk away," I said. "Not when someone tried to poison me like that. I want some answers. I think I'm entitled to them. And, yes, I'd also like to help find your husband—the job I was paid to do. Can I ask—when was your last contact with him?"

"It was the day before he disappeared," she said. "He called to tell me he was going to buy a boat, a very big one. I told him it was ridiculous."

"He called to tell you or ask your permission?"

She gave a dry, clipped laugh. "My husband does not ask for permission to do anything. Neither do I. We can have anything we want. He was just letting me know. I think he expected me to approve. I didn't. Those mega-yachts, or whatever they call them, they're the vainest possessions on earth. I find them pathetic. We'd hardly use the thing."

"So, aside from the boat, did he mention anything else? Did he sound different than usual? Was he nervous or anxious about anything?"

"Danny doesn't get nervous. He's like some kind of bloodless machine." She drank from her glass as she considered her spouse. "For some reason, that was once an attractive quality."

"Is this him?" asked a voice behind us.

Nicole Soto's face went pale. Her eyes averted.

"Eileen," she said. "I'm sorry if we disturbed you."

I turned to face a birdlike Asian woman with regal posture. She could have been anywhere between forty and seventy. Her hair was as dark as wet tar and looked freshly rinsed around a pale, unlined face. A thin, precise line of makeup was applied beneath wide, almond-shaped eyes. She wore black linen pants and a matching long-sleeved linen shirt. The sun did not shine on that skin often. There was something both ageless and sexless about her, as though she'd transcended such concerns.

Reaching us, she extended a bony hand. I stood and took it.

"I'm Eileen Chung," she said. "Danny's mother."

Chapter 18

Whatever Nicole Soto hoped to talk about, it was no longer a priority. In the presence of her mother-in-law she became a flustered, unfortunate version of herself. The confidence washed away as if she were a guest in her own home. She pushed out her chair and stepped away from me. She smoothed out her kaftan like we'd been caught in flagrante.

"This is the man that Layla hired," said Nicole.

"Are you feeling better?" asked Eileen Chung.

"I am," I said. "Thank you."

"So scary, can you imagine?"

Imagine what, I did not know. Eileen folded her hands in front of her and waited. She eyed her daughter-in-law's wineglass.

"Mr. Darley came to return the money that Layla gave him," said Nicole.

"Why?"

"He feels he didn't earn it."

Both women regarded me like a subspecies. Eileen gave a quick laugh. Nicole tried one, but it came out flat.

"How much?" asked Eileen.

"Fifty grand," said Nicole.

"Should he keep it?"

"I think he's earned it," she said. "He almost died."

"*Almost*," said Eileen. "But he is here."

I realized that I didn't quite exist to these folks, not in any legitimate sense. I was something to be purchased or set aside. My death would not have been mourned, not by them. There would have been no guilt. Alive, I was something to be dealt with, if it wasn't too much of a nuisance. They could give me money to go away. Nicole could decide she wanted to sleep with me first. Her mother-in-law could decide to have me hauled away by the agents outside the house. Or perhaps all of the above.

Or maybe they would want my help.

"How long have you been in town?" I asked.

"Southampton?" asked Eileen. "A few days. I came when I learned of my son's predicament."

"You must be very worried. Do you have any idea where he might be?"

She shook her head. "I do not," she replied. "Do you?"

"Eileen arrived from Shanghai last week," said Nicole. "When you were in your coma."

"You are very lucky man," said Eileen. "Unlike, what is his name, dear? The gentleman Danny hired for security?"

"Richard," said her daughter-in-law. "His name was Richard Gross."

"Yes, poor man, so sad."

She sounded anything but.

I looked to Nicole for some guidance in dealing with this regal creature, but she wouldn't meet my eyes. Instead she reached across the table and removed the rosé from the bucket. She held the sweating neck in one hand and took her glass in the other.

"I should leave the two of you," she said.

"Good, good," said Eileen. "I will talk to Mr. Darley. You go, have your wine."

Nicole left the kitchen without a goodbye or goodnight.

She couldn't get away from her husband's mother fast enough. Again, I considered the innumerable empty rooms that must fill this house. From somewhere far off, I thought I heard her son, Lionel, shouting and banging about. The inverse of the old kid-hating axiom: Children are to be seen, not heard. I wondered how much parenting Nicole put in herself. Her daughter seemed to be wholly self-sufficient, while the care of her stunted boy appeared to have been farmed out to their Filipino nanny.

The emptiness of the rich was not a metaphor. It was a literal reality. They surrounded themselves with room upon empty room. Sequestered inside tens of thousands of square feet, cut off and protected behind gates and acres and elevators to the sky. But what happened when those empty rooms were breached? Who could they call when a patriarch was removed from his castle?

An alcoholic investigator who once fancied himself one of them? No, I would not be at the top of any list. But then neither would federal agents or anyone in any official capacity. Danny Soto had enemies—the real kind, ones able to poison those in pursuit. The involvement of the government would only worsen a delicate situation. A private army perhaps? Why wasn't this house crawling with private-sector warriors from Blackwater?

"So, what would you like to talk about?" I asked.

Eileen looked over my shoulder, out to the dark waters beyond the house. The wind picked up. Sounds of thunder in the night. The scent of a storm stirred.

"Would you like to take a walk?" she asked.

"Lead the way."

"You stay here. I need something to cover up. Be right back."

I stood there alone with the empty bucket. Considered going to the wine fridge, opening one, and gulping it down. It wouldn't be missed. I turned my back to the booze and held my ground. Eileen Chung returned two minutes later with a fringed black shawl around her shoulders.

"You will not be cold?" she asked. "Would you like a sweatshirt?"

I glanced down at my shorts and t-shirt. "I'll be fine," I said.

"Good, okay. You are bigger than Danny. His clothes would not fit, I don't think."

She took my arm with mannered grace and led me out of the house onto a wide oceanfront deck. The wind whipped at folded parasols. Grains of sand swept across the stained white planks. She walked me to the far end where steps led to their private path to the beach. On one side were dunes and high sea grass; on the other a tamed green lawn and a large glistening pool lit from within. I heard the water moving in a languid rhythm. I saw a figure, thin arms arching up and out, slicing down the length with lazy strokes. Layla Soto, going for a night swim as her mother suggested. I wanted to trade places with her. Her grandmother didn't seem to notice.

"It is better to talk out here," she said, "where no one can listen." Then she stopped and clenched my arm. "Wait, are you carrying your cell phone?"

"No."

When she gave me a look of disbelief, I reached down and turned my pockets inside out. I held up my vape pen. "Just my medicine," I said, taking a hit.

Eileen didn't seem to mind. "Good," she said. "I knew you were smart. They are always listening, you know?"

"Who is *they*?"

She ignored my question, kept leading me down the narrow boardwalk toward the beach.

As we reached the sand, a jagged knife of lightning struck the horizon. Thunder rumbled seconds later. The scent of rain came off the ocean. It was close to low tide and the beach was wide and firm beneath us. She walked me to the water. We stopped before a dying rush of wave. I watched it retreat, waited for Eileen Chung to speak. She took her time about it. We gazed out at the black sea, lightened by the moon and the flashing far-off electricity.

"So beautiful," she said without turning. "I'm so glad Danny bought this."

She seemed to be referring not to the house behind us, but to all of creation that lay ahead.

"A storm's blowing in," I said, feeling the first mists of rain.

"Yes, not much time to talk out here. Too bad."

I turned to her. Gusts of wind whipped at her shawl; her hair flung across her face. "You know where your son is, don't you?" I asked.

She looked startled, like a bird interrupted by unwelcome human noise. I could almost envision her flapping away over the water.

"Of course not," she said. "How could I know?"

"Your granddaughter thinks you're behind his disappearance."

"Layla? She said this to you?"

"She did."

"But why? He is my son. I am her nai-nai. I don't understand."

I knew it was indelicate to lay it on her like that. However well preserved she appeared, she was an aging woman in the midst of family trauma. No amount of wealth could insulate a person from the stress that surrounded them. I decided to barrel ahead, feelings and offense be damned.

"She heard her father talking to you on the phone," I told her. "A few days before he was taken. She said he was upset, speaking loud in Chinese. She understood a bit."

"Layla still understands Chinese?" she asked, more to herself. "No thanks to her mother." Then, to me, she asked, "What did she hear?"

"Something about your husband," I said. "He and Danny were doing business, correct?"

"What did she hear, specifically?"

"She thinks she heard something about 'drugs' or 'drug dealer,' " I said. "You'd have to ask her about the exact language."

Eileen Chung looked away as she digested this information. I watched a set of waves rise and crash before she spoke. "I have been separated now for months," she said at length. "A divorce is not possible, but I no longer consider myself married."

"Do they know?" I asked, glancing back at the house.

"No," she said. "The time is not right."

"Is it possible that your now ex-husband had something to do with Danny's abduction?"

She shook her head. "That cannot be. He needed my son . . . for important matters."

"Maybe there were complications."

The mist turned to a light rain, but Eileen seemed not to notice. She turned and began to walk down the beach away from the house. I caught up, kept pace by her side. The overdose of light from the other homes on Meadow Lane looked like massive targets for an invading armada. There was not a soul visible behind any windows.

"Do you know about the fall of the Qing dynasty?" she asked.

"Very little," I said, which seemed better than the honest *almost nothing*.

"You know about the Opium Wars though, yes?"

"A bit."

"What is a bit?"

"I know that it involved opium." When that prompted

no reaction, I added, "It was between the British and the Chinese, right?"

"Yes, in the middle of the nineteenth century. It marked the birth of modern China, and the end of the imperial age. It came down to a single plant—the poppy. A strong and beautiful flower that is responsible for more human suffering than anything in the history of nature."

"The oldest high in humanity," I said.

Eileen seemed to like that; she gripped my arm. "Precisely," she said. "They made junkies of the weak dynasty rulers. Whatever the name—opium or laudanum, morphine or heroin, or the painkillers of today, it is all the same. It is what's inside the poppy. The devil's flower. Satan made it strong, did you know? It is tough as a weed, no fertilizer needed, no pests bother it. It is invincible. No military or government has ever been able to destroy it. They have all tried."

"Your son and your husband, this is the business they were in?"

"My son is a businessman and a financial genius, like his father, my first husband. Daniel has made billions with his hedge fund, he understands the biggest picture."

"And your husband—I'm sorry, your *ex*-husband—I suppose he understands the macro view too?"

"He is a billionaire too, you know? His name is Guo Gonglu, you can look him up. He is on Forbes list, same as my son. He made his money in pharmaceuticals, in China."

"Impressive."

"Yes, I have been beside so much success."

"Eileen, why tell me about the fall of the Qing dynasty?"

"For the lesson," she said.

"I'm sorry, I was never a very good student. What is the lesson I'm supposed to learn?"

"Control the poppy," she said, "and you can control all of man."

Eileen stopped walking and turned to face the ocean. We were between estates on the darkest stretch of beach. Clouds covered the glow of moon. Rain began to fall harder. When she spoke, it was difficult to hear her above the surf and the arriving storm.

"You'll deliver us from evil," she said. "Won't you, Mr. Darley? I require your help with something. It will be worth more than the few dollars that my granddaughter gave you."

Chapter 19

I was soaked and confused when we returned to the house. I wasn't feeling very savior-esque and I knew whatever high-priced task she required would not be pleasant. Upon entering, Eileen had hurried upstairs to dry off. There was no sign of mother or daughter, no more sounds from Lionel within earshot.

I decided I'd held out long enough. I deserved a drink, several. I was sliding a bottle from the wine fridge, already savoring the taste on my tongue, when Layla Soto appeared in the kitchen. She had a wet head. A towel was draped around her shoulders. She was wearing a one-piece swimsuit, cut for training. She chewed at her goggle straps.

"Helping yourself?" she asked.

"Just looking."

"Riiight."

I set the glass back on the shelf, reopened the fridge door, and returned the bottle. The roles should have been reversed. Here I was, guilty and chagrinned by a teenager catching a grown man about to have a glass of wine.

"How was your talk?"

"How was your swim?"

Layla responded by removing the towel from her neck and wrapping it around her wet hair. She squeezed and rubbed it dry. "It was awesome," she said. "Nothing like a night swim in the rain."

"You should have gotten out when you saw the lightning."

"Thanks, dad."

I looked around the expansive kitchen, perfect and impersonal in the way of many second or third homes. Or fourth or fifth, who knew how many properties Danny Soto owned across the world. The upkeep of billionaire real estate was a cottage industry.

"When's the last time your father was out here?" I asked.

Layla didn't deign to think about it. "I have no idea," she said. "He hates the Hamptons."

"Then why buy this place?"

"I told you—it was for my mom. She loves it. I suspect when I go to college, she'll stay full time and find teachers for Lionel out here."

"Where's your brother in school, in the city?"

She gave me an odd look. "He's not," she said.

"He's home schooled?"

"He's on the 'spectrum,'" she said, using air quotes around the last word. "He's not autistic or anything. He's just, like, super smart and not social, like at all. He hates big groups or sudden noises, or too much stimulation around him. Hence, the city does not work for Lionel."

"How long ago did you guys move back? From Greenwich, was it?"

"About three years ago? I finished middle school in Connecticut, then started high school in the city, so yeah, it will be three years this September."

"If your brother has these issues, why return to the city?"

"My dad insisted that it would help. Lionel was fine his first few years in school, then it started to get worse in, like, second grade. Dad decided his son was just soft. He said being a 'city kid' would set him straight."

"Let me guess—your brother refused to leave the apartment."

Layla regarded me. "You should have been a child psychologist."

"Strictly armchair."

"Huh?"

"Never mind. Just not surprising."

"Yeah, well, you're right. Lionel started throwing extreme tantrums anytime anyone tried to get him to leave. Now he has tutors come up to the clouds every day during the school year. He's doing, like, college-level calculus but can't be bothered much with books."

"Underdeveloped empathy is pretty common in minds like that."

She gave a roll of the eyes, tossed her towel on the floor by the door, and moved past me. "For an ex-con, you sure seem to know things."

I followed her across the kitchen, put my hand against the refrigerator door before she could open it. I was feeling defensive and hated knowing that a haughty seventeen-year-old could rattle me. "Remember something," I said, "before you go off to whatever fancy college: School's useless."

Another eye roll, accompanied by a pitying glance. "Like I didn't know," she said.

She brushed aside my hand, swung open the door, and removed a can of flavored sparkling water. She cracked it, sipped at the fizz, waited for my next bit of hard-won wisdom. I had nothing.

"Night-night, Duck," she said. "Feel free to pick an empty bedroom. There's plenty to choose from."

Then I was alone again in that yawning home. I figured

Nicole Soto would return at some point, if only to show me the courtesy of where to sleep. I was accustomed to the flirty energy of neglected wives. I could play her game. If she wanted to share her drugs, maybe make a hazy late-night pass, that was fine with me. But what I really wanted was to continue my conversation with Eileen Chung. After we'd run for cover in the storm she hadn't been able to elaborate on my task. I kept turning at every creak in the house, but she never materialized.

I supposed her son's abduction must have something to do with the painkiller trade. Why else her history lesson on the Opium Wars? America's opioid epidemic was the public health crisis of our time—every surviving newspaper and magazine said so. It was killing more Americans each year than the peak of AIDS; there were more overdose deaths annually than the total number of troops killed in the entire Vietnam War. I knew plenty about the pull of pills. I devoured those addiction horror stories in part to keep myself from ever sampling the stronger stuff. Vicodin was one thing; heroin was another league, cheaper and better and deadlier. I knew enough about my self-destructive enthusiasms to stay away.

Nowadays even heroin was on the soft side. It was nothing compared to the all-time killer high of fentanyl. They said that stuff was fifty times stronger than smack. It seemed every celebrity death in recent memory was linked to it. It took down Prince and Tom Petty. How good must it feel if so many were willing to risk the knife's edge between bliss and death? I didn't want to find out.

Was I supposed to be the chosen one, here to deliver the Sotos from opioid evils? I wondered if Eileen Chung knew about her daughter-in-law's medicine cabinet. I wondered what the hell she wanted me to do.

She was a strange bird, that one. The type who, upon entering a room, set off a chemical reaction in everyone else. All energy went through her. I suspected she balanced in that zone between brilliance and insanity. Genius and madness were two sides of the same coin. One could not exist without the lurking presence of the other. Which is another reason why it can often be so uncomfortable to socialize with the highest achievers. It's not just their wealth that makes them different from you and me, it's their rare and twisted genetics.

I needed to learn more about this almost-ex-husband of hers. First, I needed to remember his name. Guo something, a Chinese billionaire who made his fortune in pharma. A dubious industry even in a somewhat regulated country like the U.S. . . . A team of smart chemists, a well-funded lab, well-run distribution channels—they could be curing disease with one drug and developing compounds more dangerous than dirty bombs under the same roof.

I reached for my phone, wanting to Google-educate myself on the broad strokes. My pockets were empty. Forgot again I was smartphone-less. Those burners in my backpack with the cash were cheap, disposable models, made only for calls. There had to be laptops and iPads and assorted devices scattered about this house. I wondered if any of these women would grant me a password, allow me to unlock one. Were any of these devices safe to use? Or was everything in the Soto orbit being monitored by the feds, or whatever foreign agents were hacking on the other side?

I remembered my Gmail Drafts plan with Cass. I suspected there would be a message from her waiting. She would have been holed up at the Chamber for hours now, able to search on a secure network. I needed to check in and share our new assignment from Eileen Chung, whenever she decided to share it. Her pharmaceutical-tycoon third husband was involved. Danny Soto was doing business with him. Layla had heard her father ranting about

Guo on the phone, calling him a "drug dealer" days before he was taken. And now the mother had supplied me with a link—the poppy, and all the deadly euphoric derivatives it spawned over the ages.

What did she need me to do? How could I deliver them from evil? Then I remembered: I was an expendable servant to them. She didn't expect me to live much longer. Didn't care if I did or not. But as long as I was in their lives, she would put me to use. Spark my curiosity, flatter me with mystical expectations, send me off searching, with a mission. If I died, I died.

Chapter 20

No one came downstairs the rest of the evening. I willed myself not to open any of their wine. I'd keep their money but forgo their booze. Who knew how much more I might stand to earn from the matriarch. Ten times more, a hundred times? What was a few million to this clan? Greed was an amnesiac drug, like roofies. It could make you black out and forget all notions of safety and good sense.

Instead of drinking, I padded around the first floor of the house, hitting the vape, inspecting room after room, grudgingly admiring their taste in art and design. Perhaps it was all the product of a well-paid decorator and art consultant. Whatever, at some point the lady of the house had made judgments on what to purchase. She'd chosen well. The work on display would have been suited to any number of New York museums. The furniture and fixtures were all flawless.

Ah, to be rich once more . . .

Around midnight I accepted that everyone was down for the night and went off in search of a bed. It didn't take long. There were multiple empty guest rooms down a long hall, in another wing that felt about a quarter mile from the kitchen. I chose one with a king bed, two Stickley chairs, and oil paintings of more seascapes. I undressed, climbed beneath the covers, and took a last pull from the pen.

It was no good. No matter how high I made myself, sleep would not come. I played pillow karate for four or five hours. As the first light of dawn appeared outside the window I was finally able to drift off. My sleep was hard and brief. My awakening, rude and loud.

"Duck!" came the shouting. "Duck! Wake up, wherever you are!"

I registered Layla's voice, heard her call: "Mom, I don't think he's here!"

I roused myself, forced to prove her wrong. A clock on the nightstand read eight a.m. I stepped back into my shorts and t-shirt and staggered from the room. Weaved down the corridors until I found them gathered in the kitchen.

Grandmother and mother, daughter and son, were accompanied by my favorite agent duo—John-Jack. Eileen wore a black silk dressing gown that fell to her ankles and was cinched tight around a hipless midsection. Nicole was dressed for exercise in yoga pants and halter top. Her daughter could not be bothered. Layla's dark hair was a tangle of bedhead; an oversized nightshirt left one shoulder exposed. Lionel hovered off to the side in shorts and a Mets t-shirt, making contact with no one. He was a big kid, on the verge of puberty, but a long way from independence. He eyed the agents with agitation.

The men in suits looked uncomfortable around them at this early hour. They greeted me with crossed arms and scowls.

"Gentlemen," I said. "Ladies."

"We thought you left," said Layla.

"But here I am."

"Where were you?" asked Nicole.

I waved behind me to a doorway. "Your daughter told me to find an empty room. I did." Then, to the agents, I asked, "What's going on, boys?"

John-Jack regarded me. There was a note of sadism in their eyes. I braced to hear something ugly.

"Remember your buddy from last night?" asked one.

"That cab driver you enlisted in your obstruction in front of the house?" added the other.

"Sure," I said. "Andy. He okay?"

"No, he's not."

They looked toward the minors in the room, not sure if they should utter the D-word in front of them. I tried to force down the waves of guilt. My face grew hot. My underarms burst with sweat. I looked from the agents to the family assembled around me. The whole world seemed to await my reply. Lionel let out a squawk. It was an unnatural sound, like a bear cub caught in a trap. He covered his ears and made the sound again, even louder.

"Ida!" called Nicole.

A moment passed, another cry from the boy, before the nanny came rushing into the room. At the sight of her, he began to sob. He was bigger than his small Filipino caretaker and she almost collapsed from the weight of him in her arms. She kept her eyes averted as she regained her balance and ushered him from the room.

No one acknowledged the scene.

"What happened?" I asked.

"His car was found by Agawam Lake," said John-Jack. "About a mile from here." He turned to Nicole Soto, asked, "Do you think it would be possible for us to speak with Mr. Darley in private?"

"No," she said, without hesitation.

The agents glanced at one another. Their eyes seemed to shrug. Oh well, if these stubborn rich folks wanted to hear the dirty details, that was up to them.

"He was killed behind the wheel," said Jack-John.

"How?" I asked. "Poisoned?"

"Strangled," said John-Jack. "There were ligature marks around his neck."

"This happened down the street, by Agawam?" asked Layla.

"Who else knows about this?" asked her mother.

"No one," he said without facing her. "Yet."

"This needs to be kept quiet," said Nicole. "We cannot be connected to this . . . unfortunate event."

"Unfortunate?" Jack-John chuckled at the word.

He was too glib. He underestimated the strength of these women surrounding him. Nicole faced him. "Yes, and tragic." She took a step forward. "What was your name again?"

"Special Agent Nichols," he said. He seemed to be debating whether to stand his ground or cower.

"*Special*," said Nicole, the disdain thick on her tongue. "You are anything but. I want you out of my house, both of you."

"Mrs. Soto," interjected John-Jack. "We're here to protect . . ."

"Now," she said.

"Ma'am, may I ask your relationship to Mr. Darley here?"

"I work for them," I said.

My comment was ignored by all.

"I hired him," said Layla.

She too was ignored.

"Now," said her mother once more.

"Or what?" asked Jack-John. He seemed to have found his balls after the humiliation. "Are you going to call the cops? Not a good idea if you want to keep this quiet."

"Gentlemen," said Eileen Chung. "We are very sorry to hear about the death of that man. Our regards to his family. But now you've been asked to leave by my daughter-in-law. If you fail to follow her wishes, we can escalate this matter. Secretary Irving Stubbs is an old friend, from his days at the CIA. You report to him, correct?"

The mention of his name deflated the agents.

"I thought so," said Eileen. We watched as she picked up a phone from a countertop. She tapped and scrolled a thumbnail across the screen until she found what she was looking for, then turned it to show them. "Should I give the secretary a ring?"

They eyed each other. Eileen put her phone to her ear. A ring passed, maybe two. John-Jack blinked first. He moved for the door. When his partner tried to stand firm, he looked back and swung his head in the direction of the front door. Jack-John glowered at Nicole Soto, before relenting and followed his buddy.

"Good boy," I said. I couldn't resist.

"Mr. Darley," said Eileen, lowering the phone. "Would you be so kind as to show the agents out?"

"My pleasure," I said, leaving the ladies in the kitchen.

I caught up to John and Jack in the high foyer beneath the chandelier. I reached the door ahead of them and pulled it open. It was a heavy slab of craftsmanship, like turning a redwood on its hinges.

"Remember what I said, Darley," said John-Jack. "One way or another."

His partner was less subtle. He stepped into my space like he wanted an angry goodbye kiss. Our noses almost touched. "You're a fucking dead man," he said. "Dead."

"We'll see," I said.

I wished I had something snappier, but the fact was I suspected he was right.

The women hadn't moved much when I returned. They were positioned around the center island, each set of eyes immersed in phones in their palms. Reentering the kitchen, I regarded them from a remove. All three were striking, and aware of it. Their collective posture and grace made an intimidating trio. Based upon mother and paternal grandmother, Layla's looks were not going anywhere. She sensed me there first, looked up, opened her mouth, but didn't find words. Nicole noticed her daughter's shift in attention. Followed her gaze.

"Are they gone?" she asked.

"I saw them out," I said. "Though I doubt they've gone far."

"Such awful little men."

"Antagonizing them will not help matters," said Eileen. "It was fortunate that I know Secretary Stubbs."

I joined them around the island. "Can I ask how you know the Secretary of State?"

"Secretary for now," she said. "You know how these things change in this administration. As I mentioned, we are acquainted from his days as director of the CIA."

"Nai-nai, how did you meet the head of the CIA?" asked Layla.

"I know many people in good positions," she said. "Your father too. We meet people, you know?"

No, we didn't know, or at least I didn't.

"What are the chances that driver's death doesn't end up in the media?" asked Nicole.

She didn't seem to be addressing any of us in particular, so I supplied the first impression.

"They'll probably call it a car accident," I said. "They'll find a way to cover up the marks on his neck. That kid Andy was a local. His mom's sick. He'll be missed."

"Did you know this man?" asked Eileen. "What happened last night? That agent mentioned obstruction?"

Before I could answer, Layla stepped in.

"They were messing with Duck outside the house," she said. "He came out from the city on the train, to return the money I gave him." Then, to me, "That guy was just giving you a lift from the station, right?"

"Right. It was his bad luck to pick me up." I pictured Andy being strangled, his last gasping moments, left like roadkill by a lake, all because of his brief association with me. "He seemed like a good dude," I said. "He was just trying to help."

I searched each beautiful face but failed to find much empathy amongst them. They seemed lost in their own private considerations, calculating the personal consequences of this latest disruption. Nicole filled the silence by walking to the stove and picking up a kettle. She filled it at the sink, set it down on a burner, and lit the gas. We watched as she busied herself preparing tea. Layla looked at her phone. Eileen Chung looked at me.

"What are your thoughts?" I asked her.

"About what exactly?"

"The execution of that kid," I said. "Any idea who might be behind it?"

"Perhaps he was mixed up in some unpleasant local matter," she said. "It may have nothing to do with us."

Her daughter-in-law was the first to scoff. Nicole's hands were shaking as she removed mugs from a cabinet. "And perhaps my husband just forgot to call," she said. "I'm sure he'll come waltzing back in any moment with a perfectly good explanation for his whereabouts this last week."

"Mom," said Layla.

But her mother had held it together long enough. Maybe the morning pills hadn't kicked in yet. Or maybe the visit from those agents, and this latest murder, were the final things she could bear before blowing. She turned on her mother-in-law.

"Did you know my daughter thinks you're behind this?" she asked.

"Mom."

"Go on, Layla, tell your nai-nai what you told Duck and me. Tell her you think she's involved in the abduction of her own son."

Layla looked at her bare feet, unable to meet the eyes of any adult in the room. In that moment she wasn't an almost grown-up; she was a little girl adrift in a nightmare, who missed her dad. Her eyes began to well. She wiped at them, hunched her shoulders. Then she gave up altogether and fled the room in a rush of tears.

"Well then," said Eileen.

"She does, you know," said Nicole. "And I'm inclined to believe her."

"Mr. Darley informed me of her suspicions last night. She is a scared girl, despite her poise, but I would expect more from her mother."

"Then explain yourself," said Nicole. She crossed her arms, jutted out her chin. All brave defiance in the face of her alien in-law. "Tell us why you have the secretary of state's number in your phone. Tell us about the business you arranged between Danny and that husband of yours."

Eileen sighed. "If you must know, I have left Guo Gonglu. We've been separated for months."

"Good for you. Now answer my questions."

The kettle began to whistle on the stove. Neither woman reacted to it. The shrill sound grew louder. Steam erupted from the spout. I stepped past them and turned off the burner. The water came down from a boil.

"Tea?" I asked.

No replies. Not the moment for levity, I suppose. I made myself useful and poured the boiling water over the teabags in the mugs and let them steep. The women continued to glare at one another with dislike. Eileen broke the silence.

"They were investing in companies together," she said. "Chinese firms interested in expanding their business to the United States. They were well positioned to help one another."

"What kind of companies?"

"Drug companies," I ventured.

Eileen stiffened. Nicole turned to me. "Drugs?" she asked.

"Pharmaceuticals," I said.

"Who told you that?"

"Last night, Mr. Darley and I had a talk on the beach," said Eileen. "Which is where we should continue this conversation right now."

Without waiting on us, she strode across the kitchen, swung open the door to the deck, and stalked down the steps and across the path to the ocean. Nicole and I watched her go. She was decisive in her movements, and she did not look back. When she disappeared past the dunes and seagrass, Nicole exhaled and said, "There goes the Dragon Lady."

"Should we join her?" I asked.

"It's always on her terms," she said, more to herself. "Fucking mother-in-laws."

"Every family has its weirdness."

That got a smile, a slight one. "How reassuring," she said. "Why would we need to talk on the beach? Is she really that paranoid?"

"There's no such thing as paranoia," I said. "And you should leave your phone inside." When she raised an eyebrow, I added, "They're probably listening."

"Who is *they*?"

But it's not like I had an answer for that.

Chapter 21

It was a bright, blazing morning in Southampton, the sun low over the Atlantic. A hot one ahead, I didn't want to consider the brutality of the city on a July day like this. But out here regular plunges in water—salt or chlorine— would cure any swelter.

The storm had cleared out and the horizon was crisp and clear, with only wisps of clouds interrupting the infinite palette of blues. The ocean was calm, the waves gentle. I was reminded of that scene in *Wall Street*, when Gordon Gekko stood on this beach at dawn and told Bud Fox to get to work. It was the moment that sealed a devil's bargain, a scene so loaded with ambition and promise that it created a generation of white collar criminals who missed the moral implications. The film always made me think of my father. It had been a family favorite. I wondered if the guards ever let him screen it in prison.

Eileen Chung was down on the sand, at the spot between mansions where we spoke last night, where she asked me to "deliver us from evil" before the storm forced us inside. She stood still and straight, looking out at the water. If she saw us approaching, she did not acknowledge it. Her silk robe rippled in a light wind. We stopped a few paces from her. Waited. Her toes curled into the hard sand as if her feet were clinging to the edge of the earth.

"Did you leave your phones?" she asked without turning.

Nicole gave me a side-eye.

"We did," I said.

"Both of you?"

"Yes, Eileen, Duck advised me. Do you really expect us to believe your paranoia?"

"I don't care what you believe," she replied. "But I appreciate your listening to Mr. Darley."

Nicole folded her arms across her toned midsection. The tide rushed over our feet. "Talk," she said. "Now that no one else is listening."

Eileen gazed skyward. "Someone could always listen," she said. "There is only so much we can do. Drones—they can record us as we stand here."

"I don't have time for this," said Nicole. But she stayed put.

"It is never simple," said Eileen. "At the highest level, with so much at stake, how can it be?"

She let that comment settle between us. It seemed to contain all the wisdom she could muster at the moment. Her feet began to sink into the wet sand, but she made no effort to dislodge herself. I tried to help her along.

"So, kidnapping and killing is common among billionaire business deals?"

"Common?" she asked.

"The cost of doing business."

At last she turned to face us. Her expression was stoic, as if she were regarding a piece of art that provoked nothing but indifference. She waved a hand toward the estates interspersed at wide intervals down the beach.

"Look," she said. "Look at the homes. So beautiful, so valuable. Do you know what it takes to have houses like these?"

"You tell me," I said.

"Anything. It takes a willingness to do *anything*. Whatever is required. It is very unusual to possess this determination. So rare, can you imagine?"

When we didn't reply, she addressed her daughter-in-law.

"Your husband, my son," she said, "he is one of those rare and determined people."

"Danny is not a killer," said Nicole. "Nor would he do business with murderers."

"Of course not," said Eileen. "I did not say that."

"Is he alive?" I asked.

There was a pause. Eileen raised her arms above her head and stretched in the morning sun.

"I don't know," she said.

She yawned, pressed her hands to her lower back and arched backward. A detective may have observed her mannerisms as not unsettled enough for the situation. She appeared far too Zen. Her son was missing, people were dying, federal agents were circling, but this woman seemed at a remove from it all. She was the eye of a strange high-stakes storm that swirled around her.

"What do you want me to do for you?" I asked.

"I told you," she said. "I want you to deliver us from evil."

"You *what*?" asked Nicole.

"This gentleman has come into our lives for a reason," said Eileen. "There are no accidents, no coincidences. Layla was wise in seeking him out."

"Enough grand talk," I said. "Your granddaughter came to me because she heard of a couple cases I worked on, one involving a kid at her school. I know what I am to you people."

"Which is what?" asked Nicole.

"An expendable servant," I told them. "I want to know who tried to kill me, and I'm willing to work for an amount of money that you won't miss. Let's cut out this high-minded crap. Just tell me what you want."

My comments provoked the first genuine connection I'd seen between the women. They looked at each other.

"See," said Eileen. "Layla picked the right man, an honest man, so rare."

"I'll lie whenever it suits me," I said. "But I also care less about myself than anyone you're likely to meet."

They regarded me with folded arms and tilted heads. Another wave rushed over our ankles, but no one moved.

"Look, you don't want the government involved, I get it. I don't see any private army around, which most folks in your position would have already hired. The head of your security detail is dead. And you're putting your faith in *me*? Sorry, I'm calling bullshit."

Nicole waited for her mother-in-law to explain. Eileen stepped away from the water's edge to dry sand. She frowned at the wet fringes of her dressing gown. When she failed to speak, Nicole huffed with exasperation and said, "Just tell him what we need."

Eileen sighed but did not look up from her feet. "We've received further details," she said. "From whoever is holding Danny."

"Both of you?" I asked.

They nodded.

"Soon after Richard was killed, and you were in the coma," said Nicole, "they sent me another e-mail. They said they informed us that there would be consequences and that Danny's return would be delayed. They said further instructions would follow. I haven't received anything else since, but Eileen . . ."

"I was also contacted," she said. "In person, as I left a lunch on the Bund."

The Bund, I recalled, was the pricey waterfront district in Shanghai, a stretch lined with embassies, high-end hotels, and fine dining. A century ago, it was where the French and the British and other colonizers had used the city as a gateway to China. They built a Western republic within the city, governed by their own laws.

"Who approached you?" I asked.

"An older Chinese man," she said. "Very polite and well dressed. It did not concern me when he asked to speak in his car. I figured it had to do with leaving Guo Gonglu."

"So, you got in? Was anyone else inside the car?"

"Yes, I got in, I believed I had no reason to be worried. I did not know Danny had been taken. There were two men in front, neither looked back. When the doors closed, we drove off. The older man would not give me his name when I asked. Then he told me they had my son. I was handed a sealed manila envelope and told not to open it until I was in the air. I asked where we were going. He said the airport, that Guo Gonglu's plane was waiting and would take me to New York. I asked if my husband was involved. He said no. I was told the rest would be explained when I opened the envelope after takeoff."

"You went straight to the airport and flew here on your husband's private jet? Did he say anything else? Were you allowed to pack anything?"

"I was let off at the steps to the plane. A bag had been packed and was waiting by my seat."

"Who else was on board?"

"All new staff, unfamiliar pilots and attendants, and two men who sat in the back. Everyone was very polite. I did not ask questions. I knew they would not be permitted to answer."

"And what did you find in that envelope?"

Eileen frowned. She took a few more steps back to protect her dressing gown from the rising tide. "I will show you," she said. "It is inside. It asked for a great deal of money, in order to have my son returned. It said that my husband had also been detained, but did not mention his possible release, for any amount."

"So, it was a ransom note," I said, "and you need me as your courier."

Both women averted their eyes. It was Nicole who spoke next.

"Eileen and I talked upstairs last night," she said. "We don't see any other options."

"We need you to make contact with Danny's partner at the firm, Peter Lennox. He is the only one able to handle a transaction of this size."

"How much are we talking?"

"Two billion dollars."

"*Billion?*"

"And several million for you," said Eileen. "If you are successful in your task."

"Why me?"

"I told you," said Nicole. "You appear to be our only choice. After Richard died, the rest of our security staff stopped coming in. The information given to Eileen was clear—any interference and it's not just Danny who will be killed."

"Who else?" I asked, already knowing the answer.

"All of us."

Chapter 22

Walking back to their estate, I should have been thinking of the risk, the likelihood of surviving my role in the ransom process. Instead, I was already spending the millions I'd been promised. *Several* million—life-changing money, it was enough to buy a new apartment, maybe a little cottage by the beach, a long vacation with nothing but reading and swimming, a return to my born-rich life that I once considered a birthright.

Greed—the deadliest of the seven deadlies.

On the private path between the sea grass and the pool, Eileen took my arm and leaned close. "Some advice," she said. "If I may."

"I'm listening."

"From now on, eat only fast food."

Not what I was expecting, but okay . . . "May I ask why?"

"You've already been poisoned once," she said. "This will help ensure that it doesn't happen again."

I considered that. It made some sense. Mass-produced assembly-line garbage would be much harder to tamper with. Though the attempt on my life hadn't come from poisoned food the first time.

"You must be careful with your food and drink. That is how it happens most times. In Russia, you know, it is a regular thing. In China too, more than people think. Can you imagine?"

I could.

"People don't know this, but this is why your president eats so much McDonald's. He is afraid of being poisoned. When I heard that, I thought—smart, I will remember. So, you trust me. Only fast food while you're on this case, okay?"

"You're the boss."

Hearing us enter, Layla Soto came striding back downstairs. She was showered and dressed for the day in green shorts and a white tank top, her tears dried. She gave us a toss of damp hair and went to the refrigerator. I watched her scan its contents, reach for nothing, and close the door. A hand on her hip, she faced us and said, "So . . ."

"Layla," said her grandmother, "you know I had nothing to do with your father's disappearance, don't you?"

"Sure," she said.

"You must believe me. I could never. He is my son."

"Then what was he talking about with your husband?"

"I am leaving Guo Gonglu."

"Good for you."

"This is a difficult time."

"Okay, what was my dad talking about with your soon-to-be latest ex-husband?"

"Business."

"Drug-dealing business?"

"Pharmaceutical business."

"There's a difference? Look at mom."

Nicole Soto stiffened and strode from the room. A moment later, I heard the stairs creaking as she went up, perhaps, to her medicine cabinet.

"Guai guai, I don't know what that means, but now is not the time to be pointing fingers at your family. Not at me or your parents. We all need to focus on bringing your father back. Isn't that why you sought out Mr. Darley?"

"Sure."

"So, now we must give him anything he needs. He can help us."

"They killed Richard," said Layla. "Federal agents are parked outside. You're dropping the name of the secretary of state. There's this huge cover-up going on. What's this guy supposed to do?"

"Probably get myself killed," I said.

"He can help us," said Eileen.

"Or die trying, great." Layla turned a shoulder to me. "Nai-nai, I hired this guy, right? So, can I fire him? I don't know why he's here. It's just made everything more complicated."

"I'm sorry, guai guai, but I have rehired Mr. Darley myself. I think you should trust your instincts. I do."

"I have no say in this?"

"I always want to hear what you have to say."

"And ignore it."

Eileen pointed to me. "You brought this man to us, yes? You found him, you offered him money, you asked for his help. But you did not know the forces at work. Now people have died."

"That's supposed to be my fault?" cried Layla. "Richard's death, and that taxi driver from last night? I can't believe you're blaming *me*."

"No one is blaming you. I am only pointing out what has been set in motion. Whether you like it or not, Mr. Darley is a part of this. Sometimes it takes a stranger to help."

"Someone expendable," I added.

They both looked at me. Layla lowered her chin; her eyes narrowed. I noticed a tremble of her lips. She was trying so hard to keep it together. I wondered about the psychic damage that was accumulating in that precocious mind.

"How's he even going to make it back to the city?" she asked.

"I had a thought about that," said a voice behind us.

We turned. Nicole Soto was back. Beads of perspiration dotted her hairline. Her cheeks were flushed. Her chest rose and fell with her breath. It looked like her heart rate was still settling.

"I'm sorry, my anxiety," she said. "It's not good these days. I needed a moment."

"I understand," said her mother-in-law.

She didn't.

Nicole wiped at her forehead. Breath wheezed through her nose. She faced her daughter. "I was wondering the same thing. If someone killed that driver last night, they must be waiting for Duck to leave, as well."

"Right?" asked Layla, perking up at the commiseration.

"What do you suggest?" I asked.

"Come with me," said Nicole. "All of you."

We followed her across the endless home. Rooms seemed to wind and turn and unfold on each other in a dizzying succession. Out each window, a different postcard view, of the Atlantic, the rolling dunes, and the bay. The house had been designed for moments of contemplation, before the distractions of technology stole our attention away from natural beauty. I wanted to stop at each pane of glass and record mental snapshots. The art between these views was no less distracting. I kept falling behind as the three women strode in front of me. Layla turned and beckoned me forward.

Nicole was leading us into another, less updated kitchen at the far end of the home. It appeared to have been un-

touched from another age, where grand feasts were prepared. The kitchen for the help, where a restaurant-sized
staff assembled meals for summer parties that would be
the talk of the East End. A forgotten wing of Chateau de
Soto, they'd get around to it sooner or later.

"We don't do much entertaining," said Nicole, "so I
haven't had much need for this industrial kitchen, but
whatever, it came with the place."

"I don't think I've ever been in here," said Layla.

Eileen Chung stood waiting for her daughter-in-law to
explain.

"Maybe we'll use it for a party someday," said Nicole.

Layla gazed around, unimpressed. "Maybe," she said.

To me, Nicole added, "We Sotos are mostly homebod-
ies, I suppose. We like our privacy. Aside from the cleaning
staff and the grounds crew, I hate having too many people
around. I don't want to see them, in any case. It makes me
uneasy. Besides Ida, to help with Lionel, I prefer things
quiet and simple."

I thought of their tower in the city. There were few signs
of worker-bee life there either, yet *someone* must be
around to keep things impeccable. It wasn't the owners of
the palatial apartments.

"A historic thirty-thousand-square-foot castle on the
beach," I said, "the simple things in life."

Nicole gave a wicked grin. "Perhaps the wrong word,"
she said. "Buying this house was a way to shut up certain
folks. Those silly hens who still think 'society' should be cap-
italized." She air-quoted the S-word. "It's all such a joke. I
have fun fucking with the old guard. They lust over houses
like these. They were horrified when we bought it."

She nodded toward her mother-in-law, as if she could
explain, but Eileen wasn't paying attention.

"Especially Danny," Nicole continued. "He's the worst

type—new money *and* foreign. At least half. He didn't even go to school in the States, much less the right ones. They don't know what to make of him, and as for me . . ."

"Mom," said Layla. "What the hell?"

"What, honey?"

"When you're done, you think you can tell us what we're doing here?"

Layla flashed me a quick look. I read it. Her mom was getting loopy. On her trip upstairs, she'd probably popped a few. They were kicking in. A couple Vikes sounded good right about now. Something to numb the edge, something to slow that feeling of doom that was creeping up my spine.

I eyed Nicole. She was running her fingernails along her nose. Her lower jaw clicked. I knew the telltale signs. I mimicked her movements, but she didn't seem to notice.

"Was I rambling?" she asked. When no one replied, she continued, "Very well, would you all like to see what I have to show you? It's very cool."

She walked across the space to a large antique cupboard. Hand-carved walnut, a couple centuries old, it was over seven feet tall and looked like the sort of piece that would never be moved. It was forever part of the home, even if the current occupants seldom set foot in the room. We watched as Nicole ran her hands along the side, searching for a remembered something. She frowned. Her eyes seemed to glaze over. She had the opioid sways, a slow, silent song playing in her head. I sensed Layla about to step in to help.

Then Nicole's hand stopped on a spot high up on the armoire, almost out of reach. She straightened, her eyes opened wider.

"Aha," she said. "Here it is."

"Here's what?" asked Layla.

As soon as she said it, the cupboard began to move outwards, like a heavy door swinging slowly open. Though it must have been on ancient hinges, it made no sound. It opened forty-five degrees and stopped. Nicole stepped aside and swept her arm in a grand magician's gesture.

"Ta-da!" she exclaimed. She even added a little bow.

I doubted Eileen noticed, but Nicole seemed very high indeed. We stepped past her and peered around the moveable piece. Hidden behind it, about half its height and width, was a small arched door.

"What the . . ." whispered Layla.

"Where does this lead?" asked Eileen.

"Why don't we find out?" replied Nicole, thrilled and looped.

She stepped to the door, pulled at its latch, and pushed at it. It swayed open without a sound. Darkness came from within. Stone steps led down to a secret cellar.

"Who has a phone handy?" she asked. "We need a flashlight."

Layla lit hers. She held out the face of her phone, moved past her mother, and pointed it down the steps. They were steep. The ceiling was low and narrow. She took the first step without looking back.

"What's down there?" asked Eileen.

"Careful, honey," called Nicole.

I followed her before the grown-ups could object. I counted thirteen steps before we reached a dirt floor at the bottom. Though the cellar ceiling wasn't high, the dark room was more spacious than the claustrophobic descent. Around us were shelves of booze, some in casks, some bottled. I read the labels of the whiskeys and scotch and rum. Canadian Club, AAA, Old Fitzgerald, Havana Club . . . I recognized where we were. The hooch around us had once been contraband.

"Prohibition," I said. "A bootlegger's basement."

"The man knows his stuff," said Nicole. She took the last step and joined us in the cellar.

Eileen was a few paces behind. When she reached the dim space, she looked around, bewildered. "I do not understand," she said.

"I can't believe you never told me about this," said Layla.

Nicole gave a flighty laugh. "It didn't seem appropriate to tell my teenage daughter about a secret cellar full of alcohol."

"How long have you known about this?"

"Since we first looked at the house. It was a sales point, though the broker claimed it was secret and that she only told buyers she thought were serious. When your father made an offer, she was quite eager to share the details."

I went to the bottles, wiped away decades-old dust. I read once that before Prohibition in the 1920s, no one ordered booze by brand. Whiskey, scotch, rum, gin, whatever, you ordered liquor without specifying the maker. But when it all became illegal, requesting certain brands became a mark of quality. It was a bit like the slow road to marijuana legalization. It used to be just pot. You smoked what you were sold, and you didn't ask about certain strains or names. No longer; now weed was branded and marketed just like Prohibition-era alcohol.

"We learned that this house was built in 1925 by a man named Jack Gillis," said Nicole. "He sounds like a fascinating Gatsby sort of figure. Not much is known about him. Evidently one of his main businesses was bootlegging. This wasn't just a beach house for him, it was supposedly an important part of his distribution network."

Eileen was at the foot of the stairs looking bored. "May I ask," she said with a yawn, "why we are down here? What does this . . ."

Nicole beamed, eager to have an upper hand over her mother-in-law. "It's not *just* a cellar," she said. "There's more."

We watched her go to a shelf at the far end of the space. Layla shined her flashlight after her. In the focused light Nicole again began to feel along the side of a structure. The shelves were stocked a bit less than the others around us. She reached between two bottles. We heard a click. Then she pulled at a piece of the shelving. It creaked and swayed forward. For a moment I thought it was about to fall, destroying untold bottles of boozy relics. But the shelves stayed upright and Nicole moved out of the way.

"Another secret passage?" asked Layla. Now she was impressed.

We peered around her. No steps this time, just a dark, dank passage to God knows.

"It's a tunnel," said Nicole. "It goes under the dunes of Shinnecock Park and comes out near the inlet. The broker told us that Jack Gillis built it for his bootlegging. He'd have his boats pick up the booze at sea, from bigger ships in international waters. Then they'd pull into the inlet to unload, and bring it in through the tunnel, right into this room."

"Fucking rad," said Layla, stepping forward and staring into the darkness.

"Language, guai guai," said Eileen behind her.

"Sorry, nai-nai, but how cool is this?"

Nicole was enjoying herself. Between her pill high and her series of secret reveals, she was almost giddy. Her missing husband, the murders of Richard Gross and that driver, the dangers that lurked outside the house, all that had been temporarily forgotten.

"This guy Gillis was no dummy," she went on. "Think about it—the place is at the end of a narrow peninsula, last house on the left, next to a state park and a narrow inlet that separates the ocean from the bay. Perfect for boats to unload in calm waters and get the product safely onto his property. And this house is so big, he could constantly have trucks coming to deliver furniture or whatever. Then they'd refill them with alcohol and send it back to the city."

When she noticed our looks, she added, "After what the broker told us, I did some Googling. It's all so fascinating. The Roaring Twenties, Prohibition, it was such an interesting time, don't you think?"

"Have you ever been through there?" I asked, pointing down the tunnel.

She nodded. "Danny and I explored it after we closed on the house. Richard Gross joined us. He secured the exit with a lock from the inside, for security. I stored the key in the safe in our bedroom. The outside door in the state park is almost impossible to see, unless you know where to look."

"This is all quite remarkable," said Eileen. "But what do you propose? Are you suggesting that Mr. Darley goes through this tunnel? And then what?"

Her daughter-in-law put a hand on a hip and said, "Yes, mother, that's what I'm proposing. Unless you have a better idea?"

I stepped between them. "I'm game," I said. "But what am I supposed to do when I get out? Get in the water?"

Nicole tapped her daughter on the shoulder. Layla had been inching into the tunnel, trying to get a better look inside. "Layla, honey, didn't you say Duck was a swimmer?"

She nodded without turning. "Yeah, remember those *Post* stories from the McKay case? He and that guy used to be teammates."

"Well, then, there you go," she said, as if that settled an obvious matter.

"You're suggesting I swim across the inlet?" I asked.

"Of course. It's very narrow. Perhaps a few laps of an

Olympic-sized pool. The water is warm enough this time of year. I trust that wouldn't be a problem?"

"Of course not," I said. Though I was wondering how she expected my bag of cash, burner phones, and the ransom instructions to stay dry during my passage. Or what I was supposed to do when I reached the beach across the way.

"We have a sealable dry pack," she said, way ahead of me. "On one of his infrequent Hamptons visits, Danny decided to take up paddle-boarding in the bay. He bought a watertight bag, so he wouldn't be without his phone and belongings, just in case." She shook her head at her husband's ridiculousness. "I think he used it once. Anyway, I stored it in our water-sports room. We can fill it with whatever you need."

"And after I get through the tunnel and across the inlet with everything dry, then what?"

"Then you can use that investigator's brain of yours to find a way back to the city and rendezvous with Peter Lennox." She let out an odd, looped laugh. "I mean, really, am I expected to think of everything?"

"I guess I can manage from there."

I considered how I might appear to their neighbors across the bay, a figure emerging from the sea, with a sealed bag of essentials strapped to his back. Would I call a cab and have him take me all the way back to the city for a couple hundred bucks? Would that driver, like Andy, wind up dead, if anyone spotted me? Should I find my way to the train station and attempt to board the Long Island Railroad unseen? Should I take a walk down the beach until I reached the next town over? These did not sound like promising options.

"I can call someone," said Layla. "I know someone who can pick you up and take you back, wherever you want to go."

"Who are you going to call, honey?" asked Nicole.

"A friend."

Layla crossed her arms, challenging her mother to press for details.

"You're prepared to put this friend in danger?" she asked. "You know what happened to the last two gentlemen who were seen with Mr. Darley."

"If Duck can make it through the tunnel and across the bay without being seen, then my friend should be able to pick him up without being noticed."

"Who is he?" I asked.

Layla glared at me. A boy, I guessed. Some random local who had a thing for her was my bet, someone who would leap at her beck and call without consideration of consequence.

"We'll call him Sam," she said. "Not his real name, and no, I do not wish to discuss his identity with any of you—for the sake of security. All Duck needs to know is that he drives a blue Ford F-150. A big pickup, newer model, maybe a year or two old."

"Works for me," I said before mother or grandmother could object. "Just tell me where to find him."

"There's a restaurant and marina called Backlands," said Layla. "It's right over the point, on the bayside. You'll see it."

Nicole regarded her daughter with hands on hips. The parenting moment would have to be deferred. "We will discuss this Sam at some point in the future," she said. "You can be assured of that."

"Whatever," said Layla. "Let's get Duck ready to go."

Chapter 23

I followed the women back out of the cellar, up the stairs, through the unused staff kitchen, and we reentered the rest of the main house. Nicole closed both secret doors behind us, taking care to leave things as they were. She might have valued her quiet and privacy, but I wondered if she knew how false it was. She may not see them often, but this place had to be teeming with staff, both inside and out. Everything was too well maintained. In some part of her addled mind, she must have known they were always being watched.

I went to fetch my bag from the bedroom where I'd crashed. The distance from that cellar to this wing felt like a few city blocks. You could spend a night calling for help at one end, and no one would ever hear your cries from the other. I admired the paintings before leaving. In another home these works would have pride of place. Here at Chateau de Soto they hung, seldom seen, in one of the innumerable guest rooms. I took a few hits from my pen to calm the nerves, wished I had a Xanax to go with it. The vapor dissipated almost as soon as it left my mouth.

When I wound my way back to the center hall, I found them waiting in the ocean-facing living room. The morning sun was hard in the sky, glaring at the sea. Waves tumbled over the sand and rushed toward us, before losing energy and rolling back. Nicole and Layla sat at either end of a plush couch. Eileen was opposite them, in an elegant high-backed chair. All three gazed out the window to the water.

On a coffee table between them, there was a manila envelope. The instructions that Eileen Chung had been given in Shanghai, before she was deposited onto her husband's private plane and jetted across the globe to New York.

"Are those the orders?" I asked.

They turned together.

"In there, yes," said Eileen, nodding toward the table. "Come, take a look."

Mother and daughter watched me approach. Neither moved as I picked up the envelope and slid out the contents. They'd been typed in English.

"Layla, honey," said Nicole. "Maybe you shouldn't hear this. It could be very troubling. Why don't you—"

"I'm not going anywhere," said her daughter.

It seemed a little late to shield her at this point. From what I'd witnessed, parenting did not come easily to Nicole Soto. Her daughter possessed more resolve than she did. I wondered where Lionel was at the moment. Somewhere being tended to by the nanny, someone else's problem to handle. I considered how much he was processing in this crisis.

Nicole sighed, absently rubbing at the phantom opiate itch on her nose. "Well," she said, "have a look."

I sat on the carpet before the coffee table, pulled the papers in front of me, and began to read.

Mrs. Eileen Chung,
We have your son, Mr. Daniel Soto. We hoped to
settle a business matter without interference, how-

*ever, the situation has changed. In exchange for his
return, we now require a fee in the amount of two billion U.S. dollars.*

"Two billion," I said. "Jesus."

"It's outrageous," said Nicole.

"Relax, mom," said Layla. "Dad has, like, twice that."

"How would you know your father's worth?"

"It's called Google."

So much for being disturbed. Layla Soto was taking this
with a peculiar degree of nonchalance. Her previous burst
of tears was a momentary crack. The girl who'd come to
me days ago had been certain that her grandmother was
behind her father's abduction. Now that narrative had
shifted; people had died, yet she continued to behave in a
disconnected manner without apparent distress. I remembered the story of Amanda Knox, convicted of murder during her semester abroad in Italy. Before multiple trials and
her eventual acquittal, the cops had watched her doing
cartwheels in the police station and making out with her
boyfriend just hours after her roommate was butchered.
That behavior, more than any evidence, cast suspicion
around her. I'd read that many Italians still thought she
was guilty.

Though one's actions in the face of trauma and terror
are never consistent. There might be an expected human
response—tears, anger, panic—but it's not universal. Or
maybe Amanda Knox really was a murderer. And maybe
Layla Soto was acting so nonchalant because she knew
something we didn't.

"Should I continue?" I asked.

"I don't know how we are expected to find two billion
dollars," said Nicole.

"Mom, let him keep reading!"

"Where was I? *In the amount of* . . . Okay, here we are."

> *These funds must be transferred through Soto Capital, to an LLC called East Equity Holdings, in a trade to be arranged by SC senior partner, Peter Lennox. The full amount must be received no later than Friday, July 27. We trust this date will provide time to make arrangements. Details are enclosed. Discretion is required. When funds are received, Mr. Soto will be permitted to return to his life. If the money is not received, you will never see him again, and we will come for his family.*

Reading the last lines, I looked at his daughter, thought of his son upstairs. My chest tightened. Eileen stepped forward and took the pages from me with steady hands. She examined the instructions like an attorney reviewing a contract, focused, without emotion.

"Danny has already signed these documents," she said. "They will make this appear to be a legal trade between two parties. They will need Peter Lennox to execute. But we cannot be seen entering the offices of Soto Capital."

"Why not?" asked Layla.

"Because the government is watching," said her grandmother. "They are watching all of us. This is why we need Mr. Darley's help. We need him to deliver these instructions to Mr. Lennox. He will know what to do, where to get the money, how to move it."

"This is insane," said Nicole.

"Nai-nai, who are these people?" asked Layla.

"I told you, I don't know, guai guai."

"But you must have some idea. It must have something to do with your husband. Have you talked to him?"

"I am no longer with Guo Gonglu. As I mentioned, I—"

"Whatever, your *ex*-husband. Who cares? He was working on something with dad, something involving drugs, and a few days after I heard him yelling at you, dad was taken. Stop pretending to be so clueless."

"I am not pretending to be anything," said Eileen. "I have not spoken to Guo Gonglu. I fear he has already been killed."

"Why?" I asked. "By who?"

All three women regarded me sitting between them on the floor like a family dog who'd just barked for attention.

"In China," said Eileen, "when people are disruptive, it is common to be detained. Some are never returned. It does not matter how rich. No one is above the Party."

"How was your husband being disruptive?" I asked.

"I don't know."

"Bullshit," said Nicole.

She was shaking in her seat, filled with a rage and a fear that superseded whatever drugs coursed through her blood. The rest of us shifted away from the dark energy emanating from her. Nicole stood and approached her mother-in-law with quick, angry strides. She loomed over her at the foot of the chair. She raised her arms like a boxer's. For a second, I thought she might hit her.

"You know more than you're saying," she said. "I know it, my daughter knows it, and Duck knows it too. Now you're putting my entire family—my *children*—at risk. Goddamn you!"

It might have taken a bone-deep shock, but now this mama bear was full of fury and she was going on the attack. If it had not been a fragile grandmother before her, I had no doubt there would have been physical violence.

Eileen did not react in kind. If anything, she seemed to relax further in the face of such anger. "You are feeling irrational rage," she said. Her voice was calm, her inflection even. "It is a common response in a situation such as this, but an unhelpful one."

"Tell us what you know!" screamed Nicole.

The calmer her adversary, the more enraged Nicole became.

"Mom," said Layla. "Please."

Layla stood, took a step toward her mother. I sought her eyes, shook her off. Layla sat back down and looked at the sea. The sun was at a blinding angle through the windows, but she did not look away. It seemed she'd inherited her grandmother's genetic disposition. Nothing was fazing either of them.

"Think what you will," said Eileen. "I've told you all that I know. Danny and Guo Gonglu were doing business together. They planned to purchase a pharmaceutical company, a large firm with international interests."

"Which seems to have upset the folks in Beijing," I said.

"Perhaps," she conceded. "You must remember, in China the rich only exist at the pleasure of the Party. If one causes trouble, there will always be others enlisted to remove him. Same as Russia. Everyone in the West knows Putin, yes? Because it is an easy name to remember. But Xi Jinping, he is even more powerful, did you know? He is the most powerful man on earth, the president for life."

She placed her bony hands on her knees, pushed herself up, and tried to move past her daughter-in-law. Nicole blocked her path, then relented and let her pass. In the archway of the living room, Eileen Chung paused and turned back to us.

"We need him to get ready to go," she said. "Please, can you find that waterproof bag, so he may keep these papers dry?" She paused, then added, "Please hurry."

Chapter 24

While Nicole went off to find the bag in her "water-sports room," I had a seat on the couch next to Layla. She stiffened as I sat, scooted a bit farther away. I looked at her in profile, with the glare of the sun lighting her features. Up close, she was still a kid. Her high cheekbones still held hints of baby fat. The skin around her eyes was unblemished.

"So, who's this friend of yours?" I asked. "The one who's supposed to pick me up."

"Sam," she said without turning. "His name is Sam."

"No, it's not, but I don't care what it is. What does he look like? How should I spot him?"

"I told you, he drives a Ford F-150. Just look for his truck."

"I doubt he's the only guy in the Hamptons who drives that. This isn't the time for any mistaken identities. Please describe him for me. Answer my questions, and then please call him in front of me."

"I don't have to—"

"Yes, you do. You and your grandma are pretty good at the denial, kid, but it won't last. It's okay to be scared. I am too. Now talk."

Layla let out a dramatic sigh and swept a hand through her hair.

"He's tall with shaggy blond hair. He'll probably be wearing this camo hoodie. He's always wearing the same thing when he's not in the ocean, which is where he is most of the time. He's, like, a pro surfer."

"How old?"

"I don't know, like twenty-seven? Something like that."

"A little old for you, isn't he?"

"Did I say I was hooking up with him? No."

"You're right," I said. "I'm sure he's just a good friend, one you can trust with your life—or mine."

That last line got her attention. "What am I supposed to tell him?" she asked.

"That you need a favor."

"And?"

"Are you gonna offer to pay him?"

"Should I?"

"Probably."

"How much?"

"You tell me. As you've pointed out, I'm pretty clueless when it comes to money."

"I can't believe you're doing all this for fifty grand," she said.

"Yeah, well, we renegotiated. My fee went up a bit with your nai-nai."

"How much did she offer you?"

"We haven't finalized our agreement yet, but I was told a few million."

"Good for you."

"Given the stakes, I'd say price is irrelevant."

"I guess," she sniffed. "Considering they might kill my dad, and then us."

"You love him, don't you?" I asked.

"Who, that surfer guy? Of course not. Why would you ask—"

"I meant your dad."

That caught her tongue. She closed her eyes, nodded once. Her entire body appeared to shudder. She hugged herself. The dam was threatening to burst once more. "He's the only one who gets me," she said.

"I sort of figured that."

"Why?"

"Spending a summer in the city? Instead of this castle on the beach? Just you and him in that crazy apartment, while the rest of your family is out here?"

"I told you, I need to focus on my piano. It's the summer before senior year."

I swept my arm around the room. "You can fit a few pianos in this place. You can put up any teacher you want in a guesthouse. You're driven, just like your dad. You're more comfortable working in the city than lying by the pool. I get it."

Layla shifted in her seat, putting her back to me. Her shoulders hunched. A hand raised and wiped at her eyes. When she spoke next it was barely above a whisper. "I can't believe I didn't check on him," she said. "When I got home that night, I didn't even duck my head in his room to say I was back."

"What happened the next day?" I asked.

"He's usually out the door at, like, five a.m. When I woke up, I figured he was already at work. I played some piano, went for a run, then met up with some friends in the afternoon."

"And that night? When did you realize he was gone?"

"I didn't." Her voice broke as she relived all she might have done differently. "I didn't think anything until my mom forwarded me that encrypted email, with the video of him being wheeled away with the hood over his head."

"Layla, listen," I said. "There is nothing you could have done. You did nothing wrong. If anything, you're the only one in your family who's done anything proactive to get him back."

She snorted. "What, by hiring you, and getting a bunch of people killed?"

"None of that's on you, kid," I told her. "If anyone's responsible, it's me. Both men who've died—I was the last person they were with."

"That's pretty fucked up."

"I tend to have that effect on people."

That almost got a laugh. Nicole Soto picked that moment to return. She was holding the watertight bag and a pair of swim trunks. Her daughter got up and walked from the room without looking back. She needed to call her mystery friend, my ride back to town, if I made it that far. Her mom looked down at me.

"I found the bag," she said. "And I brought you a suit. You're bigger than Danny, but I think this should fit okay."

"Much appreciated," I said.

"Is everything okay with Layla?"

"I don't think anything's okay with anyone in this house," I said. "Does your son know what's going on?"

"Lionel? Of course not. I would never. He could never digest such a thing. I informed Ida that we're dealing with a family matter, and that it's important for her to keep Lionel occupied right now. She understood."

I stood and took the suit and the bag from her. Tried to listen for sounds of her son upstairs, but all was silent beyond us.

"I'm sure he's in good hands with Ida," I said. "Have you given any thought to your other staff?"

"I'm not sure what you mean."

"I mean that someone with access to your home must have been complicit in your husband's abduction."

"Someone who *works* for us?"

"That's almost always the case with high-profile kidnappings. I'm not saying anyone on your staff is behind this, but whoever is would have needed somebody on the inside."

"You think someone . . . in our building in the city?"

"I'm not sure if Layla mentioned it, but it seems there's been some staff turnover since Danny was taken—the doorman, the lobby manager. Did she tell you we spoke to your building's head of security?"

"Bill Willis? No. Why?"

"If they managed to hack into the tower's cameras, he might have noticed. He might even be complicit."

"If he's involved," said Nicole, "I'll ruin that sloppy bastard."

"Your daughter said the same thing."

"We're both quite capable of doing so."

"I'm sure you are."

"I spoke to your partner, Cassandra. Did you know that?"

"I did. She was at my bedside for most of the time I was out."

"She must really care for you."

"It's complicated."

"Isn't it though."

"Did she reach out to you?" I asked.

"She did. She sent me a rather cryptic direct message on my Instagram. Danny always said that I'm too easy to track on social media."

"What did she say?"

"She wrote, 'It's about your husband, please call.' She

provided a number. When I looked at the pictures posted to her account, I worried that this was some kind of sexual shakedown."

"It must have been a short-lived relief."

"It was. I soon found out that, no, my husband was not cheating with this woman, but that our trusted Richard was dead, and that the man my daughter hired was in a coma. Then, those agents visited us, the cover-up became apparent, and everything became even worse."

"Not for me," I said. "I woke up."

"Lucky you."

I looked down at the watertight bag she still held in her hand. "So, shall we get going?"

We retraced our steps through the far-flung house. Nicole led the way with her daughter by her side. Both seemed deflated and moved a bit closer together in their strides. Eileen hung back with me but did not offer any comments or conversation. She had materialized once more as soon as we prepared to go. Even after making the round-trip less than an hour before, winding through the halls I had the sense that I'd never find my way to that industrial kitchen and the secret passages below without a guide. The thought of living in a home amongst so many vacant rooms was unsettling. There were too many points of entry, for ghosts of every type.

Back inside the cavernous kitchen, no one spoke as Nicole went to the cupboard and this time found the hidden access without effort. The heavy carved piece swung open without a sound. Layla went down first; I followed, with the older women behind us, in the same procession as earlier. The cellar felt smaller than before, already familiar after one visit. The bottles beckoned. It would have been nice to spend a boozy night raiding and sampling this old contraband.

Nicole opened the entry to the tunnel. I turned on the flashlight I'd been given for my journey. I shined it down the low, dark passage. It would be a claustrophobic escape.

"About how long does it go?" I asked.

"Maybe a ten-minute walk, as I recall?"

"Just a straight shot? No turns or forks in the road I should be aware of?"

"It's a straight line, you should find the exit without difficulty," said Nicole. "Do you have the key I gave you?"

I held it up. The key that the now-dead Richard Gross had made to restrict access to this Prohibition path. "What if it doesn't open the lock?" I asked.

"Then come back the way you came," said Layla. "I'll wait here for a while to make sure you're out."

"And your friend Sam, he'll be waiting in the parking lot of that restaurant?"

"He promised he'd be there. I'm making it worth his while."

"I don't even want to know," said Nicole.

"By *paying* him. Jesus, mom, you really think . . ."

"I don't know what to think anymore."

Those were parting words as good as any.

"Ladies," I said, as I nodded farewell. "Wish me luck. I'll make contact when I reach the city."

"Use the phones I gave you," said Layla.

"Be safe, Mr. Darley," said Eileen. "Think of your fee. If you take care of us, we will do the same for you."

To the tune of several million dollars . . . No, I was not forgetting about that particular carrot of motivation. I bid my farewells to the three women, turned to the tunnel, and began to follow the glow of the flashlight.

For the first minute or two I breathed easy. The clearance was maybe five feet, so I had to move in a crouch. The breadth of the passage was about the same. The walls and ceiling had been reinforced with thick wooden planks. The ground was cool, damp dirt. The path began to turn to the right and the dim light of the cellar disappeared behind me. I quickened my pace, started to jog as my fear swelled. I thought of soldiers in Vietnam jungles, forced to patrol the dark echoes in tunnels such as this. Five minutes in and I was sweating hard. I felt an anxiety attack threatening. I sucked at my pen. Ever since the events of a few years ago, PTSD had been a lurking part of my consciousness. Situations that provoked panic and a loss of control were inadvisable. I willed myself onwards. Prayed that goddamn key would slide right in and open a door to daylight.

Fifteen minutes later and I was in a state of full freakout. I must have taken a wrong turn, I thought, despite there being no turns available. I was moving fast, much faster than Nicole Soto must have been when she explored this passage with her husband and Richard Gross. She said it was a ten-minute walk. Something must have gone wrong. I considered turning back. I stopped, gasping, put my hands on my knees and tried to find my breath. I thought I might faint. I squeezed my eyes shut and tried to count. When I reached one hundred, I exhaled and straightened up. I banged my head against the low plank ceiling and went back down. Breathed through another slow count to a hundred and pressed on.

I came to the door soon after. I swung the flashlight in search of the lock. When the beam shined on it, I grasped for the key in my pocket, then dropped it to the dirt as my hands shook. Using the light to find it, I somehow managed to bring it up and slide it in.

When it clicked, I felt the panic wash away. I slid off the padlock and pushed at the door. It didn't budge. I gave it a few more shoves, then tried kicking. Sand burst from slits in the wood. I backed up, took a running start and flung my shoulder at the door. And then I was falling out onto hot sand under a hard noon sun.

I was between low windblown dunes with the real estate behind me. Seagrass and untended flora offered little cover. The tunnel had been dug in the middle of a protected state park. It was a narrow, sandy peninsula kept from developers and monstrous spec homes. Chateau de Soto would forever be the last house on Meadow Lane. I stood to my full height, rubbed at my lower back after that hunched journey. I turned and closed the doorway to the tunnel, kicked sand over the boards. With a bit of wind, more would soon blow over it and conceal it fully. I couldn't lock it from the outside, but that was no longer my problem. Someone would need to make the same journey I did through that tunnel if they wanted to lock it again from the inside. Maybe with enough pills Nicole would be looped enough to consider it an adventure. Or perhaps she'd enlist her nanny, Ida, to do it while mother spent some time with her son.

I heard an engine, tires crunching, turned and saw a truck rumbling closer through a sandy trail between the dunes. I flung myself down. Waited for it to pass. I needed to keep moving. I orientated myself with the Atlantic to my left and tracked south. I reached the point after a couple hundred yards.

There was a sand lot full of pickups and RVs. Behind them, a jetty stretched into the surf. It was lined with fishermen scattered along the rocks. There were twenty or so, maybe more, all with their backs to me, with lines drifting in an unusual current. A couple fishing boats bobbed at the mouth of the inlet.

My passage across looked short, no more than one length of a fifty-meter pool; however, there would be obstacles. I needed to avoid being hooked. The fishermen would see me, there was no avoiding that, and they would probably object to any fool trying to swim near their lines. The current was also cause for concern. As ocean met bay, the waters swirled and then went calm, as if there were some man-made barrier just beneath the surface. That may have explained its popularity as a fishing spot; fish must have collected in that halting tide.

My best course would be to swim out into the ocean and around to the far beach in a wide arc. It would be a longer journey, but safer, and less likely to involve interaction with others.

I ran across the lot and found some cover between two empty trucks. I stripped and stepped into a pair of Danny Soto's swim trunks, provided by his wife. They were too tight and wouldn't fasten at the waist. I remembered Soto being a snake-hipped guy, leaner than I. Chances were the suit wouldn't stay on in the water and I'd emerge fully exposed. I folded my shorts and t-shirt around my flip-flops and stuffed it on top of the cash, the phones, and the envelope of instructions. I examined the bag. Waterproof or watertight? That was an important distinction. Atop a paddle board, the bag might protect one's valuables from waves, but it didn't look meant for a submerged open-water passage. I'd have to make the swim on my back, with my cargo raised dry above my chest while I kicked.

I stepped out from between the pickups and crossed to the beach with something like nonchalance. I ignored the fishermen and they seemed to ignore me. I went to the water's edge on the near side of the jetty where the waves broke and looked out to sea. Hands on my hips, bare chest thrust, just another proud Hamptonite out for a dip. I'd swim past the breakers and out beyond the last fishing boat, then turn and swim parallel to shore until I passed the inlet and was able to swim back to shore on the far beach.

Step into liquid, I thought. *What are you waiting for?* There was nowhere else to go.

Chapter 25

The sun was high and hot on my chest. The water beneath was cool and fresh, about the temperature of a competition pool. I waded and jumped through some mild surf and then I was out in the middle of the inlet on my back, dolphin-kicking to safety. Or at least some possible, temporary reprieve from the various predators on my trail.

I kept the bag raised above the surface. My arms extended straight up over my face. It helped shield some of the sun's glare from my eyes. I felt the tide trying to pull me into the bay. Fighting a current was a losing battle. It didn't matter how accomplished you thought you were in a pool. But I couldn't let it pull me into those fishing lines and dangling hooks and the questions that would follow.

I dolphin-kicked hard against the ocean's intent. The bag was sprayed with chop, but I kept it aloft. My abs began to ache with the effort. My shoulders tightened. I shut my eyes, thought of the endless laps I'd swum, all the aikido training I'd endured. This was nothing, I told myself. One more challenge faced and overcome. What an irony it would be if this, of all hardships, was the thing that finally sank me.

As I circled around and started to swim toward the opposing beach, a wave rose up and crashed over my head. Under I went, along with the bag. I clung to it, flailing beneath white water, kicking hard for the surface. Forget the cash and the phones, if the instructions inside that envelope were drenched and ruined, that could mean Danny Soto's life. Perhaps his family's too, not to mention my promised millions . . .

Surfacing, I gasped, lifted the bag, and felt my feet scrape along the rocky bottom. I scrambled up, feeling for flat, smooth surfaces, as I staggered to the sand. I scanned in all directions for any observers. All the fishermen seemed to be focused on their lines. The beach was empty. I sank to my knees, set the bag in my lap, and opened it.

The contents, thank Christ, appeared dry.

My suit, however, was long gone. I'd been so focused on keeping that bag safe that I hadn't noticed when Danny's too-small trunks had been stripped from my waist. I was a naked castaway washed ashore, his only possession somehow secure, his rescue uncertain. I took out my clothes and flip-flops, stepped into everything, still dripping wet. It wouldn't take long for this July sun to bake me dry.

Just as Layla said, the Backlands restaurant and marina was impossible to miss. On the bayside of the peninsula, across the beach road, was a cluster of fishing-related businesses. A few docks, some for commercial boats, some rich-guy yachts, a ramshackle bar called the Swan, and Backlands. The asphalt lot that connected this hub of waterside commerce was mostly empty. Evidently it wasn't a destination for midweek lunches among the Hamptons set, even in high summer. But true to the girl's word, a blue Ford F-150 sat in the center of the lot.

I saw its window lower. An arm reached out; I walked toward it.

Climbing into the cab, the AC blasted. Her friend Sam was as advertised. It looked like he spent most waking hours marinating in salt water. His shaggy blond hair was Spicoli-esque, a reference I thought he was too young to get, but probably heard all the time. His eyes were blue and narrow, burnt by the sun's daily glare over the waves. Behind us, on the flatbed of his truck, was a collection of surfboards, all well-used and caked with sand and wax. He stuck out a hand.

"Sam," he said.

I took it. "Duck. Thanks for getting me."

"No probs."

He released his grip but did not turn or put the truck in gear. We regarded each other like he was waiting for some secret password.

"So . . . like?"

"Ready when you are," I said.

"You got the cash?" he asked. "Layla said you'd have it. Ten grand, dude. That was the deal."

Clever girl. Why make things more complicated? If I had a couple million coming from her grandmother, I could use the bundle she'd given me for further expenses. I unzipped the wet bag in my lap, took out the backpack, and opened it. Handed over a stack of one-hundred hundreds. The kid flipped through them like he knew what he was doing. Satisfied at the eyeball count, he slid the bills into a pocket of his hoodie and shifted his truck into Drive.

"Rich chicks," he said, pulling out of the lot. "Ten Gs to drive a dude back to the city. Easy money."

He shook his head, smiling at his own cleverness. Maybe now wasn't the time to remind him that no money was easy. Being in my presence, the odds of his reaching his next birthday had just plunged. The last two were dead. Old Death Darley was going for the trifecta.

"So, how you know the Sotos?" he asked.

"Friend of the family."

"Good friends to have. You work for them or something?"

"Something like that."

"Yeah, well, you must be carrying some precious cargo."

I looked at this character driving contentedly down the road, thrilled by his good fortune. His left arm was extended straight and gripped the steering wheel at twelve o'clock. His right shoulder slouched over the armrest between us. The pickup's cab was wide enough for us to share the middle without intruding on each other's space, but his too comfortable manner irritated me. Hip-hop came from the radio. He turned it up. My opinion of him continued to lower.

"What else you got in that bag of yours?" he asked. "More cashola?"

I stared out the passenger-side window, waited for the silence to get awkward, then asked, "Did Layla tell you anything about me?"

"Nope. She just said she needed a favor, and that it was urgent. Offered me enough to make it worth my while. Took a little negotiating on my part. I mean, the waves are decent at Ditch today, which is rare for July. I just hang here in the summer for the chicks, and—"

"Don't talk."

"Excuse me?"

He pulled a side-eye that was supposed to look tough. Maybe he was in the surf lineup, but not here, not now.

"I said don't talk. Don't ask questions, don't tell me about your life, or act like this is some social joy ride."

"Look, dude, I'll pull over right now and kick your ass out . . ."

"You want to know what else is in this bag?" I asked. "A Glock, with one in the chamber. Among other things, none of which you want to know about. So, unless you want a bullet in the kidney, you're gonna keep driving with your mouth shut." I reached for the radio, scrolled down the options on SiriusXM. "And we're not listening to this shit."

I chose a station called Outlaw Country. Merle Haggard was singing "Misery and Gin," the live version from his *Rainbow Stew* album. Sam shifted in his seat like the music bugged him as much as his hip-hop bothered me. I sat back and savored the hard-lived lyrics. *Memories and drinks don't mix too well . . .*

To his credit, Sam managed to keep his mouth shut.

"You sound a lot smarter when you don't talk," I said.

He stiffened but didn't rise to the bait. It looked like he got the message, or at least believed my bullshit about having a loaded handgun in the bag. I was carrying nothing but my aikido to help in any matters of altercation. All I wanted was a couple hours on the road with some decent music as accompaniment. Merle's "Misery and Gin" gave way to Emmylou Harris's "Luxury Liner," another Duck-approved classic of the outlaw form. *You think I'm lonesome, and so do I, so do I . . .*

Ah, when the DJ gods smile upon us.

I could tell Sam hated my music, and that made me appreciate it all the more. I wasn't sure why he provoked such a surly reaction in me. I knew I was being a dick. I told myself it was for his own good. The less we communicated, the better. As far as I was concerned, *I'd* just paid the guy ten grand to transport me back to the city. That was my money. The rest of it, the vague millions promised by Eileen Chung, that was all contingent on some longshot shit-show. Now I was down to forty-K. Cass had ten, but at least she was working for it, and would be entitled to more if she had some success in her research. But this clown, with his beach brain and surfer ego? What did ladies see in these dude-bro wave-heads? Well, aside from the ripped physiques and perma-tans . . .

We stopped and started through the lights and the perpetual traffic of the towns along Route 27, then cut over to the 495 at Manorville. I kept an eye on the passenger-side mirror. Tried not to look back. Whatever his paltry IQ, Sam would remember—and recount—every detail of this drive. I hoped he was smart enough not to blab to his friends in some bar. Bartenders tended to perk up at tales like this. *Local surf stud gets ten grand from billionaire family to transport some angry dude back to the city* . . . It was the sort of thing that got around local beach communities, especially ones that swelled with resented rich folks for the hottest weeks of every year.

I still didn't want to hear his voice, but he needed to hear a few more things from mine.

"Listen, I know you're gonna want to talk about this," I said. "Maybe to your buddies, maybe some chick to impress her."

He shook his head, kept his lips tight.

"I need to stress this—don't. Unless you want to get yourself killed. You've signed up for more than you realize. I'm sorry to put you at risk, but that's the situation. After you drop me off, for your sake, you need to keep your mouth shut."

He started to open it.

"Just nod that you understand."

He nodded.

"Also, the money I gave you? Be low key with it. No conspicuous purchases, no whipping out that wad anywhere in public."

More nodding.

"I'm telling you this for your own safety. People have a way of dying when they spend too much time around me."

His tan seemed to evaporate as the blood drained from his face. I felt some guilt at being so brutal with the kid. I considered switching the radio back to his hip-hop station by way of apology, but I just couldn't. My nerves were frayed enough. Instead I changed the station to one called Underground Garage as a sort of contemporary compromise. They were playing Jack White.

If he didn't like that, he didn't deserve to have a radio.

Chapter 26

We made it through the Midtown Tunnel without further words, and without any sign of being followed. Not that I was adept at spotting a tail. Maybe I'd been tracked the moment I emerged from that ancient booze bunker in the dunes. Perhaps I'd been watched—with wry amusement—as I swam around the inlet with that bag aloft. Then been trailed at a careful remove behind Sam's pickup all the way back. It's not like he would have noticed. Nonetheless, I was feeling confident that I'd made it back unseen.

Now I needed to make contact with Cass.

As we exited the mouth of the tunnel into Manhattan, Sam's lips started to part. He was considering a spoken word but was still too freaked to do so without permission. I helped him along.

"Go straight to Third Avenue," I said. "Then take a right. Up a few blocks, I'll get out on East Forty-Fourth, right side."

He nodded, almost let himself exhale.

"As soon as I'm gone, circle around the block to Second and drive back through the tunnel. Go back to your normal routine. Go for an evening surf, go get drunk, do whatever you normally do, just keep quiet about all this, okay?"

"Yeah, no problem," he said.

"Look, I'm sorry for acting like a hard-ass. I appreciate your help more than you know, but bad things have a way of happening to people around me. I don't want that to happen to you."

"Thanks."

At the corner of 44th and Third, he double-parked in front of a hydrant. Didn't turn to look at me. I'd wounded his pride. The drive cost him more than he expected. I stuck out a hand. He ignored it.

"Take care of yourself," I said. Then I stepped out of the cold cab into the sweltering city.

There was an Apple Store at Grand Central. I knew Cass was nearby, holed up at the Chamber, but I didn't know the address, and wouldn't dare go knocking unannounced even if I did. I needed to check our shared Gmail Drafts account from an anonymous device. Like the ones interspersed across every Apple Store.

Walking in, I was assaulted by the usual swarm of over-helpful floor reps. The white Apple icon emblazoned at the center of every chest, the stoked-to-help smile, with that undercurrent of IT-smugness, it always felt like a cult every time I entered one of these places. The design, the layout, the worker bees, it all recalled some New Age church of the future. And I suppose it was. There was a large segment of society enslaved to living the way Steve Jobs wanted us to live. In place of a Bible was his mantra that, if a thing needs an instruction manual, it must not be designed very well.

I turned down all offers of help with a polite, no-eye-contact shake of the head. Pretended to browse a bit. I strolled over to the latest editions of MacBook Pros. Even thinner and lighter and faster than before! How much longer would we be impressed by such things?

I positioned myself in front of an open one, clicked on the Safari browser, typed in Gmail, and resisted glancing over my shoulder. I entered our agreed-upon email, lawyers gunsandmoney@, in honor of Warren Zevon, then typed in the password—Exciteableboy1978.

The Inbox was empty, but next to the Drafts icon was the number (1). I opened it and read:

Managed to ID those women, the ones who wheeled out Soto on the security vid, same ones who came by my place. They work for a Chinese billionaire named Sun Bin. And get this—he owns an apartment in the same building as the Sotos, a few floors down. An inside job indeed. No hows or whys yet but making progress. Also have some info on the guy who runs the building's security, Bill Willis. Former NSA, works for a firm called Patriot Security Services. Let me know when you get this. What's happening on your end? Remember to DELETE.

I repeated "Sun Bin" over and over in my head until I was confident it wouldn't be forgotten. Thought about how to help it stick: the sun and the trash—*Sun Bin*. Got it. Considered Bill Willis, his connections to the NSA, and his company, Patriot Security. Mother and daughter would waste no time ruining the man if we established his involvement. I deleted Cass's message, then hit Compose and typed my reply. Kept it short:

Back in town, around the corner from Chamber. A lot to share. Let me know when and where . . .

I almost hit Send out of habit, caught myself as the cursor hovered over the icon. I closed the message. Saw it appear unsent in the Drafts folder. I hoped she'd check it soon. I logged out of Gmail, tried to kill some time browsing online. I clicked on the *New York Times* site, scrolled down the bad news of the day. School shootings, tsunamis, wild fires, open-ended war, political sex scandals—I wondered how journalists managed to cope with the daily onslaught of human misery. It's not like they had job security or were even paid a decent wage. Good news wasn't news; save it for the Sunday Styles, or maybe the Sports page. I clicked on the baseball section. Per usual, the Mets were infuriating and the Yankees were overpriced.

What changed? Teams won and lost; elections came and went. People were born and died. In the meantime, they tried to survive and thrive, created and procreated, made and lost fortunes. The species continued its inexorable lurch toward extinction. The planet would soon be dead.

When an ever-helpful Apple bee tapped me on the shoulder and asked if I needed any help, I knew I'd been online too long. I suspected there was an unseen clock that timed the use of every product. Customers were welcome to come in and try things out, but this must not be mistaken for a free office. Click around, check your email, okay, but then either buy something or be on your way.

I told her I'd just be a moment. She waited with folded arms. I turned to face her. She looked like she'd come off a conveyor belt in Cupertino. An obedient, shining example of tech-ness, small and fit and bright-eyed, with an unquestioned faith in the workings of Saint Jobs.

"A moment, with privacy," I said. "I promise to buy something on my way out."

That was all she needed to hear. The sale was the thing. She smiled, even offered a slight bow.

"Take all the time you need," she said. "I'm Amy. Let me know if I can help you find anything."

I waited until she went off to bother someone else abusing their hospitality, then clicked back on Gmail, hoping to find something from Cass. She didn't disappoint. Another draft was waiting:

Hofbrau House, 3rd Ave, b/t 44th & 45th, second floor. 4p.

I looked at the top right corner of the screen. The time read 3:31 p.m. I deleted the message. The beer garden was an avenue away, right where Sam had dropped me off. Was this supposed to be some kind of sadistic test from Cass? I'd been doing so well, but there were only so many times I could be in the presence of alcohol without succumbing, especially in a venue with good German beer on tap.

On my way to the front, I picked out a new iPad. It would come in handy. I just needed a free Wi-Fi network and I could communicate with Cass anonymously through Drafts from anywhere. I gave the cashier five one-hundred-dollar bills from my bag, took back a few twenties in change.

"Does this thing come charged?" I asked.

"Sure does," she said. "But the factory charge won't be full, so you're going to want to plug it in when you get home."

Thanks," I said. "Steve would be proud."

She tilted her head, perplexed.

"He's always watching, you know?" I pointed up. "From the cloud."

I didn't wait for her to get it. It wasn't my best material.

Outside, dear Lord, this heat. Sweat leapt from every crevice before I could reach the crosswalk. The masses moving in every direction around me seemed to be operat-

ing on a slower frequency. Like those West Coast folks
who claim to feel the change of seasons in L.A., seasoned
New Yorkers can feel the pace shift based on the weather.
New York minutes are a relative thing. In winter it's ramped
up highest, because who wants to be outside in the cold
for a second longer than necessary? In fall, it's a time of
lingering, but with a purpose. Everyone's back at work or
school, there is much to be done, yet it would be rude to
deny the few moments of pleasurable weather in the city's
best months. In spring . . . well, spring doesn't exist in New
York. One day it's cold and wet and shitty, then, about
forty-eight hours later, it's hotter than hell and you wonder
why you bother to own light jackets.

But summer? Those left behind adjust their pace getting
from point A to point B. It's too oppressive to rush. I didn't
have a phone to check the temp, but I estimated it to be
somewhere in the mid-nineties. No breeze. Humidity like
the inside of a Russian bathhouse. Summer in the city—
when violence was always the highest. There must be a
corollary between tempers and body temperature.

I reached Hofbrau House surly and soaked. The blast of
AC in the entry was like an answered prayer. I climbed the
steps to the second-floor beer hall. It was faux as can be,
about as authentic as Epcot, with the requisite blue Bavar-
ian flags, and waitresses from Long Island forced to don
lederhosen.

I found a stool at the bar, eyed the row of taps with the
lust of a hound in heat. I even spotted Hofbrau's special
unfiltered summer lager. Goddamn it, Cass, this was cruel.
I caught the eye of the big-bellied bartender and almost
broke. Stayed strong and asked for water and an apple
juice, ordered the schnitzel. He grunted, poured the juice
in a thin, child's-size glass as if to mock me. I unwrapped
my new iPad. It was a fine, slick machine, so far beyond
my comprehension that it wasn't even worth marveling.

The last piece of technology that I could grasp was the compact disc. After that I stopped trying to understand. I just got in line and upgraded to each new gadget with the rest of the cattle.

It was ready to go when I felt the tap on my shoulder. I swiveled in my seat, swung around to face her. She noticed my juice and her face fell.

"Damn," she said. "I totally forgot. Do you want to go somewhere else?"

"It's cool. I already ordered the schnitzel. I'm starved."

"I'm sorry, Duck. I guess I'm so accustomed to your drinking, I didn't even think of it. This must be torture for you, sitting here."

"Here I thought you were trying to test me."

"Why would I do that? You really think I'm a sadist, don't you?"

"Can we talk about something else, please?"

"Of course. Again, my apologies. I'm impressed by your discipline, I really am. How were the Hamptons?"

"A joy."

"Everything okay at the Sotos'?"

"They're peachy. I have some news. Our rates went up."

"More than the cash the daughter gave you?"

"Just a bit."

"How much?" she asked.

"If we bring her dad back, we stand to earn several million dollars."

"Bullshit."

"Cross my heart."

"Who promised you that, the mother?"

"No, the grandmother."

"The grand . . ."

"Layla's nai-nai, the same one she suspected of being behind her father's abduction. Eileen Chung, she was there."

"There, at the house? So, she's not involved?"

"Oh, she's involved, but I don't think she has any idea where her son is. It appears to have something to do with a business deal involving her latest ex-husband."

"Guo Gonglu," she said.

"You've done your homework."

"More than you know."

"How would this Guo connect to Sun Bin? You're sure this neighbor of theirs is behind the kidnapping?"

"Positive," said Cass. "Those female bodyguards—they're always with him, like some kind of affectation. By having them pose in front of that security camera, it's clear that this Sun Bin *wants* to be identified."

"By who? Nicole Soto didn't recognize them. Her mother-in-law insists she doesn't know them either. Who else would have received that encrypted email?"

"My guess? Danny Soto's business partner, Peter Lennox. If they want money, that seems like the only guy capable of delivering it."

"About that ransom," I said.

"Did the Soto women receive something else?"

"They did. I have the instructions in my bag. You're right about Lennox. We need to see him."

"How much are they asking for?"

"Two billion," I said.

Chapter 27

I let Cass digest that number for a moment. She waved down the bartender, ordered a Grüner. I watched the wine fill her glass. Salivated, tried not to stare. I willed myself to suppress my longing. For the booze, and for her, as well. I'd be a healthier human without the lust for either. Wasn't that one of the seven deadlies? There were times when it outranked even greed. My rational mind reminded me of two things I would need to survive this and earn those millions: sobriety and the expertise of my partner.

Cass averted her eyes and took a sip. Setting it down, she turned to me and set an elbow atop the bar. She placed a palm against a pale cheek.

"So, we get a few million for the successful delivery of a few billion."

"Easy enough, right?"

She gave a sudden laugh. Heads turned.

"How in the world are we supposed to move two billion dollars?"

"By following the directions in my bag? I'm sure it's just a few clicks for a fund like Soto Capital."

"A few clicks and more than a few red flags," she said. "You think anyone can transfer that kind of money without it alerting regulators?"

"That hadn't occurred to me. Nor does it seem like our problem. We get this Sun Bin his money, he gives back Danny Soto, and we collect our fee."

"Simple."

"What could possibly go wrong?"

"What if we disclose Sun's identity?" she asked. "Let's say we pull this off. They return Soto, we get our fee, but we know who's behind it. He practically announced it with that security footage."

"Speaking of which—you still haven't told me about Bill Willis. He's former NSA?"

She nodded. "Now works for a firm called Patriot Security Services, which sounds like the go-to security company used by a lot of these towers full of powerful foreign owners. Everybody knows cybersecurity is a massive business. Well, apparently there's a lot of movement between the public and private sectors."

"Makes sense," I said. "Same as lawyers—the government job gives the prestige and access you can't get anywhere else. Then you get paid when you leave for the corporate job."

"Meaning a guy like Bill Willis is more than just a rent-a-cop, staring at a bunch of screens."

"He had to be involved," I said. "The Sotos are gonna burn that guy down."

"But why would he collude with a Chinese national in the abduction of an American billionaire?"

"Money, threats? Maybe both? There's gotta be a ton of Snowdens out there," I said. "NSA hacks who left with sensitive info. Maybe this Patriot Security plays dirty. With the threat of exposure—for treason—that would give a guy like Sun Bin plenty of leverage."

"Still, this kind of high-level fraud and kidnapping—it could set off an international incident. It seems like a play in a larger game."

"Which would make us the expendable pawns."

Cass shook her head, lifted her glass. She took an imperceptible sip. "I don't think they have any intention of releasing Soto," she said. "Why would they? They clearly have something on him. Maybe it relates to this business he was doing with his mother's husband. Maybe it's something else. Whatever it is, it makes no sense to let him go, even if we manage to get them their billions."

"So, they kill the captive, try to kill the messengers—us—and eliminate anyone who might have seen the security video?"

"No, I think Sun Bin wants his identity known, along with whatever power's behind him. Wiping the board won't erase the evidence of his guards wheeling Soto from his home."

I remembered Eileen Chung's history lesson on the beach, about the Opium Wars, the birth of modern China in the nineteenth century, fought over the devil's flower. The British had used it to even the trade gap with the Chinese, and in the process had made junkies of the Qing dynasty's ruling class.

"They're making an example of Danny," I said. "They're telling American business to knock it off, or else."

"Knock what off?"

"My guess—he was trying to do a deal with his mother's husband that angered the folks in Beijing. She said they were buying a pharmaceutical company or something. She mentioned how powerful people disappear all the time over there, how everyone is controlled by the Party, even the superrich."

"So, they kidnap, extort, and kill an American billionaire? Poison his head of security, pile up who knows how many more collateral bodies, and challenge our government to do something about it? That's pretty bold. Wars have been started for less."

"What if they have something treasonous on Soto?"

"That might excuse the kidnapping," she said, "but not the killing of innocents caught up in the case."

I looked down into my thin glass of apple juice. I took out the vape, had a puff. The bartender brought over my schnitzel and silverware. I cut into it, began to devour the battered, breaded pork.

Between bites, I said, "We can't dwell too much on the macro. It's beyond our grasp. All we should be worried about is our assignment. Delivering this ransom, somehow getting Danny Soto back to his family, and making a few million in the process."

"And staying alive."

"That too."

"So, next step—how do we contact Soto's partner, Peter Lennox? He's the guy we need to make this two billion transfer or trade or whatever it is."

"Should we swing by his office?" I asked. "I know where it is. I've been there, remember? Charlie McKay used to work for Soto. It's up on West Fifty-Seventh and Sixth, sick views, a short walk from Danny's apartment."

"Duck, there'll be eyes all over that place."

"Then what do you suggest?"

Cass glanced over at the bartender. Caught him looking. He blinked and turned, busying himself with straightening the glasses. His puffy cheeks blushed.

"I think I can catch his eye," she said. "I'll see if I can get him somewhere that we can talk in private."

"Such as?"

She tapped the bag hanging from my shoulder. "Say, the Four Seasons or somewhere comparable? We can afford a nice room."

"You're going to pick up the poor bastard."

She gave a wicked wink, lifted her glass, and tilted the wine down her throat. "He's not poor," she said. "And I'm just a gal in town from L.A., recently separated from my husband."

"They saw you too," I pointed out. "On the roof of your building. What if they see you?"

"I'll change."

I scanned her outfit. Black leather shorts that rode high on her thighs, a tight black t-shirt with THE CURE written across the chest, a pair of ankle-high black boots on her feet. Her sharp nails were painted her customary crimson. Her fingers, neck, and ears were free of jewelry. Hair as dark as squid ink. The rest of her was acres of exposed pale skin.

"Into a disguise?" I asked.

"Into something that screams rich divorcée."

"It's a risk."

"You have another suggestion?"

"Not at the moment." I shrugged. "You mentioned the Four Seasons. What did you have in mind?"

She sighed, a sound I'd heard before. It was the exhale of patience required before explaining something to a slow child. Cass crossed her legs, straightened up, and rolled back her shoulders. The tips of her painted nails clicked against the surface of the bar.

"What time is it?" she asked.

I slid my new iPad closer and touched the Home button. "Quarter after four," I said. "Why?"

She pointed at my schnitzel. "Finish that," she said. "Hurry up, we need to hustle."

I did as I was told, settled our tab, and followed her down the steps and back out into the heat. She stepped into the street, waved at a lit cab speeding up the center lane. It swerved in front of a honking UPS truck and slammed to a stop before us. There was a time when hailing a cab in late-afternoon Midtown was an impossible dream, yet ever since the advent of Uber and Lyft and other ride apps, you never had to wait long with your arm in the air. Now there were empty cabs aplenty. I tried to make a point of keeping those yellow OGs in business. Besides, we were traveling cash-only now; ordering a car was not an option.

"Fifty-Seventh and Fifth," said Cass from the back seat after I'd closed the door. "Bergdorf's." To me, she added, "Short ride, normally I'd walk, but we're pressed for time."

"Fine with me," I said. "In this heat, I can barely walk to the corner."

Not that the cab's failing AC provided much relief. I was already sweating again, anticipating the icy sanctuary of the posh department store.

"We going shopping?"

"Yep, I need something befitting a loaded lady from the Hollywood Hills."

"What canyon are you from?" I asked.

"Huh?"

"If you're from the Hills, you better have your details straight."

"Oh. Good call. Let's say Laurel Canyon, just above Sunset? I did ayahuasca once in a place around there."

"You did what?"

"You know, one of those Journeys? It was incredible. I'll tell you about it sometime. You should try it. It might help with your issues."

"My issues?"

"Never mind. Later. I need to think about what I'm going to wear."

As we inched through congested Midtown traffic, I considered Cass tripping her brains out inside some Hollywood temple of hedonism. The thought of her ingesting ayahuasca among West Coast strangers was hard to grasp. Yet another unpeeled layer of Cassandra Kimball.

At the northwest corner of 57th and Fifth, I handed another twenty over the seat, told the cabbie to keep the change, and followed her into Bergdorf's. I wouldn't have guessed she did much shopping there, but she moved with an intent that suggested she knew the place. We got off the escalator on the fifth floor, where the sign announced CONTEMPORARY CLOTHING, DENIM, SHOES AND ACCESSORIES. I wondered what she had in mind. At least it wouldn't be couture or evening wear. I had almost forty grand in cash in my bag, but I knew that wouldn't go far on certain floors in this place.

"I'm thinking a sundress," she said. "Something tasteful, something with prints, but not too conservative. Only slightly flirtatious. And heels, and maybe a pair of earrings, what else?"

"Got me."

She turned. "Sorry, I was talking to myself, not you. Why don't you have a seat?" She pointed toward a circle of plush chairs on the floor. A gray-haired sad sack was slouched in one, staring at his phone. I pictured wife number three or four swanning around nearby. I moved to join him. "I'll find you when I'm done," said Cass over her shoulder.

While I waited, I played with my new iPad. I opened the browser, found a network, and Googled "Peter Lennox Soto Capital." Aside from a few images at Hamptons events and assorted charity functions, not much popped up. Discretion for these hedgies was a prized commodity. He must have wiped his Internet presence as well. When even mid-management earned seven-figure salaries, there was reason to be wary. I wondered how often they worried about the gathering masses. There was outrage over the one-percent? Please. What about the one one-hundredth percent? Could these guys grasp the visceral hatred that so many regular folks had for them? They must. It was imperative not to be too searchable. Making a Forbes list was one thing. That was aspirational in a vague sense. The numbers were beyond comprehension. But their physical addresses, personal details, those must be guarded with care. Which was why virtually every high-end piece of residential property in this city was now owned by an anonymous LLC. Identities were sometimes revealed, in times of scandal or dumb ego or dogged reporting. The cloistered classes at the very top all knew who lived where, but it remained essential to stay unlisted when any yahoo could enter your name in a search engine and become enraged by your existence.

It was an irony of our celebrity, selfie-obsessed culture. Everyone wanted to be noticed and envied. Everyone wanted to show off their grand lives on Instagram. That is, until you *really* made it. Then anyone with any sense learned to lower the profile. The masses were closer to the castle gates than anyone cared to admit. And they were armed.

I had no luck finding any properties attached to Peter Lennox. No matter, we knew where he worked, and I had little doubt that Cass would be able to catch his eye and lure him over.

She caught mine when she appeared twenty minutes later, turned out like Julia Roberts, post–Rodeo Drive shopping spree in *Pretty Woman*. She was wearing a spaghetti-strap orange and white floral sundress that fell to her calves. The V of cleavage somehow managed to be both demure and devilish. She'd accessorized with a wide-brimmed hat fit for a Derby. Large hoop earrings dangled from her ears. A new pair of strappy heels elevated her six-foot frame even higher. She offered me her left hand and wiggled her ringless fingers.

"All that's missing is a new rock," she said. "Think Mr. Lennox will approve?"

"I don't think he'd care if you were wearing a diamond as big as the Ritz."

"Nice reference."

Should have known she'd get it.

"He's not going to be very happy to see me when you bring him upstairs to your room."

"No, I suspect he won't."

Chapter 28

We walked a block south and an avenue over and positioned ourselves across the street from Soto Capital's building a few minutes after five. There were bound to be other eyes on the entrance. Federal agents, security working for Sun Bin, who knew who else. Not to mention the cameras hidden in all the streetlights around this pocket of Billionaires' Row. Cass's disguise was impressive; I could do little better than sunglasses.

Fortunately, she was ahead of me as usual.

As I sought an empty bench in the shade, a silver Mercedes S-Class glided to a stop before us. Every piece of glass was tinted. The driver's-side window slid down a few inches. A male hand came out and waved. Cass hit my arm, moved toward the car.

"Climb in back," she said. "I found us a safe place to watch."

I didn't ask. Just followed her across the sidewalk and folded myself in the back seat, while she went around and got in the front. A smiley guy in seersucker was behind the wheel. He looked to be somewhere in his midfifties, with salt-and-pepper hair, and stretched cheeks that suggested a facelift. He glanced back at me with a smirk, then offered Cass a smile so wide I could see the caps on his molars.

"Look at you," he said, grabbing for her hand. "I didn't even recognize you at first."

She let him kiss her fingers, then turned to me and said, "Duck, this is my friend Harold. He was able to help us on short notice."

"When did you . . ."

"He was sort of on standby when we met," she said. "We've been in touch at the Chamber. When I was trying on clothes at Bergdorf's, I asked to use a lady's phone. I told her mine died."

"Such a clever girl," said Harold.

"Thank you for meeting us," said Cass.

"For you, my dear, anything." Harold kept on grinning but turned down the wattage a bit as he faced me. "We go way back, me and your partner. She's told me about you. Good to finally meet you, buddy."

Overfamiliarity sparked distrust, but this guy was so bouncy with enthusiasm it was like resisting the affections of an overgrown Labrador. He was thrilled by the adventure, clueless of any accompanying danger.

I stuck out my hand. He took it with cheer. "Appreciate the help," I said. "We don't want to be seen right about now."

"Not to worry, my friend." He waved around the darkened cabin. "Got these windows extra tinted. I like my privacy too."

I remembered Cass mentioning that real estate broker slave of hers. The one she thought might help identify the shielded owners behind those LLCs in the Sotos' tower. It appeared he had.

"So, who we lookin' for?" he asked.

"Guy named Peter Lennox," said Cass. "He's partners with . . ."

Harold was nodding. "Yeah, yeah, I know all about Lennox. The lucky stiff was best friends with Danny Soto in college. He's supposed to be dim as hell but knows how to raise capital. Danny gave him a twenty percent stake in his fund, which makes the dumb-ass worth close to a billion. Friends like these, right?"

"Yeah, well, we need to talk to him," I said.

"About what?"

I couldn't be sure how much Cass had shared, but it couldn't have been much. Before I could answer, she placed a hand on his thigh and scooted a bit closer. "I told you, Harry, we can't say. It's best if you don't know too much."

His hand covered hers, pinning it to his seersucker slacks. "Not even a clue, dear?" he cooed.

"Do you have any idea where this Lennox lives?" she asked.

He smirked. "Maybe."

"Where?"

The shift in her voice was jarring, all the more so in her current floral getup. She'd entered mistress mode and Harold would do as she asked, or else.

"Where does Peter Lennox live, Harold?" she asked again.

He didn't hesitate, an obedient slave unembarrassed by my presence in the back seat. "TriBeCa," he said. "In the Jenga building."

"The what?"

"Fifty-six Leonard," he said. "The Herzog and de Meuron tower? It looks like a giant game of Jenga. Tallest spot in TriBeCa. Lennox bought one of the top floors when it was under construction. Friend of mine brokered it."

"So, when he leaves here," I said, "he's probably headed downtown. Follow him."

Harold shrugged. "I'll follow him wherever, no problem, but he might not go straight home. Lennox has a rep, you know? Likes to party. The sort who wants to down a few before facing the home life. Besides, it's summer—

when all the wives and kids are sent packing, and all these guys pretend like they're single. You wouldn't believe—"

"There," said Cass, swiping her hand from his leg and pointing. "That's him, right?"

I recognized him from the Google images. Lennox was a stocky, sandy-haired guy who moved with the strut of wealth. He wore chinos and an open-necked white Oxford. When the temperature dropped, I imagined he added the Patagonia vest to complete the hedge-douche uniform. He scanned left and right, weaved through the crowd on the sidewalk, and made a straight line for his waiting Escalade. As soon as he closed the door, it pulled out and headed west across 57th. Harold pulled his Benz into Drive and spun an aggressive U-turn in pursuit. I leaned between the seats.

"Relax, man. Hang back. We can't let him see you."

Harold grinned at me in the rearview. "Chill, buddy. I got this. They won't see shit."

"Duck's right," said Cass, still in mistress-voice. "You need to settle down and listen to us."

His shoulders slumped. I felt him take his foot off the gas. "As you wish," he said.

He managed to hang back a few cars as Lennox's driver turned left on Seventh Avenue and began to crawl south. I respected the fact that he chose to live in a decent part of downtown, as opposed to the horror show of Midtown, but the daily commute had to be soul-sucking. It would have been faster to take the subway, though that was not an option for a man of his station. He'd say it was for security; really it was about not mixing with the masses.

It took forty-five minutes for us to reach Canal Street. The Jenga building loomed a few blocks down. For modern architecture, I had to admit it wasn't totally offensive. There was a certain originality there; it seemed to have the residents in mind more than the gawkers. The views must have been outrageous, as good as Soto's perch above Billionaires' Row, but with some neighborhood decency when you left the lobby.

I wondered if Cass had a plan, should Lennox decide to be a good boy and head straight home for the evening. Would we loiter outside his building, waiting to see if he reemerged later in the evening? And what if he left on a date with his wife? Then I remembered Harold's comment. It was summer in the city. All the wives were ensconced in some beach or country home a few hours away.

The Escalade braked and signaled right. Before it could turn on North Moore Street I guessed the destination.

"Brandy Library," I said. "Shocker."

"Know the spot?" asked Cass.

"I know it."

"Me too," said Harold. "Classy joint."

Of course he did. It was a dick-measuring whiskey bar frequented by finance types and those who catered to them. Such as high-end real estate brokers eager to close on crazy-priced palaces in the sky. I'd sipped a few there, but never on my own dime. Passed some hours at the bar, watching cheating husbands get lubricated before lurching off to meet girlfriends or pricey escorts at the cluster of nearby hotels that catered to such trysts.

Harold was smart enough to drive past and double-park on the other side of the street. The three of us watched as Peter Lennox climbed from his car and strode up the few steps beneath the iron and glass awning into Brandy Library. Empty top-shelf whiskey bottles lined the front window. A tasteful array of flower boxes was arranged beneath the burgundy sign. Like Harold said, the place was all class. I wondered if Lennox met friends there for happy hour, or if he was the type to unwind alone. I hoped for the latter. Either way, Cass would know what to do.

"Okay, gentlemen, looks like it's showtime," she said.

"Should we wait for you out here?" asked Harold.

"No, I need you to go book us a room."

"What for?" he blurted with sudden jealousy.

"So we can meet with the guy," I said. "In private."

"Ah, sorry, my bad. I'm still getting the hang of this private-eye stuff."

It didn't even warrant an eye roll.

"What's around here?" asked Cass.

While I considered the options, Harold started rattling them off. "Let's see, you got the Greenwich Hotel, the Roxy, the Soho Grand, the Thompson, the James. What else? You got the Smyth down on West Broadway and Chambers. Plenty to choose from, what are you looking for?"

"Where would a separated L.A. wife stay?" she asked. "One who wants a bit of privacy."

Harold took his time as he regarded her outfit, made a show of giving it considered thought. "I'd say . . . maybe the Greenwich? It's gorgeous, but it's popular with celebs, which means paparazzi outside. The Smyth? No, that's a bit of a walk. Why would you head all the way up to the Brandy for a drink? I'd probably go with . . . the Roxy. Used to be the TriBeCa Grand. It's real close. Nice spot."

"Okay," said Cass. "Where is it?"

"Bottom of Sixth Avenue, between Walker and White."

He had evident pride in his broker's ability to recall any address worth knowing in the city.

"We'll head over there," I said.

"How will she know what room?" asked Harold.

"Because you're gonna leave a key at the front desk for your girlfriend," I told him.

"*I* am?"

"Harry," said Cass, hand back on his thigh. "We need to stay off the radar. We can't use any cards. Duck has plenty of cash to reimburse you, but no decent hotel will let you check in without a card on file."

"True, that's true," he said, nodding.

"So, after I get out to meet Mr. Lennox, you and Duck go over to the Roxy and book us a nice suite, okay, honey?"

"Yeah, no problem. I got it. Then, we'll wait for you in the room, so you can question this guy."

Cass shook her head with a soft smile. I saw her squeeze his leg. "No, after you check in, you need to give a key to Duck. He'll go upstairs, but then it will be time for you to go home."

"Home?" he asked, like the word hurt his feelings.

"You've done a wonderful job," said Cass. "I won't forget this. I promise to make it up to you."

That put a slight breeze in his sails, but he managed to produce a pout. "When?" he asked.

"When I decide," she said.

She could control her voice like a weapon. Harold liked being stabbed with it. He started nodding again. "Yeah, okay, just let me know. I'm at your . . . service."

"I know, sweetie, I know," said Cass.

She leaned forward and grazed his cheek with hers. As she did, she looked back at me and winked. I coughed to cover my laugh.

We watched her open the door and stride across the street in her hat and sundress to meet her mark. He wouldn't be able to resist either.

Chapter 29

Her slave brooded in silence as we pulled out and circled toward the Roxy. In Cass's absence, his giddiness seemed to evaporate. The steaming TriBeCa sidewalks were mostly empty. The strollers, pushed by sweating nannies or toned moms in workout gear, were gone for the summer. The late-afternoon light gave the old loft buildings a welcoming warmth that made the neighborhood seem almost attainable. When I was a kid, these were deserted cobblestone streets, somewhere you didn't come at night. The thought of it being a land of families would have been comical. It was now the richest zip code in gentrified Manhattan.

Harold eyed me in the rearview.

"You been friends a long time, the two of you."

It didn't sound like a question. I didn't offer an answer.

"But you've never . . . like . . . been an item?"

"An item?"

"You never dated or, you know, served her?"

"It's always been platonic," I said, "and, no, I've never been much for the kinky stuff."

He didn't respond right away, just kept looking at me in the mirror while we waited at a light. When it turned green, he smiled, accelerated. "Must be tough," he said. "Pining away for an unattainable partner."

I tried to keep a neutral expression. Any protest would doth be too much.

As we approached the hotel, I told him to stop at the corner on White Street. I'd wait in the car while he went to check us in, make sure he didn't get a ticket.

"Be right back," he said.

"Harold," I called.

He turned, tilted his head in the open door.

"Nothing. Good luck."

He shut the door and jog-walked to the hotel across the street. In his absence I considered my cab driver in Southampton. What was the kid's name? Andy. A local surfer just trying to hustle some summer money while his mom was sick. Because I'd climbed into the back of his cab at the train station, he was dead. I wondered if the same fate had befallen Sam, or whatever his real name was, Layla's friend who agreed to drive me back to the city for ten grand. I had a sick sense that he'd never made it back to the Hamptons. And before that, there was Richard Gross, Soto's head of security, poisoned, now cold in some morgue, awaiting burial or cremation. His family would never know what really happened. Nor would Andy's. More lies to cover expendable lives cut short.

If you took the time to honor every unjust death, every rationalized murder, you'd never be able to climb from bed. It was an endless procession. It always had been. There would be reasons, anything from insanity to national security. The dead weren't coming back, so why dwell on the circumstances? Above us were infinite solar systems, some surely teeming with life, all indifferent to anything that happened down here. Life must be so much easier for those unbound by any sense of morality or justice. Just gaze up to the stars and remember that nothing that happened here mattered. It was only when you started putting stock in notions like karma and heaven and hell that human behavior became problematic.

Earnest worshippers made things so hard on themselves. Those at the top of humanity knew better. The ones who lived and ruled from palaces or towers in the sky, they must have been released from such things. They knew their fortunes would save them. Yet it hadn't been enough to protect Danny Soto. Worth billions, living higher than any human in history, and he'd been taken right out his front door. I doubted he'd had a moment to resist. A neighbor knocked on his door; he opened it. Then he'd been drugged, lowered into a wheelchair, a hood pulled over his head. Two ninja-esque female bodyguards wheeled him away, pausing to pose for their close-up in front of the cameras.

This neighbor, Sun Bin, appeared to be unconcerned about anyone making the connection. Nicole Soto might not recognize those women, but someone would. He or she would know who they worked for. It was a taunt, and now this Sun planned to extort two billion from his captive's fund. Cass mentioned all the regulatory red flags that would be raised by a transaction that size. Did that bother Sun? It must not. Meaning, whatever information he had about Danny Soto and his business dealings in China must be enough to neutralize any official response.

Peter Lennox would be able to shed some light. I wondered how quickly Cass could lure him to our room. Idle time alone in a hotel meant the urge to drink. The devil would whisper. The minibar would beckon. I had the vape, but that no longer felt like enough.

I was shaken from my roaming demons by excited knocking on the window. Harold was standing there holding up a hotel keycard like he'd just executed a dangerous mission. Maybe he had. His death sentence might have been sealed the moment he agreed to help his mistress. They could be waiting nearby. I pushed away the thought. I liked this goofy kinkster. He was unashamed of his desires, his shameless lust to be hurt by my partner. That was who he was. He was past the age of embarrassment. He was so eager to help. I hoped he'd survive. I'd enjoyed the company of past couriers on this case too. Look what happened to them. Better to banish such concerns. Remember the indifference of the universe above.

I opened the door and stepped out onto the cobblestones. He handed over the key.

"You're all set, buddy. Room 444. There's a key waiting for Cass at the front desk. She just has to give her name."

I took it, said, "Good work, Harold. Thanks."

I moved to go, but he wasn't ready to step offstage just yet. He bounced from one foot to the next, juiced with adrenaline, his brow bursting with sweat.

"The check-in girl, she could tell something was up," he said.

"How so?"

"Guy like me? Striding in there with no luggage, no reservation, asking to leave a key at the desk for his lady friend?"

"Yeah, she thought you were meeting either your girlfriend or an escort. You think it's the first time she's seen that?"

"No, I mean, probably. I don't know, it's a decent place. She gave me a weird smile when she handed over the keys."

"Like she was trying not to smirk?"

"Exactly! Yeah, exactly like that."

"Good. That's what we want—for her to think you're just another one-percent scumbag, checking into a nice spot to screw an expensive lady. How much was the room?"

He frowned at the characterization, perhaps realizing how well he fit the role. "It was nine hundred," he said.

"What do we get for that?"

"The one-bedroom suite. That's what Cass wanted, right?"

"That should work."

I unzipped the bag and counted out nine crisp ones. Handed them over. He hesitated for a beat, then took it and slid the cash into the breast pocket of his coat. I stuck out my hand.

"Be safe, Harold," I said. "Time for you to head home."

"Home?" he scoffed. "No thanks. I'm going back to my baby, *The Triple Mint*. Got her docked over by Brooklyn Bridge Park. When Cass called I was out in Sag Harbor. Figured I'd take the *Mint* back to town to see her. No better way to travel. Plan to do some striper fishing on the way back . . ."

"Harold," I said. "I gotta get in there."

"Right, right, I know you do, buddy. I'm rambling, I do that. Anyway, happy to help. Godspeed. Take care of that gorgeous creature for me, won't you?"

"Will do," I said.

As I walked off, I felt him watching my back, holding the open door of his Benz. I told myself that we'd been careful, that I hadn't helped kill another good man.

When I entered the Roxy, I ignored the smiling faces at the front desk and moved past a crowded lounge. The lobbies of New York's boutique hotels often doubled as meeting rooms and free office space for the laptop economy. As long as visitors spent money on the overpriced drinks and snacks, no one cared if you were staying upstairs or not. This one was a tasteful mix of leather sofas and high-backed upholstered chairs, arranged beneath an open atrium. A drum set, a couple guitars, and a mic stand were assembled on a riser beneath a neon Roxy sign. A grand piano was parked stage right. The floors above were visible in a triangular shape that matched the location's intersection. I found the elevators in the back.

I figured it would take Cass at least an hour. She'd have to make eye contact with Peter Lennox across the Brandy, exchange in flirty banter, let him buy her a drink or two, then let him think it was his idea to join her for another at her hotel. It was a sequence that could proceed fast when you looked like she did, but we had to expect that Lennox would be on guard. His friend was missing. The fund might be adrift without Soto. Lennox may have received the same encrypted email that Nicole was sent. If so, he might have recognized Danny's female captors, and their connection to Sun Bin. It was the sort of eccentricity that fellow rich guys tended to note.

He'd be wise to be wary of beautiful strangers at a bar. Though, how could rational precaution compete with hard-wired sexual attraction?

The room was a fine two-room suite, about five hundred square feet, with a desk, couch, and flat screen in one area and a king-size bed in the other. The bathroom was covered in loud-patterned blue and gold wallpaper. The fixtures were Art Deco–inspired stainless steel. I roamed the space, checking and judging all decisions in linens and decor. I was getting drowsy after the day's adventures. I considered brewing some coffee in the single-serving machine on the credenza, but the smell could alert Lennox to a presence inside as they entered. Instead I did some jumping jacks in front of the bed. Cranked out twenty push-ups after that. Smacked myself in the face a few times. That helped.

I went to the window, watched the lights below. Dusk was falling. The traffic was backed up on Sixth Avenue, queueing up for the Holland Tunnel a couple blocks north. The room was facing west, the same direction that Cass and Lennox would be coming from. I hoped to spot them as they approached. But after a couple minutes I grew impatient and began to pace the room, plotting what I would do and say when they entered.

An hour passed, then another. I began to worry.

Chapter 30

A ringing room phone made me jump. Approaching it on the nightstand, I told myself it was the concierge calling about some nonsense. No, I knew it had to be something. Someone else must be dead. I lifted the receiver, gave a cautious "Hello?"

"Duck!" boomed a familiar voice. "It's Harold, I'm just calling to see if you got in there all right. Is Lennox there yet? How's it going?"

"Jesus, man, you shouldn't be calling here."

"Cass there?"

"No, Harold," I said. "Not yet."

"You think she's okay? Maybe one of us ought to go by the Brandy and check on her."

"Not necessary. I'm sure they'll be here any minute, which is why I need to go."

"That's cool, man. Like I said, I was just checking in." He paused. When he spoke again it sounded like his mouth was away from the phone. "Well, holy shit, would you look at that."

"What is it, Harold? I really need to go."

"One of those mega-yachts. It's about to berth off the marina, not a hundred yards from *The Triple Mint*. I'll be damned, most of those monsters are cruising the Mediterranean this time a year. *The Lady Jade*, would you look at her."

"Bye, Harold."

Moments later I heard her voice coming down the hall. The fool could have screwed the whole operation with his call. Cass was speaking louder than normal, perhaps to alert me. She sounded buzzed, or at least was pretending to be. Lennox laughed at what she said. It was a deep patrician chuckle. I hated him already.

I moved quick and silent to the bedroom. I would position myself between him and the door when I stepped out. Prevent any lunges to egress. I hoped he'd resist. I wanted to use some aikido. I might accidently snap a tendon or two. *Oh well, my bad, now sit still and listen . . .*

The volume of their voices increased. They were right outside. I heard the key card slide into the lock. It clicked. A hand pushed the door open. Through the crack in the bedroom door, I saw her leading him by the hand. They passed my field of vision and went quiet. I heard the soft smacking of lips. Seeing red, I almost charged out and attacked. It took every reserve of discipline to contain myself. Instead, I stepped into the living room, blocked the door, and crossed my arms. His back was to me. Cass was facing me, her arms wrapped around his neck. She had to lean down to kiss him. Her eyes fluttered. She was putting on quite a show. You could have sworn she was enjoying herself.

I cleared my throat. She released him and stepped out of his arms.

"Sorry to interrupt," I said.

Peter Lennox sprang around and shouted. It was something unintelligible and frightened. A sound that would bring shame when he calmed down. I waited for him to rush me. Wanted it. Maybe he could sense my eagerness for confrontation, because he did the opposite. He staggered away from us with his hands up. Moving backwards, he tripped against a floor lamp and almost knocked it over. When he backed himself up as far as he could go, against the window, he glared at Cass. His instinctual cowardice was followed by an impotent rage.

"You bitch," he said. "You fucking bitch."

"Now, now," said Cass.

She smiled sweetly, took her sunhat by its wide brim, and tossed it on the couch. She ran her painted nails through her matted black hair. Shook it out and turned to me.

"Hi, Duck."

"Hello, darling," I said. "Aren't you going to introduce me to your friend?"

"Peter Lennox," she said, "say hello to my business partner, Duck Darley."

I extended my hand. He glowered at it. I turned it up and shrugged. His work bag sat in a heap in the center of the room, where moments earlier he'd had different expectations. A middle-aged gut spilled from his untucked Oxford. His sandy hair was thinning. His face was puffy and had the sheen of daily whiskey intake. He was the sort who might be able to dress up nice, but when stripped of his threads was just another schlubby ruin. He tried to straighten up and regain some dignity. It didn't work.

"Enjoy your drinks?" I asked Cass. "You sounded pretty loose coming down the hall."

She stuck a thumb at Lennox in the corner. "This guy made me have scotch," she said. "I hate scotch, it goes straight to my head."

"You seemed to like it a few minutes ago," he said.

She stepped toward him. I swear, he cowered. "I can *pretend* to like a lot of things," she said.

"What do you want?" he asked. "This is about Danny, isn't it?"

We were impressed. "You're smarter than you look," I said. "When you're not thinking with your dick."

"I know who you're working for," he said. "If I go missing next, I've left instructions. I'll take everyone down with me. This is America, you can't just snatch citizens without consequence. Danny and I are *Americans*."

Proclaiming his nationality seemed to give him the boost of strength that his character lacked.

"So are we," I said.

"Disgraces. That's what you two are. Traitors. You work for the enemy. That's called treason."

"Peter," said Cass. Her voice modulated to maximum threat. "You need to settle down. Who do you think we're working for?"

"You know damn well."

"I want to hear you say his name, just to be sure."

"Sun Bin," he said. "There, you happy? Tell me I'm wrong. I got the email, okay? I saw Danny being wheeled out of his own building, between Sun's bodyguards. Everyone knows they work for him."

Cass couldn't suppress a smile. Neither could I. Confirmation, as we'd hoped.

"Very good," she said. "That's very good to hear. Thank you, Peter."

She took another step toward him. I noticed her hands. They were tense and wide at her sides. Her nails looked like bloody claws sprouting from her fingertips. I thought she might slash him. I'd seen her do it before. It was effective. When she was within arm's reach, she raised her right arm and traced those claws lightly against her pale cheek. Her stance was wide, her shoulders squared. She appeared to be longing for action as much as I was. But Lennox was not the sort to fight back, at least not physically.

"We're not working for Sun Bin," I said.

He seemed not to hear me. His eyes were locked on Cass, and hers on him.

"We've been hired by the Soto family," said Cass. "We're

here to help. Well, not you. You're likely fucked. But we're going to try to bring your friend back, if that means anything to you."

"Nicole hired you?" he asked.

"Technically, their daughter, Layla, hired us," I said. "But not to worry, I got her mother's permission first."

"You're working for a seventeen-year-old?"

"Not anymore. We were at first, but now we're in the employ of Eileen Chung, Danny's . . ."

"I know who she is."

"And?"

"And what? If you're working for Danny's mother, it proves what I said—you're a couple of traitors."

"You don't think she has her son's best interests at heart?"

He let out an ugly, clipped laugh. "Whatever she's paying you, I can top it. Name it."

"You don't seem very interested in saving your friend," said Cass.

"He's my *best* friend," said Lennox. "Has been for more than thirty years, so don't tell me what it *seems* like. Eileen Chung cannot be trusted. Danny would say the same thing himself. His mother's trouble, always has been. When I got that email, I thought she was behind it. Still do."

"Layla agreed with you," I said.

"She's a smart kid."

"She doesn't think so anymore."

"Why not?"

"Because Eileen denies it. She's staying at the Sotos' place out in Southampton," I said. "I just got back from there. We all talked. There's been some developments in the case, Pete. You care to hear about it?"

"Tell me."

Cass turned, asked, "You want to show him the instructions she gave you?"

"He's not gonna like it," I said.

I went to the bedroom to grab the bag. It was getting lighter. I was spending the cash rather quickly. I had an awareness that this might be all the payment we received. The promised millions from Eileen Chung felt far off. I removed the ransom note and the financial instructions. Cass and Lennox were still positioned as I had left them by the window. Now, instead of lust, he emitted loathing. I set the papers on the coffee table in front of the couch.

"Have a seat," I said.

He took a step to move around her. Cass moved with him, holding his eyes.

"Relax," I added. "She won't bite."

"I might," said Cass.

With a grin, she relented and let him pass.

Lennox took a seat at the center of the couch and leaned forward to examine the documents. Cass and I remained standing, flanking him on either side. He was tense as he read, his expression focused, and then disgusted. He was shaking his head hard as he finished.

"She gave this to you?" he asked, looking up at me.

"She did. She told me she received it from an older stranger in Shanghai. She said she was approached on the Bund as she left lunch and was asked to get into a car. There, she was informed about Danny's situation. The guy gave her these papers and took her to a private airport where her husband's plane was waiting. It flew her to New York, and she went to see her daughter-in-law and grand-kids in the Hamptons."

"You believe all that?"

"I'm telling you what she told me," I said. "Whatever her sins, I'm having a hard time believing that she would abduct, and then extort, her own son."

"Well, if *you* believe her," he scoffed.

"Why should we believe his friend over his mother?" asked Cass.

Lennox hung his head in his hands. We watched him rub his chubby cheeks. When he peered up, he had the look of a beaten boxer who coasted through the early rounds and thought he had the fight won. Too late, he realized he was on the verge of being knocked out.

"I'm screwed," he said. "So is Danny. If he's not dead already."

"Why?" I asked.

Cass answered for him. "Because if he makes that trade, Soto Capital is going to have regulators up its ass with both fists."

Lennox liked that. In spite of the moment, he seemed to appreciate the analogy. "What she said," he said.

We let him stew for a moment. He scanned over the documents again. He stood and moved back to the window. Cass let him pass. His reflection in the night glass looked pathetic. No matter how much he'd managed to amass, the bill had come due.

"She's got us trapped," he said. "Goddamn clever lady. Guess that's where Danny got the brains."

"Talk to us, Peter," said Cass.

He gave a withering look, not appreciating the tender tone from a woman who'd just manipulated him.

"She's gonna blow up our fund," he said. "I make this trade, Soto Capital is fucked. If I don't, I could be letting my best friend die. She knows Danny's a brother to me. He's family. I care about him more than his own mother. She's gonna try to take two billion dollars off us, set herself up nice, and she'll probably leave it to her grandkids, which is how she'll rationalize it. And she'll own her son again. She's always hated Nicole. She'll tell him, *Not to worry, our family still has money, but now it's mine and you must listen.*" He turned and searched our faces. "You guys see what I'm saying?"

We did, though we didn't want to admit it. He was making a strong, if improbable, case. It was a difficult thing to admit, but I'd been witness to parental treacheries. The bonds of our makers weren't always as tight as we told ourselves. Sometimes it was easier to believe in the bonds of friendship. That relationship was chosen. I didn't doubt that Lennox believed what he was telling us, but I also knew that he was a long way from innocent. Anyone who accumulates a near billion has much to atone for. At that level, every hand has blood on it.

"What does Sun Bin have on you?" I asked.

He hesitated, enough to express guilt in the pause.

"C'mon, Peter," said Cass. "He wouldn't leave a calling card like that, showing his women on camera taking Soto, if he was worried about being caught."

Lennox gazed up at the ceiling. His eyes fell shut as he exhaled. "I tried to warn him," he said, more to himself. "There was too much downside. I told him just to buy his damn boat and take a breather."

"Let me guess," I said. "He was doing business with his mother's husband. The deal had something to do with pharmaceuticals, painkillers specifically."

"How . . ."

"She told me," I said. "In so many words. Prefaced by a history lesson on the Opium Wars, how the British enslaved the Qing dynasty. They made junkies of the ruling class and brought down imperial China."

"That sounds like Eileen."

"You've spent time with her?"

"Of course. I've known her since Danny and I were freshmen at St. Andrews," he said. "She was my best friend's mom. I knew she was nuts even then, so did Dan."

"But he was doing business with her? Even if you both thought she was crazy?"

"Every once in a while. Money's the only way she knows how to communicate. The fund would involve her in a few plays a year. Danny would say it was the only relationship he had with his mother. It was always small-time stuff, just a few million here and there."

Small time, you know, just a couple million . . . Jesus.

"But this latest pharmaceutical deal with her husband," said Cass. "That wasn't so small-time, was it?"

Lennox shook his head. "It was pretty major. It could have made us a lot, but like I said—I told him there was too much downside."

"Such as kidnapping and ransom," I pointed out.

"That wasn't the initial concern, but yeah, now that."

"What was the deal?" asked Cass. "Explain it to us."

He snorted. "You wouldn't understand."

"Try us," she said. "How was Sun Bin involved?"

Again, I marveled at the way she used her voice as a weapon. If Cass Kimball asked you to explain, in the right tone, you would damn well start talking.

"He wasn't," he said. "Not at first."

"What changed?"

Lennox agitated. He blinked and looked down at the street below. The life of a downtown summer night hummed beneath us. I went to the minibar.

"Want another scotch?" I asked.

"Please."

"Neat?"

"That's fine."

"Darling?" I asked. "Anything for you?"

"Water," said Cass.

I leaned down, opened the door, and examined the beverages. I took out a Fiji for Cass and two mini bottles of Glenlivet for Lennox. Twisted them open, held each to my nose, and sniffed. I could allow myself that much. I poured them into a tumbler from the shelf and walked across the room to deliver the overpriced spring water to my partner and the amber to our new friend.

I waited until Lennox had a few sips. Watching him, it was clear he was a man who savored the whiskey burn. I could see him holding it on his tongue, letting the spirit dissolve and work its magic, before he swallowed it down.

"What changed?" asked Cass, impatient. "How did Sun Bin enter into all this?"

"Guy's connected up the ass," said Lennox. "Way up."

"We know," I said. "Eileen mentioned how every rich guy in China is controlled by the Party. They all work for Xi Jinping, just like every Russian works for Putin."

"Beijing must have gotten wind of this deal, between Soto Capital and Eileen Chung's spouse," said Cass. "They didn't like it. Sun's acting on orders from high up."

Lennox looked at us. The defeat in his eyes was striking. "I didn't mean connected in China," he said. "You've got it backwards."

He lifted his glass and drained the scotch. Then he surprised us. As Cass lowered herself onto the couch and I processed his comment, he made a rush for the door.

Chapter 31

He almost made it. He managed to turn the handle, even opened it an inch. It was a respectable effort. More than I expected from him. He'd chosen his moment well. Cass was seated, I was confused, and he was done answering questions. He must have realized just how screwed he was. Whether Eileen Chung was behind her own son's abduction or not, Peter Lennox had few options.

My apprehension of him was not elegant, but it was effective. There was no time for any aikido. If I'd tried to grab him from behind he might have managed to pull open the door. He wouldn't have made it across the threshold, but he could have been seen by a passing guest. He might have cried out for help. I couldn't let that happen. So, I lowered my shoulder and rushed at his lower back. The door slammed shut as we collided. He pressed against it with a grunt. I delivered two rapid kidney shots to take any remaining fight out of him. Lennox sank to the floor.

I hovered over him, right fist raised. He held up his hands in front of his face.

"Okay," he said. "Okay!"

"Where do you think you're going?" I asked.

He curled on the floor, clutched his side, and gasped for breath. I offered the humiliated man my hand. To my surprise, he took it. I helped him up and steered him back to his seat. Cass scooted over, patted the cushion next to her. He settled beside her with a grimace. She eyed the documents on the table until Lennox looked back at them.

"So, Sun Bin is working with the U.S. government, not his own?" she asked.

Lennox rubbed his side, remained quiet.

"When can you execute this trade?" I asked.

"I can't," he said. "I told you . . ."

"Your fund is fucked if you do," I said. "You mentioned that. And your friend is dead if you don't."

"Probably already is."

Just as Layla had believed when she first involved me in this mess.

"Is that a chance you're willing to take?" I asked.

He ignored my question, faced Cass. She crossed her legs, folded her hands over her knees. Smoothed out her sundress. It covered more of her than he would have liked. Beneath the loathing, his longing for her still simmered.

"Let's say we believe you," she said. "Say Danny Soto's mother betrayed him and helped facilitate his kidnapping. That would mean she's working for Sun, whom you say is working for American interests?"

"I didn't say that," he claimed. "I said you had things backwards."

"You're going to have to be more specific, Peter."

"They must have flipped her," he said. "Same as Sun. You think anyone with real money cares about *patriotism*? Please, they're on whatever side is willing to play ball. You know how many Chinese citizens are taken every day over there? You become a problem, or even a perceived problem, and they just grab you. Ever hear about those booksellers from Hong Kong?"

I remembered the stories in the *Times*. Publishers of books deemed offensive to the powers-that-be were taken with some regularity. Some were returned to their families after time away in places unknown. When they came back, they kept their mouths shut. Others were never seen again. The Western press could report on it all they liked, which wasn't much, but no one could do a thing.

"I've heard about it," I said.

"Well, those were *booksellers*. Free speech nuts on the fringe. What do you think they do to folks who can make real trouble?"

"Kill them," I said.

"Exactly."

"So instead the guilty parties cast their lot with the other side?"

"Even if it means sacrificing a son?" asked Cass. "I'm not sure I believe that."

"Maybe Eileen thought it was the only way to *save* her son," I said. "And herself. Sure, Soto Capital goes down, and two billion disappears, but her family lives. They'd still be plenty rich."

"You give that woman too much credit," said Lennox. "She'll be destroying untold life savings, bringing down a major firm, and she's getting people killed."

"Play this out, Peter," said Cass. "Say you refuse to pay. You go about business as usual and write off your best friend as dead. Say someone sends you his severed head in a box. Say you can live with all that. You don't think they'll come for you next?"

"Not if I drop the deal," he said. "Anyway, in the event of my disappearance, I've left instructions to—"

"You don't have the leverage," she said. "Washington will release what it knows about your shady hedge fund. Who's going to miss you? You'll be portrayed as white-collar criminals trying to profit off the opioid crisis."

"Doesn't get much lower than that," I said. "With the purchase of that pharma company, did you plan to flood both Chinese *and* American shores with painkillers?"

"It wasn't like that," he said.

"You sure? I'm all for the libertarian legalize-everything argument, but that's some cold shit. That's like Mexican cartel level."

Lennox motioned toward the mini fridge. "You got any more Glenlivet left in there?"

I didn't get up to check. I no longer had the capacity to see or smell alcohol without sampling it. "Nope," I said.

"You're planning to run," said Cass. "Aren't you?"

His eyes went to his lap and stayed there.

"You thought you could find a way out of this," she continued. "But now you know for certain that you're cooked. That's why you tried to get out of here. You're gonna run. Solo, is my guess. Leave your family behind, wish them the best. There's probably a safe with a few million stashed somewhere. Your wife will have to scale back her lifestyle, your kids will grow up without a father, but they'll be fine. No one will want to hurt them once you're gone. That's what you're telling yourself, isn't it?"

He didn't nod; he didn't have to.

"What was the plan?" I asked. "Fire up the jet at Teterboro? Access some offshore accounts? Live out your days as a rich outlaw on some Central American beach? Can't say I blame you."

"It must be liberating to embrace one's cowardice," said Cass. "Easier than trying to save a friend or be there for family. I'm sure the Sotos will understand, his kids, especially."

"It was grandma's fault anyway," I said. "It's Eileen Chung who's guilty, not you. Maybe your buddy is too. You tried to warn him, right? There was too much downside. He should have just bought a new toy, gotten that boat like you advised, taken the summer off. Not your fault this all went to shit, is it?"

"Goddamn right!" he shouted. "The hell with both of you."

He stood, swept the documents off the table, and stalked back to the window. We let him stew in front of his reflection for a bit. It was Cass who spoke first.

"Peter," she said, "if you're going to leave, why not make the trade first? If it goes through, maybe they'll return Danny. If you're gone, what do you care if the company comes under scrutiny?"

"You want me to destroy the business we've built, abandon my friend and my family, and *then* leave?"

"Who said there's no honor among thieves?" I asked.

"I know," said Cass. "There's much more dignity in fleeing in the night and signing your friend's death warrant in absentia."

"I think Danny's already dead," he said again. "At least this way the firm might have a chance to survive."

"You'll never know for certain. While you're watching some perfect sunset on a white sand beach, all alone, I'm sure you'll never think of how you might have saved your best friend. But you're right—he's probably never coming home, so why take the risk? Too much downside."

"Motherfucker," muttered Lennox.

He slid his phone from his pocket and tapped at the screen. His body language changed as he watched what appeared. In the seconds that passed, we watched him transform from a craven man, about to flee, to one with a resigned sense of purpose. "My God," he said. "Look at this."

Sun Bin, or whoever controlled him, had tired of waiting.

Lennox handed it to Cass. I came over and sat next to her on the couch. She positioned the small screen so we both could get a look. Her crimson nail clicked the Play icon.

We were looking at an odd-shaped room of glistening teakwood, lit from above around the perimeter. There were narrow, oblong windows on either side. It was night out. In the center of the room was a king-size bed. Danny Soto was pushed into the frame. He stumbled to the foot of the bed and turned to face the camera with a questioning look. He was wearing boxer shorts and a torn white t-shirt. He looked like a morning-after version of himself. His legs were thin and hairless. Uneven stubble scratched his cheeks. His mouth was tight and turned down. His eyes were charged with indignation.

Another figure appeared in the frame. Or more accurately—another limb appeared. It was the leg of one of Sun's female guards and it shot out and up in a powerful strike. The heel of her boot caught Danny under the chin. His head rocked back, and his body followed, as he fell backwards onto the bed. His assailant came after him. She was wearing the same dark fatigues that we'd seen on the previous video. In one hand she held a small black piece of rounded leather, a sap. She straddled Danny, raised her arm, and whipped it down across his face. Raised it again and added a backhand to the other cheek.

The beating may have continued, but that was the end of the clip.

Cass tapped at Lennox's phone. She read aloud the email that accompanied it. It was succinct:

Transaction must be processed by noon tomorrow. Or we kill him.

"So, he's still alive," I said. "For now, anyway."

"What are you going to do, Peter?" asked Cass. "Still want to run? There's proof—your friend isn't dead yet."

I took the phone from Cass, opened the video again, and examined that room, searching for a connection at the edge of my consciousness. I paused it as her kick made contact with his jaw. Between that blow and the sap strikes that followed, Danny would be needing reconstructive surgery to his once fine face. I figured the woman's partner had done the filming. Maybe she joined in the beat-down after she stopped recording. I thought of Cass's work at the Chamber. There were men who paid for such masochism, extra for two at once. But Danny Soto didn't look to be enjoying himself. There was dungeon play torture, and then there was the real thing.

"I'll make the trade," said Lennox. "As soon as the markets open tomorrow, I'll do it."

"Good choice," I said.

"Can I go now?" he asked.

"You may not," said Cass. "You may, however, have the bedroom. Go on, get in there, get some rest. Tomorrow is a big day for you."

The beaten bastard searched our faces. His life force seemed to be seeping out of him like a slow leak in a football. This time tomorrow, his business would be facing ruin; he would be in legal jeopardy; but, just maybe, he would have saved his best friend.

Chapter 32

After Lennox trudged to the bedroom and shut the door, Cass and I settled into an uncomfortable silence. I went to the window, pressed my forehead to the glass, and stared down at the night. It started to rain. Umbrellas were up along the sidewalks and movement beneath them was brisk. A couple raced through the crosswalk as the light changed. A cab honked. Middle fingers were exchanged. These coursing city streets, these charged lives, all of us convinced that the world should stop and start on our watch, and no one else's.

I remembered my conversation with Nicole Soto out in Southampton, before her mother-in-law announced herself. What had she said about her husband? That he was a bloodless machine who did not ask for permission. He could have anything he wanted, and so could his wife. They took what they desired, when they desired it. One day it might be a yacht, the next a new plane, or another beautiful home in some charmed locale. Danny Soto had reached a station, amassed so much wealth, that the word *aspiration* no longer applied. With billions in the bank, you didn't long for things. You saw, you liked, you bought. Repeat.

It made sense that folks like these developed delusions

of invincibility. Everything in their physical existence reinforced that belief. Through brute capitalism, they'd conquered humanity. They would still die like everyone else,
yes, but not before they exhausted all options, with the
best medicine money could buy. It was all illusion. Any
one of them could be struck down at any moment. No
matter how high the gates, how extensive the security,
everyone could be reached. Much as they hated to admit
it, they were mortal. And all of them had enemies.

"The couch pulls out," said Cass. "We can share it if
you want."

I turned. "Huh? Oh right, it's not like either of us can go
home."

"How do you think this is going to play out?" she
asked.

"You mean, do I think they'll release Soto after Lennox
executes that trade? Maybe."

"That, but I also meant with us, with our own lives. Are
we going to be able to return to them? Are they gonna decide we're better off dead?" She frowned, sighed. "Whoever *they* are . . ."

"I don't know."

We couldn't look at each other. The future, even a sun-
rise away, felt impossible to comprehend. Outside of this
hotel room, there was nothing that made sense. I thought
of my apartment, my little garden pad, with old Mr. Petit
upstairs. When was I last there? He might have died. I
might have already been evicted. I remembered I left the
AC running. It was all too abstract to consider.

"I meant it, you know," said Cass. "I do want to be
partners. Business partners with a proper investigations
firm. We can do it, Duck."

"You think?"

"I'm sure. You've built a reputation, people trust you
with their troubles. But you're unprofessional. That self-

destructive streak is going to catch up with you. You need me, not just to help keep your head on straight, but on the research end. I'm more methodical, more organized, and through my contacts from the Chamber . . ."

"Holy fuck," I muttered.

"What?"

"Hang on a sec."

I leapt up and crossed the room and threw open the bedroom door. Lennox was lying on top of the covers, fully dressed, staring at the ceiling. He turned his head on a pillow to face me.

"Peter," I said, "that boat that Danny wanted to buy, what was its name?"

He yawned. "I can't remember. Jade something. *The Lady Jade*, I think?"

I flung the door shut and went to Cass.

"Your contacts," I said. "Call Harold Lester. I need to talk to him, right away."

"Why? What just occurred to you?"

"They're holding Danny Soto on a goddamn boat. That room in the video? It was a cabin room on a yacht. Those narrow windows, the shape of the space, the teakwood? It was within the bow of a boat. And Harold has . . ."

"*The Triple Mint*," she said. "He's always asking to take me out on it. But why . . ."

"When you left to meet Lennox at the bar, Harold told me he was staying on board tonight, in some Brooklyn marina by the bridge. Then, before you arrived, the jackass called the hotel phone to check on us."

"He did what?"

"I know, but before I could hang up, he mentioned seeing some mega-yacht pulling into the harbor. He was excited to see it, said most of the big ones are in the Mediterranean this time of year."

"You think that's where they're keeping Soto?"

"*The Lady Jade*," I said. "It's the same name that Harold mentioned. And I just remembered—the last time Nicole spoke to her husband, the day before he was taken, he told her he was buying a boat, a big one. She didn't approve. It was the last thing she mentioned before her mother-in-law appeared."

"Who was he buying it from?" asked Cass. "Sun Bin? Is that why he welcomed his neighbor to his apartment that night? Not to talk business, but because Soto thought he was buying a new toy."

"Danny would have known it was docked here. He was probably excited to see it."

"But not like this." Cass stood and approached the window. "To catch a big fish . . ."

"You need some big bait."

"What do you want Harold to do?"

"I want him to pick me up on his boat," I said. "We won't be able to reach the *Jade* from land. The marina is bound to have a ton of security. But from the water . . ."

"You think you can just hop aboard? You think Harry can just pull up next to it, in the middle of the night? C'mon, Duck. Why not wait for Lennox to make the trade tomorrow? Who cares if it blows up their fund? They probably deserve it. Maybe then they'll release Soto, and his kids can see their father again. That's what this is about, isn't it?"

"What, Soto's kids?"

"Please. You don't care if a man like Danny Soto lives or dies. But you *do* care about his kids having a father. You don't want to see him murdered, or in prison, because . . ."

"Don't give me this projecting crap," I said. "You said you wanted to start a business? Well, here's the way to start—by solving a case worth a couple million dollars. We get Danny back, and we get paid. They release him after rigging a multibillion-dollar, dubious trade, then what happens? All accounts, all assets, frozen. Maybe some of the money eventually reaches Eileen Chung, but it's not like she'll be in any position to pay us at that point."

"You want me to call off Lennox?" she asked. "That seems like a hell of a reckless risk."

"Just stay with him and wait to hear from me," I said. "I'm not convinced they have any intention of releasing Danny. If I'm in their position, I wait for the trade to go through, then I kill the captive, dump him in New York Harbor, and set sail. They'll be in international waters by the time he's found. They'd *want* him to be found. Soto Capital will be exposed, the fund exploded, and then the founder washes up in the East River, looking like a suicide, or the deserving victim of foul play. Either way, no one's going to spend much time mourning him—or investigating further."

"Aside from his children."

"They'll adjust," I said.

"Look how well you turned out."

"Crack goes the whip."

"I'm sorry," she said. "That was cruel."

I shrugged. "It's your nature."

"Fuck you, Duck."

"So, are you gonna call Harold for me?"

She pretended to think it over. Hands on her hips, stance wide, steady glare, she reverted to mistress-mode, the way she'd learned to make men cower. I didn't bite. She let out a dramatic sigh and placed the call.

Harold was thrilled to hear from us. He claimed he knew we'd be in touch, had a premonition that we still needed his help. I asked if the mega-yacht was still berthed at his marina. Goddamn right, he replied. He'd been trying to get a closer look from the deck with his binoculars.

"The *Jade*," he said. "She is one gorgeous lady."

Jade—the imperial gem of China. It was thought to bring luck and protect one from evil. Or in this case, perhaps, to protect one while committing evil. I wondered if Danny Soto planned to rechristen it with a new name when it came into his possession. *The Pain Killer*, perhaps? As a prisoner on board, did he still covet it? Had he been permitted to tour its opulent interiors? Or was he kept in that single cabin room, humiliated and beaten by Sun Bin's ladies? Either way, he was learning some hard lessons in humility. The final lesson would be coming soon enough.

Harold agreed to pick me up at the North Cove Marina, next to Brookfield Place, near the World Trade Center and 9/11 Memorial. It was about a mile and a half south of the hotel, a short cab ride down West Street at this time of night. It was almost as close for Harold by boat, a loop around the southern tip of Manhattan.

"What are you going to do when you get there?" asked Cass.

"We'll see."

"Don't be a fool. Tell me you have a plan or I'm not letting you walk out this door."

"I have a plan."

"What is it?"

"You just said to tell you I had one. Now, can I go?"

"No."

She crossed the room, positioned herself in front of the door, and folded her arms like a bouncer. Maybe she could physically restrain me, maybe not. I wasn't about to find out.

"I'm not going to fight my way past you, Cass."

"I know that."

"Will you please step aside?"

"I thought you wanted to be partners?" she asked. "Real ones. If that's the case, then *we* need to come up with a plan. I'm not letting you blunder into your latent death wish."

"Okay, you have any ideas?"

She allowed a smile. "I might."

It wasn't a bad one. I thought it might even work. We talked it through, I added a few suggestions, got her approvals. Unlike Danny and Nicole Soto, we would need to ask each other for permission before we went about our business. Communication—they say it's key to any long-lasting partnership. But they say a lot of things, and most of it is worthless.

I bid my farewell with a hug at the door. She opened it for me and wished me luck. It was a little after eleven. Harold had agreed to meet at 11:30 p.m. The marina closed at ten, so he said he'd pull up just north of it, alongside the Battery Park Esplanade in Rockefeller Park. I could hop aboard and then we'd spin around at the mouth of the Hudson.

The rain had stopped. The night was sticky with humidity. A mosquito buzzed close to my ear as I raised my arm for a cab. I swatted at it. The driver took my lowered arm as a change of mind. He sped on. I moved west across White Street to the corner of West Broadway and found another. I didn't know the closest cross streets by the marina, so I told him to drop me in front of the Goldman Sachs building, on West between Murray and Vesey. I could find it from there.

The destination seemed rather appropriate. If Peter Lennox planned to execute a multibillion-dollar trade tomorrow, chances were high that Goldman, the vaunted vampire squid, would have its blood funnel jammed into the deal somehow. Every time I found myself near its headquarters, I remembered that vicious *Rolling Stone* story some years back. The writer, Matt Taibbi, had become a folk hero to the legions of Goldman haters. His coinage of "vampire squid" stuck. "The Squid" was now shorthand for the bank's relentless greed, even by those that worked there.

"Gotta work late," I told the cabbie. "Money never sleeps."

He didn't get the reference, but that was okay. The sequel wasn't very good anyway.

Chapter 33

Squid tower was all lit up. The ever-present fleet of Town Cars and Escalades idled out front. Behind the glass, the soaring lobby was dominated by an eighty-foot piece of abstract art that had been commissioned for five million dollars when the building opened. It was an incoherent, colorful mess, like a low-rent Kandinsky in a very high-rent place. Whatever happened upstairs was a mystery to me, but I knew the decisions made on those floors guided world markets more than any other institution. Would the fall of Soto Capital impact them? The sudden implosion of a multibillion-dollar hedge fund must send ripples far and wide.

Someone would profit. Someone would get shot. It was a zero-sum game, like life itself.

I handed a twenty over the seats, told him to keep the change, and got out in front of the building. Just another blithe banker headed back to the office late at night, except I didn't look like anyone who would be allowed inside, even at this hour. I could smell myself. A rank mixture of sea water, sweat, and adrenaline, it wasn't pleasant. Maybe I'd go for a dip in the Hudson after Harold picked me up.

I turned on Vesey Street and walked toward the river.

The sidewalks were mostly empty. It was a stifling summer night, after a hard rain. Those in town were hunkered indoors with AC blasting, but most of this neighborhood was checked out of the city. The wives, the kids, the bosses, they sat on porches a hundred miles away, proclaiming that they never wanted to go back. Maybe after all this, I'd convince Cass to join me on a beach getaway. We could discuss our new business over cocktails, after dips in the sea. It would be a worthy end to the booze cleanse. Even if we never saw those promised millions, I still had plenty of cash in my backpack to afford somewhere decent.

I turned left on North End Avenue and walked to the dead end. A few doors down, a couple drunks were spilling out of P.J. Clarke's, firing up cigarettes and talking loud. I didn't need anyone to see me. I stayed in the shadows and moved through the narrow park that bordered the marina. Most of the slips were occupied by commercial craft. Tourist cruisers or city sailing clubs, for folks who took advantage of the oft-forgotten fact that we lived on an island. I positioned myself at the corner and searched the waters for approaching lights.

Harold didn't keep me waiting. I spotted *The Triple Mint* coming up slow, hugging close to shore. He had on enough lights to guide him, but no more than necessary. I raised an arm; he flashed his lights. He cut the engine and guided the boat in front of me. I stepped over the single chain fence that separated pedestrians from the water. Waited for it, leapt out, and landed clean on the stern.

"Welcome aboard," he called from the wheel.

I went into the covered cockpit and shook his hand. "Thank you, Harold," I said. "You ready to have some fun?"

"Goddamn right," he said.

He swung the wheel to the left, turned us around, and gave it some juice. The bow lifted as we sliced south, out of the Hudson and into the harbor. The *Mint* was an impressive forty-two-foot Chris-Craft that Harold maintained in spotless condition. I knew boaters could be obsessive with their toys, especially ones who took pride in running their ships without help. Those mega-yachts required a full crew and some serious professional expertise. Boats like Harold's could be managed by a single individual, provided he or she had enough time and disposable income to devote to this notoriously wasteful hobby.

"Beautiful night," he said, sweeping his arm toward the passing skyline. "Would you look at that? I swear, it never gets old."

The southern point of Manhattan rose up on the port side. One World Trade Center poked highest in the sky, its spire lit red, white, and blue at 1,776 feet. Further north in Midtown, standing higher than the Empire State or any of its neighbors, was Danny Soto's tower, a long, thin stack of cubes that rose and rose with astronomically priced apartments. The lights at the very top were off. Its owner was indisposed at the moment. His wife and children were hunkered in at their castle in Southampton. Perhaps the two fools on this boat, close to midnight in the middle of the harbor, would help restore order to their lives.

As we turned the corner at the bottom of the island, I considered the varying vantage points. This was where the city first came into being, as a port town positioned with perfection within a protected harbor, alongside a river that stretched over three hundred miles north, ending in the Adirondacks at Lake Tear of the Clouds. This city didn't need Henry Hudson to "discover" it; its future greatness was preordained by its geography. But its conquering—by men like Danny Soto—in the four hundred years since was difficult to fathom. On the ground, Manhattan was not a large place, just thirteen miles long and less than two and a half miles at its widest point. Yet those weren't the dimensions that mattered. Its size and ambition came vertically, pushing through the clouds.

What did Danny Soto see when he looked down from the top of his tower at night? Lights—endless, infinite lights, all beneath him, and black sky above. There were few stars visible above New York City. The lights from below blinded them. He looked down into the tamed light, not up into a vast unknown. He'd managed to reverse the natural order. The first settlers of this city must have marveled at the stars above this rich, untapped land. Now the rulers peered down at the glittering lights.

Would a man at that vantage point ever realize when he was weak, that it could all be taken away by a knock at the door?

Sun Bin's ancestors, they knew. They didn't come from a childish land, a few centuries old. Theirs was a culture that went back thousands, not hundreds, of years. Rises and falls of empires, these things were as inevitable as the sun rising and setting. It was all temporary. I wondered how many Americans knew that over the last one thousand years China had had the largest GDP on Earth for nine of those centuries. The twentieth century was a blip, a passing stumble, while the USA rose with false, teenage confidence. That was being corrected in the twenty-first, whether Americans were ready to admit it or not.

We reached the neighboring marina quickly. By land, by day, it could take an hour to get from Battery Park to Brooklyn Heights. By boat, at night, it was a couple minutes, a short ride around an empty stretch of water.

The Lady Jade was visible from far off. It was a floating fortress of polished fiberglass, eschewing the traditional white for a gunmetal-gray finish, with dark tinted windows. It rose up three stories and must have stretched over two hundred feet. Emerald lights glowed along its base at the water's edge. Of all the innumerable ways to spend a fortune, this would be any billionaire's prize possession.

"Would you look at her," said Harold. "Isn't she something?"

"How much you think something like that goes for?" I asked.

"Maybe two-fifty, three-hundred million? Plus, seven figures a year in upkeep, when you factor in crew, gas, and maintenance. Hell, just your dockage fees are probably around four hundred grand for a boat like that. It's about the most expensive thing a man can own. More than any plane or mansion."

"I look forward to a tour."

"You think you're going aboard that thing? Good luck. We're talking military-grade security. I read that most of these suckers come with bomb-proof windows, motion sensors, even escape pods, not to mention an arsenal of weapons. You need to remember—there's no law out in the open ocean. It's every boat for itself. They're designed with Somali pirates in mind, missile attacks, hurricanes, you name it."

"I'm impressed."

"You damn well should be. Now you gonna tell me what you have in mind?"

"If we can't get in," I said, "then we'll have to have them come out."

"How do you suggest we do that?"

Cass's plan was a simple one, involving loud music. If all went smooth, I just needed to make a visual ID, make a call, and enjoy the racket.

"How's your sound system on board?" I asked.

"Pumping," said Harold. "Got a set of Kenwoods, best marine speakers out there. The *Mint*'s seen a few parties, my friend."

"You ready to violate some noise ordinances?"

"I thought we wanted to be discreet?"

"Not anymore," I told him. "Now it's time to spook our prey from its nest. We need some music."

"Whaddya like?"

"The driver deejays," I said. "You tell me."

Harold was already reaching for his iPhone, pleased. "Oh, I got just the thing. An album made to offend." He eyed the screen, scrolled for his selection. "You realize others are bound to call 311? What if we get hassled before anyone appears outside the *Jade*?"

"Then we turn it down, take the ticket, and come up with a better idea."

"And if someone *does* poke their head out of there?"

"Soon as I can make a positive ID, we call it in, report the location of a kidnapping, and we wait for law enforcement to do its job."

"Who are we looking for?"

"A pair of tall Asian women," I said, "in military fatigues. They were seen on a security camera wheeling Danny Soto out of his lobby."

"Know who they work for?"

"A Chinese billionaire named Sun Bin," I said. "Also a resident of the Sotos' tower."

Harold was nodding. "Eighty-eighth floor," he said. "Paid a little over sixty million."

"Man knows his high-end real estate."

"It's my job to know."

I gazed across the dark waters at *The Lady Jade*. It looked more like a sci-fi warship than a vessel of luxury. "How long would it take a boat that size to start up and pull out of here?" I asked.

"This time of night, with the crew down? It would take a couple minutes to get everyone in position, pull up anchor, and get the engines humming, but after that, you'd be surprised how fast that beast can move. Soon as it's out of the harbor, it could start flying. My guess—it can probably top fifty knots. The *Mint* can move, I topped her out once at forty-five, but don't ask me to chase 'em. They'll fire on our ass. You ever hear of a sonic gun?"

"Nope."

"That would be a non-lethal best case—they fire a focused sonic wave at us that would blast our eardrums deaf and throw us off course. I hear that's standard on every mega-yacht these days. More likely—they'll fire actual bullets and sink my baby, if they don't hit us first." Harold looked up from his phone. "Remind me again why I'm out here with you?"

"Because you're involved in a matter of national security," I said. "You're helping to save a life, a rich and powerful life, that could one day repay you. And Cassandra Kimball will also be forever in your debt."

"A persuasive case," he said. "But if that beast pulls out, I'm still not chasing it."

"Fair enough," I said. "Now, about that music. What did you pick?"

Harold beamed. "*Never Mind the Bollocks*," he shouted as the sound of marching boots and a beating drum filled the harbor. "*Here's . . . the Sex Pistols!*"

It was an inspired choice, the defining scream of punk chaos, the inspiration of anarchy itself. The boots gave way to ripping guitars and Johnny Rotten's signature snarl: *A cheap holiday in other peoples' misery!* "Holidays in the Sun"—it sounded like a threat to all that the rich held dear. Who cared if it was being cranked from a rich broker's boat in New York Harbor? The important thing was where it was directed. At the inhabitants of *The Lady Jade*, at Sun Bin and his female ninjas, and at Danny Soto himself. I hoped they all could hear it.

I held up my thumb and raised it a few times. Harold

turned it up. He wasn't wrong, his speakers could sing. By the end of the first verse I could see lights coming on inside other boats at the marina. A nautical horn gave a warning shout. There were shouts of protest almost audible beneath the Pistols' outrage. But nothing yet from the *Jade*.

Harold was enjoying himself. Head-banging, he pulled down the throttle and got us even closer to Sun's ship. The song "Bodies" came next. It was even angrier than the first. The opening chords sounded like a horror movie soundtrack, or the warning cries of an invading army. Either way, it announced that death and destruction were imminent.

I saw a head emerge from the top deck. It wasn't the one I was looking for. It was that of an anonymous crew member that neither confirmed nor denied anything. More lights from other boats were coming on, more shouts trying to break through the disturbance. I knew sound was amplified when it traveled across water. I wondered if the residents in those waterfront Brooklyn condos could hear our party yet. I hoped so. I wanted it to outrage the entire borough. I wanted these songs of rage to infiltrate every dream and awaken everybody in panic. But not before someone I recognized stuck his or her head from *The Lady Jade*.

My wish came true with the start of the third song: "No Feelings." I saw a light flicker on the second deck, then movement across a room, and a female form emerging outside.

"There!" I shouted to Harold. "Shine your light!"

He turned his searchlight and pointed it in the direction of my finger. It landed on one of Sun's ladies. Just for a moment, but it was enough. Positive ID confirmed. The moment the bright light hit her face, she dove back inside and shut off the interior lights.

"That her?" called Harold.

I nodded and motioned for him to lower the volume. He gave me a confused look, so I extended my pinkie and thumb, as in *I-gotta-make-a-call*. Harold handed over his phone. I entered 9-1-1, waited for the voice to ask for my emergency.

When she did, I said, "I need to report a kidnapping at a marina in Brooklyn Heights." I turned and asked Harold, "What's the name of the marina?"

"The One Fifteen," he said. "Off Pier Five at Brooklyn Bridge Park."

I repeated the information to the dispatcher. Added, "A man named Danny Soto is being held inside a large yacht called *The Lady Jade*. They could leave any moment, please hurry."

"Sir," asked the voice, "where are you calling from?"

"I'm on the water, on another craft, about ten meters from the boat in question."

"And you've made positive identification?"

"You think I'd be calling you if I hadn't?"

"Copy," she said. "Stay where you are."

"Just get here!"

Harold called in the emergency on his VHF radio. After we ended our reports, he set down the receiver and asked, "Should I put the music back on?"

Before I could answer, we saw what looked like a garage door swinging open by the base of *The Lady Jade*'s stern. A powerboat was reversing out of the yacht by the emerald light. Three forms were visible aboard, one hooded. As soon as it cleared the exit of the mothership, the smaller vessel pivoted and accelerated toward open water.

Chapter 34

"Follow it," I said.

Harold hesitated. He'd refused to chase the big boat, but neither of us could have known there was a sleek speedboat hidden within its body.

"Fuck it," he muttered. "Let's go."

The bow of the *Mint* raised and turned and pointed after them. Perhaps it was a decoy, to send us running after harmless cargo, but I doubted that. If Danny Soto was being held captive and they realized we'd found them, they'd be getting him offshore—and away from their boss—as fast as possible.

Where they intended to take or leave him was another question.

Killing and dumping the body, and outrunning whatever was behind them, that seemed the likely option. Maybe they weren't ready to write off the billions due tomorrow just yet. If they could get their captive out to sea, clean up all evidence of his stay aboard the *Jade*, and wait it out for one more night, they might pull it off.

Once the cops boarded the boat, it was possible they might not find anything, not the prisoner nor the women who took him. In which case, all they would have was the claims of an unstable snoop who'd withheld video evidence of a kidnapping, and then insisted he saw one of the perpetrators on the ship of a respected Chinese tycoon. Sun Bin would have questions to answer, but even if anyone believed me, nothing would stick.

The small craft ahead sped between Governors Island and Red Hook and raced south. If they managed to get under the Verrazano Bridge, it wouldn't be long before they were out into open ocean. They'd fly past Brighton Beach and the Rockaways, with nothing but the Atlantic ahead.

Harold pushed down the throttle and kept pace. The harbor narrowed between Bay Ridge and Staten Island as we approached the bridge. I looked back for Coast Guard coming to help, but there were neither sights nor sounds in pursuit, not yet. We pressed on after them. The lights of the city began to recede behind us. Then we were passing under the Verrazano and their boat was turning away from shore, headed southeast into darkness.

The searchlight on the *Mint* captured movement on board, a figure turning and raising something on her shoulder. Realizing what it was, I ducked and tried to yell for Harold to get down. It was too late. The weapon burst with rapid fire. It sprayed his baby with bullets. I heard the glass of the cockpit shatter above me, a billion shards exploding over my shoulders. I looked up for Harold at the wheel. He wasn't there. I swung my head around and saw him flung back, slumped against the cabin door. A bullet had ripped through an eye and exploded his brain. On his face was a mask of confusion.

Without him at the wheel, the boat veered off course. The firing paused a moment. I peered over the shattered glass. At that exact moment I saw a figure stand and stumble and leap into the water. The last, desperate act of Danny Soto, he'd waited until that volley of distraction to make his move. It appeared his hands were tied; it looked like the hood was still affixed over his head. A man must be convinced of his coming death in order to throw himself into the ocean at night, bound and blind.

There are times for weighing rational options before taking action. This was not one of them. A thinking man with a sense of his own mortality might have tried to take control of the craft. Tried to turn it around and get away while he could. I did the opposite. I lunged from the cockpit, scrambled across the stern, and flung myself overboard.

The water welcomed me with a shock. Midsummer in New York, the ocean was in the low seventies—not bad, but surviving the chill was not my primary concern. It was escaping the bullets I knew would soon spray again in my direction. They would be coming around to find Danny—and to make sure their pursuers were dead.

I scanned over the surface, watching as the speedboat made a looping turn. They hadn't accounted for the *Mint*'s new passenger-free course. The bow of Harold's boat broadsided theirs as it swung around, capsizing it in a crush of colliding fiberglass.

A moment later, flames sparked from the battered vessels. I dove under water for what I knew was coming next. The sky exploded in a fireball. The surface burst with white light over my head. Shrapnel fell into the sea around me like burning hail. I breaststroked away from it, about a meter deep, pulling and kicking in the opposite direction until my lungs ached and I had to come up for air. Gasping, I searched across the wreckage, the smoldering boats and simmering surface fires, looking for bodies.

I heard his cries.

Soto had somehow ripped the hood from his head. He was roaring to the heavens, a man raging against the dying light. Through a nearby flame I could make out his face. It was tossed back, eyes beseeching the stars above.

"Danny!" I called out.

Hearing the sound of his name silenced him. He picked up his head, searched in terror toward my voice. It took him a moment to realize that it was not the tone of his captors, but a male voice, a stranger's, who knew his name.

"Who's there?" he cried. "Who are you?"

Instead of answering, I swam toward him with a heads-up freestyle, avoiding burning boat pieces. When I was about a body length away, I said, "My name is Duck, your daughter hired me to find you."

"Layla?" he asked. Saying her name seemed to confuse him. Shock was setting in.

"Are you hurt?" I asked.

"No," he said. "I mean, yes, my face."

I saw through the moonlight what he meant. His face was a ruin. I remembered the video. He looked like a pummeled fighter who might die in the dressing room after an inhumane beating.

"My hands," he gasped. He tried to show me but couldn't get his bound wrists above the surface.

"Your legs, are they tied too?"

"No," he said. "But I can't swim without my hands. I need help. I'm drowning."

"No, you're not," I said. "I'm going to get us to shore. I just need you to relax and stay on your back."

I swam under him, came up and wrapped one arm around his chest. With my free arm, I began to pull us in the direction of shore. I scissor-kicked beneath him. I tried to control my breathing, conserve my energy. Remembered those lifeguard training courses from my youth. We'd practice rescue techniques in the deep end of my team's pool. My Red Cross certs had expired about two decades ago. I did the best I could. The shore lights looked a long way off.

"If you could kick a bit," I told him, "that would be helpful."

He gave a few weak flutter kicks. It didn't help.

"I don't want to die," he said. "Please don't let me die."

"Neither of us is going to die," I said. "Now keep quiet. Talk will tire us out."

It was slow going. My free arm ached; my side cramped; my kick was awkward, inefficient beneath his weight. An hour or so passed. The land looked as far as when we started. Danny didn't speak. I wondered if he passed out. I slapped at his cheek. Forgot about the broken bones in his face.

"Ow!" he cried. "What the fuck?"

"Making sure you're still with me."

"You told me not to talk."

"Just stay awake."

He grunted. I went back to my inching progress. The night continued to pass. At some point I became aware of a presence, something large and shadowy, nearby. Perhaps it was my imagination, perhaps something more. Baby great whites had been spotted off the Rockaways on numerous occasions. I remembered reading in the *Post* about a fisherman catching one; another story about a surfer being bit in the leg. These were shark-infested waters. City beachgoers didn't like to consider it, and on summer days in crowded shallow waters, they had little to fear. But out here, a mile or so offshore, in the middle of the night, with blood in the water?

I waited for a strike. Wondered what it would be like to die that way. After all of this, to be attacked by a beast of nature, confused for a struggling seal. Sharks don't target people. *Jaws* was full of shit. I reminded myself that shark attacks are the most minuscule of risks. But on occasion, sharks did mistake a human form for its preferred diet of seals and sea lions. We were struggling. We trailed the scent of blood. It was feeding hour. In situations such as these, one's risk goes up quite a bit.

The shadow, the weight—whatever it was, at some point it went away. I kept waiting for it to return. With every shift of the sea, I envisioned a tall, jagged fin breaking the surface and slicing toward us. It gave me strength. It made me swim faster. The lurking, potential presence of a great white shark in the darkest waters of night will do that.

Chapter 35

The sun was flirting with the horizon when we reached the surf break. A slim parenthesis of orange peaked over the ocean. *We made it*, I thought. I exhaled. Pride was already replacing my bone-deep exhaustion. This was followed by a high wave that lifted us and broke on our heads. It tossed us without regard onto the sea floor. I lost my grip on Danny Soto, felt him tumbling over me, felt my shoulder slam into the sand and rocks. I let myself go loose like a rag doll, waited for the white water to have its way with me.

Then I was staggering to my feet in waist-deep surf. There was no sign of the man I almost saved. I saw two surfers standing with their boards at the tide line. They gazed at me with incomprehension. One of them pointed to my right, dropped his board, and started to run into the water. I watched him high-knee it through the inner break and dive through another rising wave. He came up clutching Soto and dragged him the rest of the way in.

We were a sorry sight collapsed on that dawn beach. It was difficult for either of us to form words. One of the surfers ran off to phone for help, while the other kept asking if we were okay. I managed to nod. I asked for water. He called back to his friend. The guy gave a thumbs-up.

The minutes passed in a once-removed way, like someone flipping through pictures on a phone of what was unfolding in the present. I heard Danny Soto groaning next to me. He began to vomit across the sand. The surfer and I gave him some room. When he finished, he sat back on his heels, wiped at his mouth with his bound wrists, and lifted his face to the brightening sky.

"Where are we?" he asked.

"Rockaway Beach," said the surfer. "Where did you guys come from?"

I pointed toward the horizon. "There was an accident," I said, "between two boats. We crashed in the middle of the night."

The surfer waited for me to continue. My mouth was parched from the salt water. I felt an overwhelming need for hydration. Looking up to the street past the beach, I hoped to see his friend returning with large bottles of water. I fantasized about gulping it down, like one of those Looney Toons episodes when a famished Bugs Bunny sees a mirage in the desert. When I opened my mouth to speak again, I felt the corners of my lips cracking.

"You need to call your partner," I said to Danny. To the surfer, I asked, "What time is it?"

He shrugged, motioned to the rising sun like it was a watch. "About six or so?"

"My partner?" asked Danny.

"Peter Lennox," I said. "He's your friend and business partner, correct?"

After a couple weeks in captivity, the hamsters were running slow in that brilliant mind of his. "Peter? Yes. Why?"

"Because as soon as the markets open, he's going to blow up your fund," I told him.

That got the rodents moving on their wheel. Danny's eyes widened. His shoulders straightened. I was now very much in focus, no longer an abstraction who'd rescued him in the night ocean. He tried to stand. He wavered on his feet, then stumbled backwards before collapsing on his ass in the shallow surf. He tried again, this time managed to steady himself.

"Where's your phone?" he asked the surfer.

The guy shrugged again and pointed back toward his car. Poor dude had been up for a quiet morning surf, and instead he'd come upon this mess. I remembered Harold Lester, shot through the eye as he gave chase at my behest. Another casualty of coming into contact with Death Darley. I hoped these surfers wouldn't suffer a similar fate.

"I need to make a call," said Danny, voice clear despite his ruined face. "It's an emergency."

"My buddy'll be back in a sec. Just chill. He's probably getting some water like your friend asked."

"I need a phone, not water!" cried Danny.

He started to run up the beach. It was a pitiful sight. He weaved and stumbled and tripped over the sand with his hands tied before his battered body. His spindly, hairless legs were almost useless, just as they had been in the water. He was dressed only in white boxers and a white undershirt, both soaked through and clinging to his sagging skin.

Why was I helping this man? There was no purity of purpose. The roots of motivation were always tangled. Was it simple greed, the promise of millions? Partly, that couldn't be denied, but money had never been my main motivation. Was it some kind of psychological transference, as Cass implied? An effort to bring a rich and criminal father home to his kids, as no one had done for me? I hated those half-bright stabs at armchair psychology, but it didn't take a PhD to find the parallels. Perhaps it was about having power over someone so powerful. If I succeeded in rescuing Danny Soto, it would be a debt his billions could never repay. That was a valuable commodity to store away, something that could temper the envy of his endless possessions.

What about the hardheaded honor in finishing what you started? That old noir fiction of a singular man braving the mean streets in pursuit of truth . . . Please. That came down to pride. I was a whole grab bag of deadly sins.

I spotted the other surfer returning. Danny ran toward him. They met about a hundred feet from us. Danny ignored the bottled water in his hand and pointed, frantic for the phone in his other. The surfer slipped a small leash-cutting knife from a forearm pocket of his wetsuit. He sliced through the binds around Danny's wrists. Then he tapped at his phone, handed it over, and looked over Soto's shoulder. I waved him on. He hesitated, not wanting to leave his phone with this deranged man who'd just washed up in the morning surf.

Reaching us, he said, "I called 911. They should be here any minute. I tried to tell your friend but . . ."

"He has other calls to make," I said.

"What happened to his face?"

I looked into both of theirs. "The less you guys know, the better. Okay?"

They nodded, didn't press the issue.

I grabbed the water and gulped at it. Felt my insides replenish with each swallow. I lowered it at the sound of the sirens. Two cop cars and an ambulance screamed down the road in our direction. I saw Danny stick a finger in one ear as he shouted into the phone. The cavalry came to a stop with wheels on the sand; six doors flung open at once. They raced toward us.

Danny ended the call and lowered his arms. One paramedic and two cops stopped with him, while the other three came to me. I tried to explain. They already knew about the accident at sea. I remembered Harold making the call on his radio. The wreckage was being recovered as we spoke. It appeared the current was strong last night. We'd been pulled east as I swam with Danny to shore. Seeing no survivors in the surrounding area of the crash, the Coast Guard had not yet widened a search. Everyone was presumed dead.

"Who else was aboard, sir?" asked one of the cops.

Seeing minimal injuries on me, the other paramedic went back to help his partner with Danny, who was now collapsed on the sand and not moving. Whatever money-fueled adrenaline was coursing through him moments ago, it was spent. The call had been made, the doomed trade called off, and now the accumulated horrors he endured were descending. I saw another ambulance and a few more cop cars approaching.

"A man named Harold Lester," I said. "He was a real estate broker helping in my investigation. One of the boats was his."

"*Your* investigation?" asked one of the cops. "What agency are you with?"

"My own," I said.

That earned a pair of frowns. "Was there anyone else involved in the accident?" asked the other.

"Two women," I said. "Anonymous. I don't know their names or identities, or even any aliases. Asian descent, believed to be in the employ of a Chinese businessman with a residence here in the city."

"What is the name of this businessman?"

"I'd rather not say."

"We're here to help, you do realize that, correct?"

"I do, and I thank you. But it's better if you don't know too many details."

The surfer kicked at the sand, scoffed, and looked at the officers. "He said the same thing to me, man."

"If you were involved in the commission of a crime, we'll know the details soon enough," said a cop. "Could you come with us, please?"

The other moved to take my arm. I pulled it away. "I was *involved* in saving that man's life," I said, pointing to Soto, who was now being lifted and strapped onto a lifeguard's stretcher. "All respect, guys, but this is beyond your grade. I suspect federal agents will be here soon. You can ask them. Now, can I join my client at the hospital? He's suffered some serious injuries."

Danny was taken to St. John's Episcopal in Far Rockaway. It wasn't where a billionaire would choose to have his face reconstructed, but it was the closest major medical center. He was unconscious by the time he arrived. The shock of it all was too much. I was given an IV with fluids to rehydrate and was treated for burns I hadn't noticed as I swam through the flaming waters. Aside from that, I was unscathed and feeling rather well under the circumstances. I asked a nurse if I could use a phone. She gave me hers and shut the curtain around my bed for privacy.

I called the Roxy Hotel, asked for room 444. I knew Cass didn't have her cell and didn't know where else to reach her. Maybe I could leave word at the Chamber if she'd already checked out. On the second ring she answered.

"Hello?"

"It's me."

"Duck. Thank God."

The sound of my name on her voice, that was all I needed. I told her about the previous evening, how her plan had worked until that speedboat emerged from *The Lady Jade*, carrying Soto and his captors. I told her about our chase, Harold's fate, the crash, and then my long swim with Danny to Rockaway Beach. She already knew some of it. Danny managed to catch Peter Lennox before he left for the office. Cass and Lennox were still holed up there, awaiting further details.

The markets would open soon. There would be no red-flag trades to satisfy billion-dollar ransoms from Soto Capital this morning. The boss was safe in a Queens hospital. I wondered if Danny's family had been notified. They were not his first call. I wondered if they were still hunkered down in Southampton. I wondered if Eileen Chung was still with them.

Our conversation was cut short by the arrival of John-Jack at my bedside. Their presence was as unsmiling as ever. They flanked each side like I might be tempted to rip the IV from my hand and run.

"Darley," said John, or maybe Jack, I still couldn't tell them apart.

"One way or another," I reminded him, "I'll wind up dead. That's true for all of us, isn't it? But not on this case, boys."

"How did you make the connection between Soto and Sun Bin?" asked one.

"He wanted us to make the connection," I said. "A video was sent to Soto's wife and his business partner. It showed him being wheeled out of his building by two female bodyguards. They worked for Sun, which was apparently a well-known fact among those who did business with him. Lennox knew right away who took his friend. Sun *wanted* them to know."

They stiffened. "You saw the video?" asked the other.

"I did."

"And you failed to disclose it to us, or to anyone in a position of authority?"

"Wasn't my decision to make," I said. "His family and his friend feared for his life. They were warned not to share it."

"Yet they shared it with you."

"Danny Soto's daughter, Layla, hired me at first. But after our run-in on Meadow Lane, I was rehired by Soto's mother, Eileen Chung."

The agents communicated something with their eyes across the bed. I remembered Lennox's conviction that Eileen was behind the abduction. Recalled Layla's suspicions when she first sought me out.

"You have something to tell me?" I asked.

"Not at this point," said one.

"The Sotos must be very grateful," said the other.

I wanted to sit up and hit them both. I recalled Peter Lennox's words: *You've got it backwards.* Did that mean it wasn't the Chinese government pulling the strings, committing these crimes, but our own? Rationalized for the sake of national security, for the good of the people. Free markets could flourish, but only to a point.

A mother hadn't betrayed her son. She was caught up in a new opium war, one of the few to appreciate the way history was repeating. To her husband and her son, it was business, a deal that made sense in the most sober, soulless terms. What was another multinational deal among billionaires? When had Soto's neighbor, Sun Bin, inserted himself? It appeared he was working on behalf of American interests, not his country's, or maybe it was both.

At least that's the way it looked from my hospital bed.

Trade between the world's two mightiest superpowers would never be simple. Sometimes billionaires needed to be put back in line. Sometimes faceless white men like John-Jack needed to restore order, even if it meant playing assassin.

"Gentlemen," I said. "Do me a favor?"

"Sure. What can we do for you?"

"Get the fuck out of here."

I noted their haircuts as they left. The hair on the backs of their necks was trimmed with precise care. It was rather like the head on that suit, as he hurried through the crowd after jabbing me with his umbrella.

Chapter 36

Cass and I were invited to the Soto apartment at the end of the following week. For payment, we presumed. A bit of thanks was in order too. There had been no communication with anyone in the family since I helped Danny wash up on that Rockaway beach. Calls to Peter Lennox and Soto Capital went unreturned. I made noise about confrontations in lobbies, but Cass talked me down. She assured me that they would be in touch. They were. Nicole Soto's email sounded as breezy as an invite to a casual dinner party. I supposed she'd gotten my address from her daughter.

I didn't recognize the doorman, or the new man stationed at the front desk, but we were greeted like honored guests. Heavy doors and swift elevators were held open for us, buttons pressed so we wouldn't dirty our fingertips. *And a good day to you, sir!* Order had been restored to the top of the food chain.

As we elevated, our ears popped. I looked at Cass beside me. She was dressed for provocation, in a black leather tank top, matching miniskirt, and stilettos. Her black hair was tied atop her head in a swirl. Makeup was applied with maximum severity. All that was missing was the whip.

"Did you know this is the fastest elevator on earth?" I asked.

She gazed around the sleek, speeding cube. "Why would people live like this?"

"For the views," I said. "Wait till you see."

"I wouldn't live here for a view of heaven itself," she said.

We glided to a stop 1,396 feet in the sky. For the time being, there was no family on earth that lived higher. Cass had Googled the tower. The record would soon be surpassed by other supertalls in development, but at present the Sotos resided in the highest residential apartment on the planet. *Think about that*, she'd said. *In a literal way, they look down on all of humanity*. I supposed Danny's recent experience must have injected some perspective into his lofty existence, though any feelings of vulnerability would soon recede. As long as a man could survey his domain from this height, his confidence wouldn't waver.

The elevator doors opened onto the grand gallery of Asian art and antiques, alongside old masters of the West. There was John Singer-Sargent. There was Johannes Vermeer. There were rooms in the Met with less. Before I could go back to them and gawk, Nicole Soto was rushing toward us, bejeweled and gowned, the lady of the house.

"There they are," she gushed. "It's so good to see you." She offered me her hand as she regarded Cass without approval. "And you must be Cassandra. It's a pleasure to meet in person. You look . . . lovely."

"As do you," said Cass.

She mimed a curtsy. Nicole tried not to cringe.

I recognized the Rachmaninoff coming from the living room, Layla at the keys. Nicole Soto led us toward the sounds. Danny was standing at the high center window, his back to us, looking over the lights and the dark expanse of Central Park below. He gave a theatrical, well-timed turn as we entered.

"Duck, Cassandra," he said. "Welcome."

His face was heavily bandaged, his eyes were bruised, but his speech was clear.

"What can I get you two to drink?"

"A glass of wine would be fine," said Cass. "Whatever you have open."

"Sparkling water," I said.

I tried not to gloat at my sobriety, though I was stoned as can be on the vape. That was as high as I cared to get for the foreseeable future.

Danny led us to a sitting area near the grand piano. Layla smiled at me over the ivories, but did not stop playing. A server appeared with our drinks. I hadn't seen anyone else, and Danny had not relayed our order, but there they were on a silver tray, a white wine for Cass and my sparkling water with a lime wedge. The server was a small Southeast Asian lady, Thai perhaps, her demeanor and dress in quiet deference. Taking the glasses, we gave our thanks. She did not react, just turned and moved briskly out of sight.

Danny crossed his legs and draped an arm over the couch. He was a thin and lethal man, despite his injuries. In his other hand, he held a few inches of amber in cut crystal. His expression was inscrutable beneath those bandages. He was either wincing or grinning. I hoped it was the latter. There was business to be settled.

"How's your mother?" I asked. "Is she here?"

He looked over his shoulder at his daughter. "Layla, honey, would you mind taking a break and helping your mom in the kitchen?"

Her fingers lifted, the Rachmaninoff ceased. "Help mom? Like she's doing anything in there herself?"

"Please, darling. You know what I mean."

Layla stood, approached, and stopped before us. She offered a deep, formal bow. To me, she mouthed *thank you.* To Cass she gave a devilish wink. Seventeen, going into her senior year of high school, she looked older now. The precociousness and certainty replaced by something heavier.

"I'm afraid my mother had to get back to Shanghai," said Danny. "I'm sorry you missed her. She spoke highly of you."

"Nice to hear," I said. "At first, some were convinced she was behind your abduction."

"So I've been told."

"Who was?" asked Cass. "Besides your neighbor, Sun Bin. Was he working for our government?"

Danny was shaking his battered head as she spoke. "The *U.S.* government? Ridiculous," he said. "I understand you've tried to investigate my business dealings, and perhaps you've learned a bit, but I assure you that my mother had nothing to do with my recent . . . situation. Nor did any American interests. In this country, our government does not abduct private citizens."

"You sure about that?"

"Quite."

"Tell us about this deal between you and your mother's husband," I said. "Something regarding a pharmaceutical company and opioid manufacturing?"

"Where did you hear that?"

"From Eileen, and then from your partner, Peter Lennox."

He sighed, set his glass on the table between us, and leaned in. "It should have been a simple transaction. My mother helped connect me with her third husband, who's done quite well in China in the pharmaceutical space. That was the extent of her involvement. Unfortunately, the deal proved more problematic than anticipated, due to the manufacturing of certain drugs."

"Painkillers," I said. "What, you didn't realize buying a fentanyl factory might be frowned upon?"

"Don't be trite," he said. "There was much more to it. As I'm sure you're aware, there is considerable tension between China and the U.S. these days, particularly with regards to trade. My business, however, knows no borders, and nor does my blood. I'm half Chinese, after all. My father, may he rest in peace, was first-generation American. His family came from Spain after the Second World War. So, you see, it's in my genetic makeup not to recognize anything as arbitrary as flags or lines in the sand. All borders are temporary, and blood will be mixed. As it should be—just look at what happens to thoroughbred horses and British royalty after too much inbreeding. You produce dim, brittle animals."

Pleased with his soapbox soliloquy, his bandages turned up into something like a smile. He lifted his glass, toasted us, and took a sip. We did not lift ours in return.

"Fascinating," said Cass. She crossed her bare legs and let a point of stiletto stick out in his direction. "From up here, you're above it all, aren't you?"

"It helps to clarify a different perspective, yes," he said. "I realize my lack of nationalism can be unpopular in times like these."

"Where's Sun Bin?" I asked. "That was quite a boat he had you on."

The bandages turned down. "Mr. Sun will not be returning to this country anytime soon. After it was searched, while you and I were bobbing like shark bait in the ocean, *The Lady Jade* left the harbor and presumably set a course for international waters. They managed to clear any evidence of my stay before allowing the authorities aboard." His black-and-blue eyes looked into mine until I returned the contact. "I thank you, Duck. You saved my life. I'll never be able to repay you."

"Which brings us to the subject of our fee," I said. "Your mother promised me several million dollars for finding you."

"I'll have to ask her about that," he said.

"Or," said Cass, "you can do the honorable thing and settle it yourself. As you noted, you'll never be able to repay us, but, say, four million dollars may be a step in that direction."

"Very well," he said. "Where would you like me to wire it?"

Just like that. We were millionaires, or at least had a verbal agreement to be ones soon. It occurred to me that we should have asked for more. Greed, it really was the deadliest of the seven. As Danny noted, his debt was forever. These few million were just a down payment. If we ever needed anything again, anything of a fiscal nature, we could always go back to the well.

"We'll send the wiring instructions later tonight," said Cass.

"Wonderful," said Danny. "You'll have your funds in the morning. You've both earned it."

He stood, extended a hand. We took it.

"Now, unless you have anything further to discuss, I'd like to get back to my family. It's been a difficult time, as you can imagine. I can't tell you how much it means to be back with them."

"Go," said Cass. "Spend time with your beautiful wife and kids. You'll receive the wiring details shortly."

As she turned to go, Danny grabbed my arm. I hung back. He hesitated for a moment, and then flung his arms around me, hugging me tight. "Thank you," he said in my ear. "Thank you." I returned his embrace until he was ready to release me. His bruised eyes were damp as he stepped away.

His wife and kids were off in other parts of the home. I

thought I heard Lionel shouting. They did not come to say goodbye. We let ourselves out.

That night was among the best I'll ever live. We took a cab downtown. I called ahead and booked a reservation at the Strip House, a few blocks south of Union Square. It was the dead of summer; reservations were easy to come by. We had a table for two waiting.

The steakhouse was the sight of milestones celebrated, always had been, even when I couldn't afford it. This would be the first time I dined there without drinking. It seemed unnatural not to order a martini or a bourbon before dinner, and some good red wine with my meat, but I'd made it this far. I was starting to enjoy the dry life.

We got out in front of the crimson awning on East 12th Street between University and Fifth. STRIP HOUSE glowed in neon above the entrance. The interior was a rich burgundy palette, with framed black-and-white photographs of burlesque ladies from another age. We were shown to our table in the back. I let Cass slide in first, and took the chair facing her. She was at her loveliest. Beneath the leather and the severity of her style, her heart was open. She smiled and laughed with ease.

"You know, in all our time together," I said, "I've never seen you eat anything."

"What are you talking about?"

"I mean, besides energy bars. I've never seen you use a knife and fork, I swear."

"Well, you never asked me to dinner before. I tend to lose my appetite seated at the bar. Which was where I always found you."

"No longer."

"I'm proud of you."

"One day at a time," I said. "Isn't that what twelve-steppers like to say?"

"Well, today I'm impressed," she said. "We'll see if the same is true tomorrow."

"Four million dollars is going to hit our account tomorrow, and I'm not even going to have a drink to celebrate."

"Now that will be impressive."

After the waiter took our orders—bone-in ribeye for me, petite filet for her, the creamed spinach and goose-fat potatoes on the side—Cass had a surprise for me. During my time in Southampton, she'd left the Chamber for an errand. At a nearby branch of Chase Bank, she went in and opened a new account for us.

"After we incorporate, we can switch it over to a business banking account, but this will work for now. I'll get your information and get it set up as a joint checking that we can both access. Tonight, I'll send Danny the wiring details."

"Four million," I said. The number still didn't seem quite real. Perhaps because it wasn't, not yet. "That will give our firm a nice start."

"What should we call it?" she asked.

"D and C Investigations?"

"Boring."

"Okay, what did you have in mind?"

"What about Saint and Sinner?"

I laughed. "Who's who?"

"Take a guess."

"Saint Darley, at your service."

We toasted. The sparkling water didn't even taste so wrong.

After our feast, we walked southeast at random leisure. On Broadway and Bleeker, I pointed out where Pfaff's beer cellar once resided beneath the sidewalk, in a vault that birthed bohemianism in America, where Walt Whitman and the boys used to laugh and live without restraint. A little farther on, we lamented the loss of downtown dives

now dead. The International Bar, Mars Bar, Max Fish . . .
an endless wake for alcoholic temples. I hit the vape at regular intervals and tried to push down the urge for something stronger.

When we reached Cass's apartment on Orchard, I didn't
pine for any invitations inside. I offered a professional hug
on the sidewalk, turned around, and returned north without looking back. I reached my garden pad on East 17th
feeling lighter and happier than I thought possible. Then I
climbed into bed and slept a full eight hours with dreams
that didn't haunt.

In the morning I awaited the news that the funds hit our
account.

They didn't.

Calls, emails, and texts went unreturned. Cass came by
and we paced and cursed across my floor. I got more
stoned by the hour. It failed to calm me. Late in the afternoon, around five p.m., we decided to show up at the
Sotos' building. We'd wait in the lobby and refuse to leave
until Danny returned and provided some answers—and
paid us what he promised.

The doorman was frowning as we approached. The
heat was miserable. The air reeked of rotting garbage and
car exhaust between the towers. No matter how gilded
and temperature-controlled the environments inside, no
matter how much one paid, nothing could be done about
summer in Manhattan.

"Is he okay?" asked the doorman.

"Is who okay?"

"Mr. Soto," he stammered. "That's why you are here,
yes? He was rushed out, early this morning, in an ambulance. Very scary."

"Fuck," said Cass.

The doorman was gracious and allowed us to wait inside the chilled lobby. We were there for two hours. We

didn't say much. Early in the evening, we saw Layla getting out of a cab in front, alone. Her shoulders were turned inward. Her chin pressed to her chest. Her face was a blotchy ruin of tears. We stood as she saw us.

"He's dead," she said.

"How?" I asked.

She raised air quotes, and said, "Heart attack."

She swept past us and rode that high-speed elevator up to her empty home.

Epilogue

News reports in the business sections failed to note Danny Soto's abduction. It didn't exist, not in any official sense. His sudden death was a tragic case of a successful man cut down in his prime. It was the stress, some speculated. A hedge fund founder faced untold daily pressures. His heart gave out. He was survived by two children, a wife, and a mother in Shanghai. Peter Lennox promised the investment community that Soto Capital would continue to thrive. His closest friend and partner hired only the brilliant. They were well positioned for another quarter of double-digit returns.

Not that we believed any of that. Someone, somehow, had gotten to Soto in the days after I saved him, after his surgeries, after he was released from the hospital. It could have been anyone, in any number of ways. A slow-acting poison, slipped into a lunch, a brushed-up bit of contact at a crosswalk. I knew who I suspected: that faceless federal agent duo, John-Jack. The same ones who, I was convinced, poisoned me on that sidewalk.

I'd never have proof, just conviction.

I considered the building's head of security, the former NSA agent, Bill Willis. There was always the man on the inside, who helped facilitate these things. Mother and daughter had vowed to ruin him if he was involved. I wondered how long he had to live.

Would the rich ever realize how easy it was to reach them?

Cloistered atop their towers in the sky, surrounded by their art and their beautiful music, traveling to and fro between their collection of homes, it was a rarified existence that would never be touched by earthly concerns, until it was.

Cass and I could be touched too. If someone decided we needed to be taken off the board, it wouldn't take much. They would get away with it.

Until then, Saint & Sinner was open for business.

Don't miss how it all began . . .

in

UNDER WATER

and

AGAINST NATURE,

available now from

Casey Barrett

and

Kensington Books,

wherever books are sold.